Ian Ross Vayro was born in Townsville, North Queensland, Australia. He was raised in a farming community near Dalby and attended a one-teacher primary school.

On leaving 'the bush', he was educated in Brisbane and for a time returned as a working cowboy on a station near Roma. He later served in the Royal Australian Air Force, which allowed him to travel extensively and instilled the discipline he has utilized in most endeavours since.

Ian Ross was a musician and a DJ and studied Electronic Engineering, then Classical Ancient History and Archaeology, a somewhat unusual mix, and tempered this with a lifelong interest and personal research in Theology.

He actively created a successful business life, becoming the best in his business field, culminating in his own hugely successful Outdoor Advertising Company. Ian achieved greatly through a commitment and focus and somewhat perfectionist attitude which he has transferred to his research and work as an author.

Ian Ross now lives on acreage with horses and dogs, near Lake Wivenhoe…an hour from Brisbane in Queensland, Australia, and enjoys the peace and tranquillity of this beautiful location.

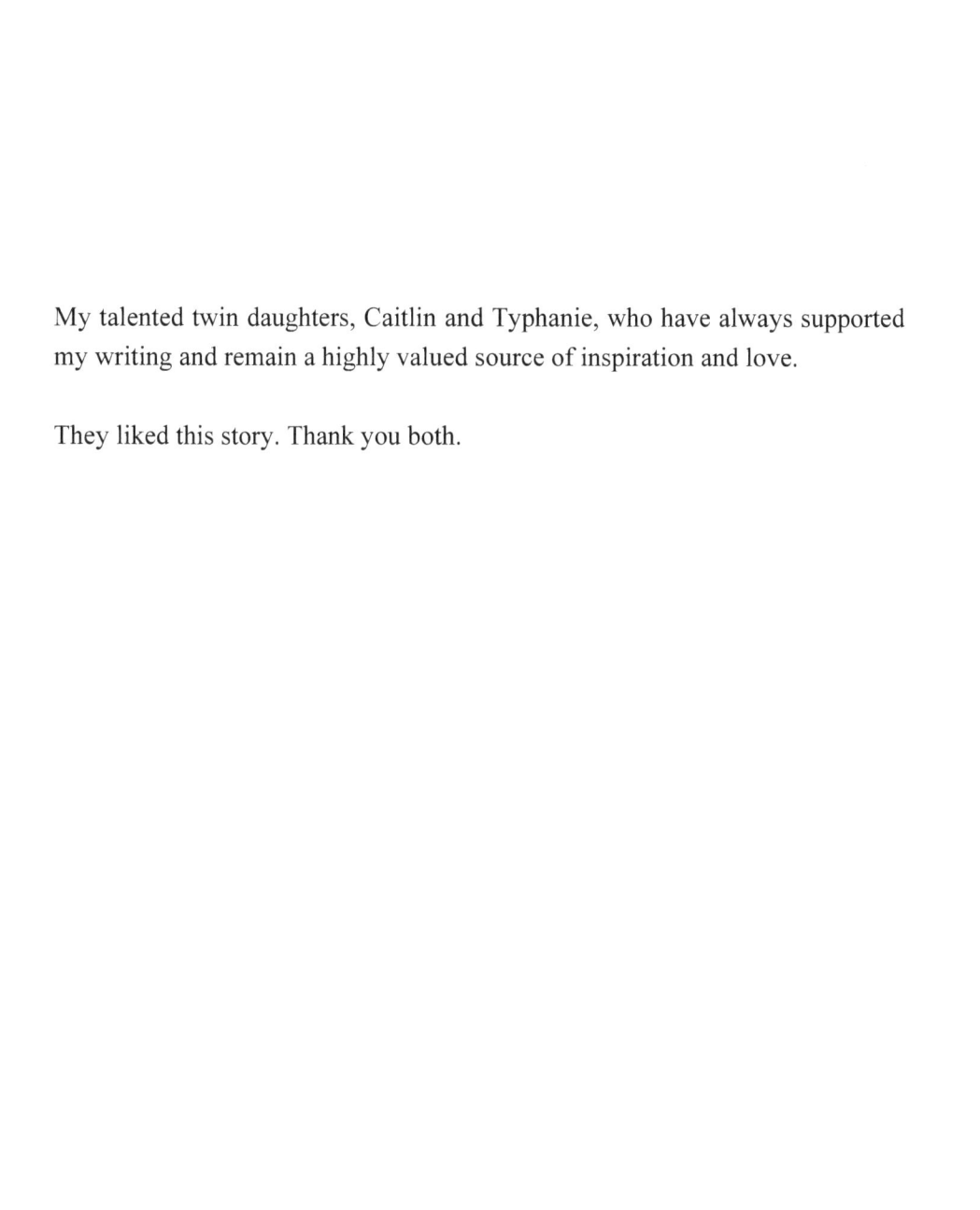

My talented twin daughters, Caitlin and Typhanie, who have always supported my writing and remain a highly valued source of inspiration and love.

They liked this story. Thank you both.

Ian Ross Vayro

# SUICIDE OR MURDER

AUSTIN MACAULEY PUBLISHERS™
LONDON * CAMBRIDGE * NEW YORK * SHARJAH

Copyright © Ian Ross Vayro 2023

The right of Ian Ross Vayro to be identified as author of this work has been asserted by the author in accordance with sections 77 and 78 of the Copyright, Designs and Patents Act 1988.

All rights reserved. No part of this publication may be reproduced, stored in a retrieval system, or transmitted in any form or by any means, electronic, mechanical, photocopying, recording, or otherwise, without the prior permission of the publishers.

Any person who commits any unauthorised act in relation to this publication may be liable to criminal prosecution and civil claims for damages.

This is a work of fiction. Names, characters, businesses, places, events, locales, and incidents are either the products of the author's imagination or used in a fictitious manner. Any resemblance to actual persons, living or dead, or actual events is purely coincidental.

A CIP catalogue record for this title is available from the British Library.

ISBN 9781398444942 (Paperback)
ISBN 9781398471696 (ePub e-book)

www.austinmacauley.com

First Published 2023
Austin Macauley Publishers Ltd®
1 Canada Square
Canary Wharf
London
E14 5AA

The author would like to acknowledge Dr Donald Harper-Mills for the initial story that he originally purported to be true.

In addition, he acknowledges the wonderful people of Australia's Northern Territory, including the Manilakarr people of Arnhem Land.

The author has flown with Lufthansa and thanks all the pilots, flight attendants and ground crew of this professional airline.

Thanks go to the folks from Los Angeles and the romantics of Paris. This story is also for all those, everywhere, who are in love.

# Table of Contents

| | |
|---|---|
| **Main Characters** | 13 |
| **The Role of the Coroner** | 15 |
| **Chapter 1: A Stupid Incident** | 16 |
| **Chapter 2: A Busy Week** | 31 |
| **Chapter 3: Aussie Philosophy** | 74 |
| **Chapter 4: Girls and Apples** | 85 |
| **Chapter 5: Seeking Tranquillity** | 101 |
| **Chapter 6: It's All Happening** | 105 |
| **Chapter 7: Emerald Springs** | 126 |
| **Chapter 8: It's About Respect** | 157 |
| **Chapter 9: A Few Loose Ends** | 173 |
| **Chapter 10: A Neat Surprise** | 184 |
| **End Notes** | 207 |

*Truth is stranger than fiction, but it is because fiction is obliged to stick to possibilities, truth isn't.*

– Mark Twain

**With its somewhat ominous 'Murder Mystery' title, one might wonder how this book could be based on the romantic and sometimes humorous, exploits of a young student detective, Adam and a Lufthansa flight attendant called Mina. Despite the odds, they establish a loving relationship in this astounding sequence of events, in a scenario that was initially purported to be true. A case that supposedly boggled Police investigators and Medical Examiners in LA.**

**The story was originally reported in 1994, by Kurt Westerveld for Associated Press. And talks about the legal complications associated with a bizarre death that was chosen as the most unusual case on record, for presentation at an anniversary Awards Dinner of the American Association of Forensic Scientists, back in 1987. The situation was explained by AAFS President, Dr Don Harper Mills, and in this context, was later featured in 'Duty First' Magazine in the Spring of 2006, as a factual report.**

**This story then began to circulate on the Internet and attained the status of urban legend, until Mills himself, finally announced that he actually made it up as an illustrative anecdote, "to show how different legal consequences can follow each twist in a homicide inquiry." He went on to express little surprise at the story's acceptance, calling it 'a fabulous story'. He has fielded numerous inquiries about it, in the years since. It is indeed an interesting story, however, today's modern detection methods and the use of DNA technology would possibly help solve this case much more quickly and efficiently, than in the version from 1987. Because back then, no amount of technology could ascertain if the conclusions reached in the final summation were, in fact, the correct ones. It is quite possible that they weren't.**

*Dr Don Harper Mills and the original character's names are included in this story, but for this work, the characters themselves are of course fictional. The narrative is built around this coincidence riddled case, recorded in a way that shows how the story might have really unfolded.*

*– Ian Ross Vayro*

# Main Characters

**Adam Mills**—As a trainee police detective in the criminology study program at California State University, Adam becomes embroiled in unfair charges and receives only token support from his Lieutenant. As a fitness disciple, he also teaches Martial Arts at the police youth club and is immersed in the I Ching philosophy of Tae Kwon Do. Searching for the deeper lesson amidst the disorder, Adam discerns that as a legitimate proponent of Yin and Yang, he is possibly being tested. The circle of life dictates that like all those who consistently try to do what is right, sometimes you are punished, sometimes you are rewarded.

**Dr Don Harper Mills**—Adam's father is the chief medical examiner in charge of forensic science for the inner Los Angeles area. He is a medical doctor specialising in forensic science and also holds a law degree, and as such is a veritable asset to the county in this position. A loving husband and a caring parent, he resides in a comfortable home in the LA hills with his wife Sarah. The well-respected Doctor Mills is a long-term Rotarian and president of the American Association of Forensic Scientists. He is a spiritual individual with an interest in theology and is well versed in ancient scripture.

**Mina Jenkins**—A sophisticated Los Angeles girl originally from Oklahoma, Mina has a dream job as a flight attendant working out of Europe with Lufthansa. She has studied ballet and classical piano, but remains very much the girl next door with an easy country charm. She is a striking and vivacious person, but for some reason can't seem to attract nice guys and her relationships tend to be pretty disastrous. As a result, her confidence wavers. Mina is an intelligent and sensitive individual and possibly a true romantic, who trusts in her 'Guardian Angel' and lives for the day, her dreams will find some fruition.

**Leah Suffolk**—The blonde Leah, is a confirmed 'party girl' and Mina's co-worker and best friend. She is a happy-go-lucky, city-girl who is high on life. The ultimate people person, she loves flying and enjoys meeting new people.

Life is a very big box of chocolates for Leah, and she wants all the soft centres. Leah and Mina are opposites as individuals, but together form a cohesive team. Over time, they learn to adopt some of each other's attributes, which is hugely beneficial, and ultimately leads to greater fulfilment for both.

**Gordon 'Mack' Mackenzie**—Subtle as a train smash, Mack is an 'old school' police lieutenant, loud and coarse without much imagination or any manners. He can be a bulldozer when the situation requires it and quite often even when it doesn't. Mack has Neanderthal views on dealing with people and is still unaware that new hi-tech detection methods are on the way, requiring a new breed of detective to operate within this advancing technological system. In this time of manpower shortages, Mack is merely classed as 'adequate' but he fits into the department surprisingly well. This book is about Mack's strangest case and the way it was investigated. It is a bizarre story.

**Dr Barry Hannaway**—A down to Earth, soft-spoken Australian with a vocabulary from the Aussie outback, he brings humour and credence to the story. He is crusty and unsophisticated, but can be resourceful and original. He hates subterfuge and cuts through departmental politics to get the job done with a philosophy that is all his own. Hannaway has seen a lot of life in the Northern Territory of Australia and has learned a thing or two from the Aboriginal natives. He is a natural egalitarian, which gives him a low tolerance and very little respect for many in authority. His manner is quite disarming, but he proves to be considerably more astute than he appears.

**Ronald Opus**—Although quite reasonable looking, Ron has a surly nature and is an opportunist, and a user. He is a very misguided person who believes that the world owes him a living. His involvement in drugs and God knows what else, is leading him on a collision course with disaster. Ron is at a crossroads in his life and has one last shot at choosing the right path. The best day of his life was when Mina, suffering a touch of 'mother hen' syndrome, agreed to go out with him. Ron should have recognised that this was something special, but he acted like a total retard and even blew that one. He didn't learn from the opportunities he was presented with, and missed out as a result.

# The Role of the Coroner

A coroner is an official responsible for investigating deaths, particularly those occurring under unusual circumstances. The coroner's job is to determine the precise time and cause of death. Depending on the jurisdiction, it is usual for the coroner to adjudge the cause himself, but at times, he may act as the presiding officer of a special court.

Coroners in the United States at county-level, are sometimes elected, rather than appointed and do not necessarily need to hold any medical qualifications. In larger cities (for instance, Los Angeles) and more populous counties, the post is actually filled by a 'Chief Medical Examiner', who unlike a coroner must be a licensed physician and is most often a specialist in pathology or forensic medicine. In several jurisdictions, a Medical Examiner is required to be both a doctor and a lawyer, to handle the elevated position. The Medical Examiner is most often an appointed, qualified, official. This has been part of a fairly recent move toward professionalising the job, which today is increasingly involved with more advanced technology and scientific requirements.

Coroners are often depicted in police dramas as a source of cleverly deduced information for detectives, and it is true, they often work together. But in reality, the official duties of the Coroner or Chief Medical Examiner usually don't go much beyond determining the cause, time, and manner of death. Despite what is shown in TV dramas, only a small percentage of deaths require an autopsy to determine these criteria. The role of the Coroner or Medical Examiner can employ similar investigatory skills to a police detective, but their answers are most often extracted from the circumstances, scene, and recent medical records of the deceased. When a body cannot be identified, the detectives rely more heavily on the Coroner or Chief Medical Examiner.[1]

# Chapter 1
# A Stupid Incident

**Saturday Evening**
**LA International Airport**

Bright landing lights penetrated the fog as the Lufthansa 747 cruised gracefully into LAX, just after dark.

It seemed to hang in the air like a giant condor, hovering, searching for prey, then with the roar of its powerful engines, swooped in for a perfect landing and the final dash along the runway. The passengers were pretty docile after the tiring flight from Europe and many stared out the aircraft windows at the lights that resembled glow-worms in the enveloping fog.

Oblivious to this, a nattily dressed, 'too cool for school', blonde guy in 17A was getting down to his favourite rap. His ultra hi-fidelity Sennheiser cans were plugged into the aircraft system, while the elaborate designer case sat on the vacant seat next to his big screen iPhone, and 'genuine calfskin' gold embossed, Dunhill passport holder.

The heavily loaded airliner moved from the runway to one of the many taxiways picked out by subdued blue lighting. This illumination criss-crossed the field, creating a surreal coloured fairyland in the fog. The spectacular rotating green and white beam from the tower reflected the mist to join with the kaleidoscope of colour from flashing red and blue safety lights on a myriad of fire trucks and the sporadic amber of the baggage carts and refuelling vehicles. A hive of workers went about preparing for the turn-around, but it seemed to take forever for the giant craft to taxi all the way to Gate 52.

Two, tired but sweet, flight attendants commenced saying goodbye to 356 disembarking passengers as they wearily filed out of the aircraft in a zombie line.

"Have a nice stay."

"You take care now."

"Hey! Enjoy your time at Disneyland."

"Hope you'll fly with us again soon."

"Here, let me help you with that."

A couple of times, these two cheekily poked faces at each other, when there was an opportunity to get away with it, and not get sprung by the passengers.

"You made the flight a real pleasure for me." The blonde European guy thanked her so sincerely and profusely, it caused Leah's eyebrows to almost touch her hairline. It also caused Mina to shake her head in mock consternation. Did she really give him that much pleasure on the flight? Oh hell! Did she really give him her cell phone number? Here we go again! Mina shrugged, rolling her big dark eyes.

She could never be like Leah. They were opposites in so many ways and yet were able to work brilliantly together and remained the very best of friends. "Three days stopover," Leah whispered between final greetings, "three days break…Wowee!" Mina's face broke into an attractive smile, which she turned on the next alighting passenger, who just happened to be the fat, ugly grouch who had put on a performance in Business Class over the inadequacies of the wine selection.

"Thank-you for flying Lufthansa, Sir." She winced just a little at his responding grunt, while Leah smiled at the irony, and showed Mina the tip of her tongue again. Finally, when all the passengers had alighted, the flight attendants left the aircraft together and walked smartly through the boarding tunnel to the terminal, pulling their wheeled carry-ons behind them.

Mina and Leah still called Los Angeles home, but flew for Lufthansa out of Europe, so a stopover in LA, was considered pretty special since they had family here. The girls stepped off the travellator and moved into the commercial area. Something in a Duty-Free shop caught Mina's eye and she pointed almost imperceptibly at the magnificent Ralph Lauren casual jacket in a men's wear display. Leah didn't miss the gesture and shook her head causing a few errant strands of her long blonde hair to escape the way she wore it up when working.

She knew it was about Ron. Well, not really about him specifically. Ron Opus was a drop-kick; in fact, he was a total retard, creepy, loser, drop-kick. How did that particular sperm ever win the race? Leah had sort of loathed him from the start, because he was ignorant and viewed women as sex objects. (Vanessa: "Mr Powers I would never have sex with you, ever; ever! If you were the last man on earth and I was the last woman on earth, and the future of the human race depended on our having sex, simply for procreation, I still would not have sex with you." Austin Powers: "What's your point Vanessa?")

17

Mina was the type of young woman who needed someone to care for and fuss over, and as a result, she was also a master at attracting 'lame ducks'. Leah, on the other hand, was single, footloose and fancy free. It seemed that Mina just had to be attached since she couldn't function as a single unit. No, that wasn't really true; on second thoughts, she could function just fine because she was an ultimate professional and the best friend Leah ever had. The girls had known each other since high school and lived in the same neighbourhood. Leah thought about it for a moment. Terminally lovesick? Possibly true; but it's just that there are some horses that perform better in double harness and Mina was a lot like that.

Most times, she was the warm and cheery, girl next-door type, who in time could become the perfect wife and wonderful mother, but she also had a sophisticated side that exuded intelligence and a quick wit. Maybe this is what the guys sensed and couldn't handle or maybe Mina simply hadn't met the right ones. The reality was, that she didn't need adventure like Leah did, she needed family. She didn't need exploits, she needed relationships. Yet, somehow, together, the girls clicked and were mutually supportive, their personal strengths and weaknesses seemed to complement and overlap.

They passed the lines of passengers waiting at customs and immigration, which presented a mere formality for flight crew, and quickly proceeded towards the taxi ranks outside the LAX terminal. Bristling at the cold, they exited to the roadway and looked for a taxi to share. How good it felt to be home!

The parting of ways hadn't gone well when Mina had terminated her short relationship with Ron, on her last visit home. God! Was it three weeks ago? Things might still be a bit awkward, so Leah was determined to be there for her friend, come what may. With any luck, they wouldn't see the obsessive creep at all. It wasn't that Mina had really missed him, she only missed being in a relationship and that's what her look at the Polo jacket had been about. 'In love with being in love', Leah recognised it.

Although the girls enjoyed flying, and loved the exotic destinations, it was not the sort of career that was conducive to forming lasting relationships. Leah thrived on this aspect, but knew that Mina didn't, so she made up her mind, to ensure her friend was not going to have an instant to mope or be miserable on this home break. Actually, a new relationship is what she really needed, and Leah, a matchmaker at heart, was seriously on the lookout. Even the ethnic cabbie didn't escape a quick appraisal, as the taxi sped off into the night, lights whirling like ghosts in the LA fog.

## The Apartment

The taxi passed an apartment block on the main arterial road, not far from the city centre and the girls barely gave it a glance. Observed from the street, the complex appeared to be a tired, old brownstone, but at least inside unit 9/3A it was newly painted, comfortable, tidy and immaculately clean. Ironically, the happy animated chatter of the homecoming girls, was in sharp contrast to the harsh discourse being exchanged within this unit. The language was not at all comfortable, tidy…or clean.

"You're a low-life bum Clive Opus! Did you ever think of getting a job or doing any work? No! You've always been a bum and now you're teaching our son to go the same way." Maggie Opus was on the wrong side of sixty, but still a tidy package of trim, good-looking woman, even though the hair was greying and there was weariness showing in her eyes. Thank God wrinkles don't hurt, she often reflected. They had moved into this apartment almost eight years ago, when she had a windfall in the form of an unexpected inheritance from an aunt she had nursed for years. The surprising thing was, that no one knew the old lady had money stashed away, and Maggie was the only one selfless enough to support her with no ulterior motive.

She now stood in the kitchen, scrubbing a saucepan with a brillo and maintained a calm dignity, despite the situation she had been forced to endure. Sure, she was tired and world weary from life with the unkempt Clive, but she maintained a quiet decorum that neither her husband nor son possessed. Neither of these two reprobates had worked in living memory, more than happy to sponge off her inheritance. Not usually one to indulge in self-pity, right now, Maggie couldn't prevent a thought flashing through her mind, about how much more fulfilling her life might be with a responsible husband and a loving son.

Clive's stained singlet and slovenly ways were an outward manifestation of the turmoil in his mind. He had always wanted to be somebody and had a thousand excuses ready, to explain the rotten hand that fate had dealt him, circumstances that had always somehow prevented him from getting ahead. In his mind, a thousand other people were to blame. He was never at fault.

Maggie's hopes and dreams and all ambition were long gone and now she just wanted peace and quiet and an escape from the constant antagonism and shame of her husband and her son. They had been quietly whispering together just out of her hearing, planning more trouble, no doubt. She controlled the money and saw that Clive was making this point angrily to his son. She had then watched Ronnie storm out, seething with anger. Maggie was over it all, but still couldn't come to terms with how she had failed as a parent.

Ronnie was an only child and she didn't have him until later in life, and now wondered if this was where she went wrong. She had tried so hard with him but nothing seemed to work. It was the same old thing, he always wanted more money, and historically, she had found it difficult to deny him anything. Lately he had become so secretive, that she was reticent to give in to him anymore. He would disappear for days at a time, even for a week and never tell her where he was going or what he was doing or ever discuss where he had been. Running away from responsibility and integrity at the speed of sound, without a parachute. It couldn't go on.

He'd had a lovely girl for a short time, Maggie had met her once. She seemed so sweet and Maggie hoped she might settle Ronnie down, but he hadn't treated her well and they had broken up after a couple of weeks. Her son was tall and apart from the scowl that now appeared to be permanent, could have been an attractive young man. But, despite all her work with him, it just seemed he held no idea of how to interact with decent folk.

She had tried so hard to raise him right, to instil some social skills and values of respect, but the rebellion and overbearing influence of his father, was something stronger than a mother's love and caring. Father and son seemed to share an anger that bordered on madness, which she simply couldn't fathom. There was no hardness or cruelty in her nature and she was plainly not equipped to deal with it in others. They were leeches, she finally admitted to herself. Blood sucking leeches.

"Don't you ever talk down to me like that again!" Oh God! Clive was back from rummaging in the bedroom. She had been lost in her thoughts and had almost forgotten about his anger at her words. As if to punctuate his outburst, Clive produced a double-barrelled shotgun, raised it to his shoulder and slowly, purposefully pulled back both hammers. He saw the disgust in her eyes, edged with an element of fear and this is what he lived for. He savoured the feeling for a long moment. Life had dealt him a lousy hand and now he fought back with intimidation and control. "Don't you ever talk to me like that again," he repeated enjoying the feeling of power pumping through his body. "Bitch!"

Time had slowed down. She clearly heard the screech of tyres as her son pulled out from the apartment block.

She wasn't to know if the gun was loaded or not, thought Clive as he finally hammered down. She heard the violent acceleration of Ronnie's car as the barrel of the shotgun slammed against the side of her neck. She didn't even feel it. Her husband hadn't existed in her life for a good many years, and his juvenile power displays really didn't bother her much. Now Clive stormed out heading for a bar and grill, without even changing his dirty singlet.

Good riddance! He didn't matter much. Now she was forced to admit to herself that she didn't know her own son anymore. That actually hurt her far more than the blow had done. Why couldn't Ronnie see the lonely road he was taking? She thought of the joy they had shared when he was a little boy and the tears came.

## Sunday Ron Opus

Breakfast in Unit 9/3A resembled a sick parade. The two ungrateful patients were both unwell with self-inflicted illnesses procured from dubious liquor in two different sleazy bars. They maintained silence except for the sucking and slurping sounds, as orange juice, toast, bacon, eggs and coffee disappeared. Feeding time at the zoo. They left the table without a word of thanks or appreciation; Maggie had not even been acknowledged. She was the ATM and house slave, nothing more. If it wasn't for the money, they'd throw rocks at her. She had thought late into the night about this situation and resolved that it could not continue; she was fully over it.

Maggie hadn't had a victory in a while. She was standing at the sink with a plunger, earnestly continuing an on-going battle with the prehistoric plumbing in the apartment block. Finally, the sink gave off a sulky gurgle, manifested some brackish liquid with a revolting smell that fortunately drained away fairly rapidly. Maggie resisted the temptation to punch the air, rejoicing that she had finally triumphed, regardless that it may be short lived.

Again, she heard the screech of tyres as Ronnie left, signalling that once more her words had not got through to him. His red car raced into the morning sunshine, his erratic driving telegraphing the rage seething inside him. He had used up his credit and had to get some money. He pulled out his cell phone and called 'the man'. Something was written in permanent marker pen on the case of his cell phone, but his hand covered it as the call connected. "Ron here; do you have another job lined up?"

Flynn was a total thug and sounded it, "Benny Franklin's, Ronnie Boy. Bring me the money first."

"Be cool man, it's happening, I'll bring it tomorrow," Ron lied.

"OK, I'll stay cool, but don't let me down," Flynn snapped. Nobody let him down—not ever. As Ron went to replace his cell phone, it made noise. He noted the caller ID, made the connection, and then briefly smiled as he listened. It was a momentary wicked smile, before the anger reappeared, and the scowl got deeper. How dare that slag break up with him? He dug in the glove compartment, dragged out a packet and snorted a nose full of coke as he drove.

Light glinted on the butt of a pistol concealed there, and he lovingly stroked the cool metal as he replaced his stash. He could have any girl he wanted. It was those pilots in their fancy uniforms that had turned her head…bastards! His mother had cut off his money…Jesus! Was the whole world against him? "I'll show her," he breathed aloud. A mad look showed in his eyes. It wasn't certain whether he meant the ex-girlfriend or his mother. Perhaps in his turmoiled mind, it was both.

## The Dojang

The simple sign out front read 'LA City-Police Youth Club'. A large glossy coloured photo mounted on the Dojang wall showed a tall, muscular young man with sandy hair and a square chiselled jaw, in the act of throwing a larger competitor. There was a lot of animation captured in that frozen sixtieth of a second, but the memorable feature, was the young man's startling, steel blue eyes. At the far end of the polished timber floor, those same blue eyes were focused on a much smaller opponent. She was going through various kicks and blocks when he sprang into action.

God, he was like a well-oiled machine, smooth and fast. His demeanour was usually that of a serene, relaxed guy, but when he was involved in martial arts, it was total concentration and focus, every moment. The reflected overhead lighting glittered on the platinum and gold thread embroidered on his black belt. It spelled out 'Adam Harper Mills' in English and depicted Korean symbols for his third dan rating. Effortlessly, he relaxed from his fighting stance, snapped down his sleeves, and bowed to the girl, and dismissed her.

At a command, "Chul Sa," the Tae Kwon Do class lined up quickly. Adam addressed his young students and they listened intently, hanging on his every word. Many came from pretty tough neighbourhoods and several commenced martial arts training for protection against the local gangs. Adam had good reason to be proud of them all. At first, it had been incredibly difficult for him, but now every new student was pulled into line by the positive peer pressure and integrity of the collective group. The respect and self-esteem he had instilled in them was more than evident. It seemed to be a palpable thing that reverberated with his words around the Dojang.

"We follow the two 'Rs'…Respect and Responsibility." They heard it every week, but still listened intently. "Respect for ourselves; respect for others. Responsibility for those we can help; responsibility for our actions." The message was slowly getting through to even to the toughest ones there. "We learn about life here. We learn about strength of character and good living here. We learn martial arts for fitness and for self-defence," he told them for the hundredth time, "…not to fight, but rather, so we don't have to fight." This caused a few to swallow or wince slightly. Subconsciously telegraphing, that this was a real-life situation for them.

Adam relaxed a little and a grin split his animated face, "OK, you did well today. Take care now. Be strong, train hard and remember; Eat right. Think right. Live right." He dismissed the class. They bowed to each other.

Adam's build was deceptive, as he moved out after a hot shower, dressed in Levis and sneakers, with a California State University tracksuit top. He was tall and trim with an air of confidence. But hidden, was the muscular chest, the firm biceps and the hard whipcord muscles of his 'six pack' abs, honed from many years of discipline and training.

He certainly didn't exhibit male model looks, but all his attributes seemed to blend in a classical way, creating a very pleasing persona that was set off by those amazing eyes; clear windows to the soul. To even a casual observer, Adam exuded an aura of warmth and friendliness but his easy graceful walk certainly belied the deadly focused instrument he had been on the mat some minutes before.

A car screeched to a stop right next door to the Youth Club, but he paid no attention as he concentrated on locking the front door, until the girl screamed.

# The Sidewalk Café

"Isn't it great to be home," Leah exclaimed. "My neurotic cat still has separation anxiety and shows her affection on my return by dragging headless carcasses into the house and depositing them at my bedroom door. She seems to have trouble understanding my less than enthusiastic response to her generous gifts and consequently, continues to upsize. I am expecting to find an albatross or a pelican or perhaps even a pterodactyl at my door any day soon." Mina had been sharing a blueberry muffin with Leah in their favourite coffee shop, while untouched café latte's cooled in front of them.

"I don't recall, have I met your cat?" Mina asked.

"Nuh. Don't think so. We got her from the shelter and she was tentatively called 'Green' in reference to the green ID collar they put on her, but my pesky brother named her 'Gang'. Somehow, the name stuck before we twigged that it was 'Gangrene'. Silly, but it really doesn't make much difference, since she doesn't come to either name."

Mina smiled, and brought up the subject of the hot European guy on the flight. "So, what precisely did you do to make his flight so memorable? Are we talking 'mile high' stuff or what?" Refreshed after a good night's sleep in her own bed, Mina was the picture of loveliness, her shoulder length, dark-hair gleamed, and her tall, tanned body, oozed fitness and good health. Her dark eyes held Leah's gaze but a smile touched her generous mouth. "My lips are sealed."

It was Leah's standard answer; still, she did laugh at the suggestion. She wore her blond hair long, with a few streaked highlights and projected an equally fit and healthy appearance. Hers was an angular attractiveness that could not rival the classic beauty of her friend. Nevertheless, men found her striking, and on the job, she was hit on more frequently than Mina. They both wore black Versace jeans with designer tops, that complimented their trim figures. Both girls cut a very smart, casual profile, but somehow, Leah always seemed the more approachable.

Not so long back, they had answered an advertisement, had applied together and had been selected as flight attendants with Lufthansa. They had trained together in Europe and were inseparable ever since, usually flying in the same crew. The job wasn't quite as glamorous as they had first envisaged, but they certainly had no complaints. The work on the long-haul trips was repetitious and tiring, however, this was more than compensated by the travel they so much enjoyed. In fact, they had toured exotic places, seen much of Europe and indeed a lot of the world. They often joked that it was certainly much better than a real job.

"It is so good to be home," Leah said again, "we'll see if the girls want to go for a swim." She pulled out her cell phone. In reality, flying out of Europe had been perfect for Mina, and her horizons were broadening as a result. She was becoming a more robust and rounded person. Both girls' high school German was improving daily, but on the aircraft, they mostly spoke English anyway.

The screech of tyres made Mina turn her head sharply, cascading curls around her face. Her big eyes dilated.

"Tell me this isn't happening," she breathed, as she saw Ron Opus leaping out of the car and rushing towards them, yelling incoherently. Jesus!

The entire scenario seemed fully surreal. Ron had been a mistake, a bad one. She had heard of girls being attracted to 'bad boys', but this guy was a maniac. What a loser he had turned out to be. God! What had she ever seen in him? He harboured enough issues for a psychiatrist's convention and all his accusations were so juvenile. Mina was a naturally open and honest person, and yet he had always been so secretive and distant. She was tired of it all. Tired of his insecurities, tired of the abuse, tired of him, period. She was so totally over it; it wasn't true. "Why do I always end up with losers and liars," she thought aloud "What's wrong with me? Am I a 'moron magnet'?"

Then he was in front of her grabbing at her handbag. Leah tried to intervene and copped a hard slap across the face for her trouble. The table went over spilling coffee everywhere. The hand closed into a fist and it was coming right for Mina when a minor miracle occurred. At lightning speed, another hand intercepted the punch, twisted sharply and Ron slid along the sidewalk on his face, taking out the next table and two unoccupied chairs.

Bellowing like a bull, he regained his feet with a stupid look on his bleeding visage. He charged the agile stranger, who anticipated the move and easily avoided the attack, throwing out an arm to protect the girls and move them out of the way. "Come on, calm down; this isn't helping anybody. Don't be stupid." He tried desperately to reason with the enraged tough.

There was no place for reasoning with Ron Opus. Traces of madness showed in his eyes, and he attacked again, this time wielding a metal chair he had grabbed in his forward movement. Saliva and blood dribbled to his chin as he opened his mouth to curse. He would now pound this interfering bastard's head in, then deal with the girls. He moved forward, this time more calculating and more treacherous. Adam instinctively recognised the inherent danger in this situation and his eyes became pinpoints of focus.

Sun Tzu's, *'The Art of War'* suggests that if a man is your enemy, aim to kill—not to wound. Adam had always thought this was a bit excessive and over dramatic. He would never fully subscribe to this philosophy. However, now he found himself standing toe to toe with a man devoid of scruples, devoid of reason, devoid of compassion; a man he didn't even know, who nevertheless, wanted to kill him. When he eventually moved to disarm this enraged psychopath, it was straight from the manual, delivered at a speed that was difficult to follow. Side step, block, spear hand, block, front kick, punch, side kick, swivel turn, roundhouse kick. It was a combination he had practiced many, many times, but never to disarm a live opponent and the impact was devastating.

When Ron finally regained consciousness, lying in the gutter, the shaken girls and their rescuer were gone. Carlo, the chubby little Italian proprietor was still busy picking up his broken crockery, mopping up spilled coffee and righting his overturned furniture. His wife had already called an ambulance.

## Dark Green Mustang

The girls proved they were fairly resilient and determined to enjoy their break, because not much later that morning, they were driving undeterred in Leah's elder brothers immaculately restored, dark green Mustang. Her brother Steve was away overseas with the U.S. Air Force, and allowed her to drive his car when she was home. Their school friend Caitlin, had joined them as they toured through Orange County towards North Long Beach, chatting happily.

"Hey! 'Spray on Pants', I love this song," Leah said, as she turned up the car stereo, until the heavy bass lines rattled the windows. "My young brother plays a Fender P-bass and I love the bass riff in that introduction bit." She sang along, *"They…try to get up to dance, but they're all wearing spray on pants…"* She winced as the singing pained her sore cheek.

"Oh my God! He was incredible!" Mina exclaimed to her friends for the third time; this time actually running on the spot, while sitting in the leather passenger side, bucket seat. Kicking her feet up and down certainly emphasised the point and seemed to get rid of some adrenalin. "He just came out of nowhere and the fight…OMG! He was so fast."

"He was amazing," Leah agreed, "I never saw anything like that before in my life. Definitely way more Chuck Norris than Justin Bieber."

"But he was so kind and gentle, checking your poor cheek and he calmed us down and got us out of there," Mina said dreamily.

"But remember one small detail, girlfriend, he left no forwarding address," Leah stated, "probably married with about ten kids…but then he did say his name was Adam."

"Yes, Adam! The original man," Mina said in a throaty voice.

"Maybe, he is looking for an Eve," Leah breathed, ever the matchmaker, but somehow, sounding more like a midnight to dawn D.J. making a breathy announcement.

"He certainly beat off the snake," Mina added, staying with the silly theme.

"After he hit me, the moronic, low-life creep!"

Mina winced, still visibly shaken, "Oh my God, don't remind me. You poor thing, does it still hurt?"

"Yeeees! Hello! My bottom molars have just been bent out of shape by a woman beating weirdo and you ask if it hurts?"

"You girls are slipping," Caitlin observed, "You mean to say, you didn't even give him your phone number?"

"It happened so quickly. I was too shocked to even thank Adam properly," Mina admitted.

"Well, if you like, we could just use up the rest of our break driving up and down all the streets calling out…Hey Adam!" Leah teased, getting Mina's mind back to Earth and causing Caitlin to chuckle.

## Adam's Apartment

Adam spent the rest of the day back in his apartment, working on an assignment. He tapped furiously at the computer keyboard and consulted a myriad of books spread out around his work area. He certainly took his studies seriously, and did each assignment to the best of his ability. For just one moment, he stopped work and re-lived the events of the morning. "Stupid!" He whispered aloud shaking his head from side to side.

Stupid—that the assailant would attack women in broad daylight.

Stupid—that someone actually let this creep off his chain.

Stupid—that he wasn't able to reason with him.

Stupid—that the creep had attacked using a chair as a weapon.

Stupid—that Adam couldn't render him immobile without that last series of damaging kicks. The whole thing was so damn stupid!

Stupid—that Adam hadn't got the scared, dark-haired girl's phone number.

## Dinner at Lo Stivale

That evening, Mina and Leah along with Caitlin, met up with some old school friends at a little Italian restaurant, that had long been a favourite for great food, at a reasonable cost. It was appropriately named 'Lo Stivale' the Italian words for, *'The Boot'*. Describing the well-known boot shape of the Italian peninsular.

The globetrotting girls were the centre of attention as their friends sought to know every detail of their little jaunts around the world. The designer clothes picked up in the country of origin or duty free, for a fraction the cost in America, made the other girls just a tad envious. Both Mina and Leah were not the sort of girls who caused jealousy or resentment over trifles, and their friends were actually very proud to see them living the dream. Of course, the presents of duty-free perfume samples and airline give away stuff, were appreciated too. But their friends genuinely wished Mina and Leah well, and believed these two absolutely deserved everything they had achieved. There was a lot of 'girl talk' and the meeting with Adam was discussed and dissected in the finest detail. Most agreed with Caitlin, that they should have exchanged phone numbers, no matter how intense the situation.

"Oh God, I just love Boy meets Girl stories," one of the girls exclaimed emotionally, with a quiet, alcohol-induced sob in her voice, "Like Rhett and Scarlett in Gone with the Wind."

It must be a chick flick thing as others chimed in around the group.

"Like Bonnie and Clyde."

"Richard Gere and Pretty Woman."

"Heathcliff and Catherine in Wuthering Heights."

"Cinderella and the handsome Prince."

"Arthur Dent and Fenchurch in The Hitchhikers' Guide."

"Scully and the big blue chick in Avatar."

"Roy Rogers and Trigger."

"What…?"

"Are there ever any hot prospects among your passengers?" One of the girls asked cheekily, while putting down her wine glass. Leah responded negatively about the wine list grouch, and Mina gave a hilarious outline of the European guy whose life had been immeasurably enhanced by meeting Leah on the flight into LA. Their friends adored these stories and frequently interrupted with hilarity and some banality.

"Last week, I actually had a lady tell me that her new boyfriend was meeting her, so could I reallocate her away from the window seat to the aisle, so her hair wouldn't get messed up," Mina shared. "She was so sweet and so serious. Weird, some passengers haven't flown before and simply have no idea."

"A lady on one flight wanted to know how it was possible that her flight from Munich left at 8:20 a.m. and got into Paris at 8:33 a.m. I tried to explain that Munich was in a different time zone, two hours ahead of Paris, but she couldn't grasp the concept of time zones at all. Finally, I told her that the plane went really fast, and she seemed happy with that!" Leah added.

"Actually, on this trip to LAX," Mina shared, "I had a lovely lady who was a bit overweight. Who said she was really upset that the man had written FAT on her luggage slip. She thought it was to identify her when she picked up her luggage from the carousel. I checked it out and nearly burst out laughing. She was through connected to Fresno and the city code for Fresno is FAT (Fresno Air Terminal). I had to explain that it wasn't derogatory; the airline was just putting the standard destination tag on her luggage."

"What about that weird guy in Frankfurt," Leah exclaimed, "He wasn't even on our flight; he grabbed us at the airport, complaining because the desk had said he needed a visa to fly to China. We confirmed that, yes, he would indeed need a visa. Well, he didn't like Visa and thought they'd accept his MasterCard." Mina and Leah both cracked up at the memory. "I don't know what the desk said to him," Mina laughed.

"There was an interesting guy out of Paris," Leah reminisced, "He looked great and gave me a wink…but he was wearing Crocs and that totally didn't do it for me."

"What's wrong with Crocs?" someone asked.

"Hello! We saw 'The Dictator' as an in-flight movie and I can't help but recall the line, 'Crocs are the universal symbol of a man who has given up hope.' Come on, you guys, I can forgive anything, but not Crocs. I believe Crocs with socks could be effectively used for birth control." The wine kept flowing.

"Yeah, I agree," Mina laughed, "printing nutritional data on a bag of Twisties is pretty much like putting 'Dating Tips' on the box the Crocs come in."

Smiles all around, as more drinks arrived. What had started out as a quiet dinner was now threatening to advance into a full-blown party, until Caitlin reminded everybody that it was Sunday night, and although 'some people', were ladies of leisure, most had to show up bright eyed and bushy tailed at the 'Salt Mines' in the morning. "Maybe so," Leah slurred, "but I bet the Okie milk maid will be up at dawn, to milk the cows and feed the hogs."

"Them's fighting words, Yankee," Mina said. "Prepare for a duel. Milk stools at ten paces."

Amid some laughter, the group reluctantly broke up.

# Chapter 2
# A Busy Week

**Monday**
**Police Headquarters**

"Well, Mills, what have you got to say for yourself?" Lieutenant Mackenzie bellowed on Monday morning, at 9:00 a.m. sharp. "Brawling, like a common hoodlum."

"It wasn't like that, sir," Adam tried to explain. He had been summoned to the headquarters of the Los Angeles Police Department situated, in the Parker Centre, located in Downtown LA. Adam attempted to relay the way the altercation had unfolded. Mack glared at him from under brows, bushier than a muskrat. "Well, one Ronald Opus has facial lacerations, some concussion, severe bruising and three fractured ribs," Mackenzie roared, "Suppose you tell me how it was." Mackenzie softened a little, remembering that Adam was the son of a colleague and he was a good recruit who achieved high grades.

Nevertheless, after inviting his input, the bulldozing Mackenzie didn't give Adam any opportunity to get in a word of explanation. "I was called in yesterday. Opus had a doctor's report; he is suing the Department and he provided a circus for the media. You, my lad, are suspended until further investigation." He scratched his sizable ear. "Now, I want a full report on what happened, including everything you know about the witnesses. Look son, you'll be a good detective and you have a great future, but one slip up like this and the public are all over us. You can write your report then go home and stay quiet. You got that!"

He swivelled around for no apparent reason, "Arrange it with Briggs, and then go home." It was a sign of dismissal. Adam was stunned, that so much was being made of the stupid incident. For goodness's sake, he had only tried to help. What was going on here? Regardless of everything, wasn't he innocent until proven guilty?

It took nearly two and a half hours before Sergeant Briggs was satisfied that the statement was complete with nothing left out. Adam then spent more time going through the report with him, confirming each bit verbally. Briggs checked out details over and over, made notes, asked questions, until Adam's head began to swim. Finally, he signed the report and got up to leave, still feeling a bit confused.

He'd been called in to explain to the Lieutenant but hadn't really got a word in. Suspended, Jesus! What had he done to deserve that? Mackenzie was a salty character, but probably his bark was worse than his bite. As Adam walked down the hallway, Mack turned to his sergeant and grimaced. "Christ knows what will be on TV by tonight." He was shaking his head with a faraway look in his eyes.

Adam wondered how his dad would take this. He left the building.

## Chief Medical Examiner

As he passed a bakery on the busy street, that wonderful enticing aroma of hot bread drifted tantalisingly from the premises, and Adam realised it was nearly lunchtime. Commercially induced hunger…He chose a salad sandwich on fresh rye and a mineral water, then walked the two blocks to the forensic science building just down the street.

The building was huge and ancient, its rooms had high ceilings and magnificent old windows that looked out on absolutely nothing worth seeing. Pretty much, a brick wall and the chimney stack of the heating plant next door. The sills had been overpainted multiple times but fitted in to the overall décor, if you liked that 'old world' look. The polished brass plate on the dark timber door he approached, read, 'Dr Don Harper Mills—Senior Medical Examiner.' Inside the room, Dr Mills was on the telephone, listening intently. He was a family man and several photos held pride of place on his desk.

Dr Mills was a remarkable judge of character and divided people into four categories; peacocks, hawks, doves and owls. No! Actually, five if you included 'vultures', which was reserved for the very worst of the worst. Mills was a self-confessed owl. These days he didn't wear the white lab coats, he now had an administrative role, that replaced that of the former Coroner. As such, he only became involved in the actual medical examination of a body in a training and supervisory role and he did this so well. His department was highly respected and he was seen as a thorough professional.

Many difficult cases had been solved by his brilliant forensic detection and autopsy work and with an 'open door' policy, all his staff knew they could call on him at any time for assistance. He also had a law degree and was completely familiar with the legal implications of homicide, which made him invaluable in this position. He certainly gave good service to the county despite his little idiosyncrasies. No one else would dare come to work in brown brogues, corduroy trousers and Tweed jackets with those suede elbow patches, but on Dr Mills, this looked right and he actually blended well with the spacious, high ceilinged office, built in the 1950s.

Dr Mills was the President of the *American Association of Forensic Scientists* and their monthly Journals littered his desk. Competing for space was a photo of a pleasant matronly woman and next to it an attractive blonde, female student, in a University of Southern California sweater. Pride of place, however, was held by a picture of his son, photographed in a snow-white dobok at the Olympic Games, looking so much younger than the worried young man currently knocking on his door. Adam entered his father's office at his call. The doctor hung up the phone with a concerned look and moved to switch on the TV set at the end of his generous room.

As if it had been cued, the story came on, *'Olympic medal winner involved in downtown brawl,'* read the newsreader. The doctor motioned for his son to sit and watch. What followed was Ron Opus' accusations, reported with pure media sensationalism but very little substance and almost totally devoid of fact. Adam was forced to endure it all the way through, under the withering gaze of his sire. Carlo and Maria, the Italians who owned the sidewalk café had seen nothing, and no one had come forward to explain what had happened. Jesus, were they all blind? Adam began to feel insecure and very alone.

"Dad, it just wasn't like that…you know I always try hard to do the right thing. I only wanted to help. No; not even that. What I did was instantaneous, an automatic reaction to combat all that is wrong in this city…in this World. It's ironic, I had just finished telling my students that fighting is always the last resort and a moment later was dragged into all this mess. This guy was a jerk. He was loaded and he was trying to assault two girls." The doctor nodded for Adam to continue.

"Look Dad, you know I have despised bullying all my life, having seen my share in grade school. I see it with my class. They come to the club to learn martial arts believing it will combat their problems, which nearly always involve some form of bullying or intimidation. I believe it's my job to firstly teach them that's not the purpose of Tae Kwon Do. It thrills my heart and soul when they finally understand that we learn to fight so that we don't have to fight."

"It's a joy for me when they realise that the respect and the self-esteem is what matters; not the colour of someone's belt or the colour of their skin or how they part their hair…Now, for God's sake the media is saying I beat up some guy as if he was a saint and I was some creep who did it for no reason. It just wasn't like that…" He trailed off, but his stare softened somewhat as he thought of the pretty girl and her friend. Despite the seriousness of his predicament, a wry smile touched his lips thinking about the shock he had given to the swaggering, overconfident thug who attacked them. A sound ass-whipping was the last thing he had expected.

"Dad, I did what I had to do. There wasn't time to think, I just reacted. I believe I did the right thing, and I guess in a similar predicament, I would do the same thing again." The senior Mills slowly nodded his understanding. The phone on the desk made noise; Dr Mills slammed the receiver against the side of his head, appearing to be at risk of knocking himself out. He listened intently for a minute.

"Good God," he groaned. "Just what we didn't need; thank-you for letting me know, Kelvin. I'll be right down."

He gently replaced the receiver letting it slip through his fingers as if compensating for the previous rough treatment.

"Sorry Adam, duty calls and this is important, can you wait ten minutes. I'll show you where to get coffee. We'll finish our talk," he said mechanically. "The darnedest case I ever heard of…" he muttered as he squeezed his son's shoulder. It was a gesture of silent support.

**Examination Room**

"This body just came in and it looks a bit weird," announced the young Medical Examiner importantly. "The cops say the DA is taking a personal interest in this one, Chief."

"Peacock," breathed Mills to himself, "Yes…yes…Kelvin, you told me that, on the phone." A bit of impatience was showing through.

"He was killed by a shotgun blast at close range and fell from the top of a ten-story building." The young doctor pulled back the sheet. The shotgun had done terrible damage to the man's face, but Mills' experienced eyes looked beyond that in an instant.

"Something is a bit screwy here all right," the senior Doctor said, "No compound fractures, this body has not fallen from ten stories. Check it out, will you?"

"Warren is still out there, Chief, so he hasn't reported in yet. We don't have the pictures of where the body was found, so everything now is just preliminary, but I thought you'd want to know."

"OK thanks. Tell me when his report is in."

"It will be interesting reading," predicted the young examiner.

"Who was he?"

"No identification yet Chief, and it appears that he had his hands up to his face when he was shot. His fingers are shredded from the blast of pellets, so I don't think we'll get any decent fingerprints." Mills took a look and winced.

"Try anyway. Check him out, just don't get too fancy," warned Dr Mills. "Remember; cause, time, and manner of death." He looked at the body. "Try the usual dental records and check for drugs too, will you?"

"Sure, Chief."

Mills turned to leave; he was anxious to get back to Adam. "Is that a tattoo on his forehead?"

"It's a number '6' written in marker pen Chief. Looks like he had '666' written across his forehead, until some was removed by the shotgun blast."

Mills studied it carefully. "Mark of the Beast," he said under his breath. "Jesus!"

## Shopping Mall

The girls were enjoying healthy chicken kebabs and fruit smoothies. They were settled in the mall, with Leah's younger brother Brad tagging along. "Crazy! We spend all our time in Europe and come home to shop," Mina said.

"It's a fun place to hang out," Leah said, "I just love the top I found." Mina remained silent and Leah knew she was still a little shaken from the previous morning. "Hey Brad, do that French joke," she begged. Leah's younger brother had a day off school and used it as an excuse to join them.

"You do it on a bass guitar, you can't just tell it."

"Come on please try, Mina needs cheering up." Brad would do anything for this babe. God she was HOT.

"OK. I'll try…but you have to picture a bass guitar and imagine the sound of a slide down the strings and back up again. Here goes; This American dude was in a Paris restaurant see, and he didn't know what to order so he looked around and saw this Frenchman eating something that smelled good, but didn't belong to any recognisable food group. He saw this guy dig his fork in…Bling." Brad plucked an imaginary bass string. "He put it on his tongue…Blonk," (another string) "and it went…Blooooong!"

Brad was a real showman and gave a good vocal rendition of a bass string, descending slide. "So, when the waiter came over, he pointed to what the French guy was eating. 'Oui. Oui Monsieur.' When his food finally arrived, he wasn't too sure about it so he took another peek at the Frenchman. He dug his fork into another one…Bling. He put it in his tongue…Blonk; and it went…Blooooong! So, this dude gave it a try. He dug his fork into one…Bling. He put it on his tongue…Blonk; and it went: Blooooong…Buuuuurp!"

They howled with laughter, more at the delivery than at the joke. People at nearby tables had seen Brad's performance and were all smiling. Brad was quite good looking, with crazy, wild blonde hair and a naturally funny demeanour. He had actually begun to manifest the attributes of a rock star. Walk the walk, so to speak; fake it 'til you make it. He was likely destined for success and stardom and in his own mind this was never in doubt. A few teenage girls at a nearby table kept sneaking looks and giggling. They apparently thought he was pretty cool, right about now.

**Talk with Adam**

Mills apologised to his son, although he had not been away as long as he had anticipated. Adam felt he had covered all there was to say and now remained silent.

"What does Mack say?" The older Mills asked.

"Well, I'm stood down pending investigation. I'll still do Uni."

"What are they investigating, precisely?"

"The jerk has claimed 'Police Brutality', but honestly it wasn't like that."

"How did he know you were a Police Detective?"

"I don't know, Dad. I guess he saw me come out of the Police Youth Club and made inquiries."

"You should have got the girls' contact details," Dr Mills stated, "They could have cleared you."

"Yeah, I wish I had, but they were pretty shaken up. I just got them out of there…to their car. Dad, this guy was a raging bull; he was hopped up on something. He was really crazy and dangerous! He wanted to beat them up or…or…maybe even kill them."

"Think hard Adam and write down everything you know about the girls…and get it to Mack. He'll find them."

"I've already done that, Dad," Adam was waving his copy of the report he had so laboriously compiled with Briggs.

"What did Mack say?"

"I gave it to Mack's assistant. He said, 'White Caucasian females, early-twenties, one blonde, one brunette, that narrows it down to a few million,'" said Adam, taking off the gruff voice of Briggs.

"Alright, go home now and take it easy, Adam. Drop in tonight for dinner, I'll call your mother now, she'll be frantic if she caught the broadcast."

"OK, Dad."

"Don't worry, we'll sort this out. See you tonight, champ."

## Mack Mackenzie

Mackenzie suffered from sleep apnoea and as a result, didn't achieve restful slumber and seldom awoke refreshed. After a coffee fuelled rush to the office each morning and squirming in his chair all day, his suit was so rumpled, it could have doubled as pyjamas. He actually took on the appearance of an unmade bed. His bloated jowls and awkward body looked like they had come from the same designer who did Alfred Hitchcock's.

Mack was a drinker and had 'liver spots' on the back of his hands indicating that his liver probably looked something like a Navajo blanket, caused by the sustained abuse he had inflicted on it over a long tenure. From his blotchy skin and outward appearance, he could almost be described as a heart attack going somewhere to happen.

He spent a lot of time chasing his own tail and had become a fairly unproductive, habitual workaholic. This was initially down to his ex-wife, from around three years in the past. Olivia Mackenzie had an acid tongue and was the sort of woman you didn't go home to, until you had exhausted every other option. She had finally left him a few years back, and after he recovered from the instantaneous relief, it never occurred to him at any stage since, to upgrade his wardrobe, employ a decent ironing service or even a hair stylist for his thinning patch.

He was a bachelor and certainly looked it. His evening meal usually consisted of a counter meal washed down by a few beers from his local tavern or a six-pack from Wal-Mart and this lifestyle had certainly promoted the unhealthy pallor he wore to the office. At times, after a bit of a session, he was left in dire need of a makeover and a proper shave and actually, some mouthwash would not have gone astray.

There were mornings when Mack could be forgiven for thinking a small furry animal had camped in his mouth overnight and even his tongue might have benefited from a quick shave as well.

Wal-Mart was Mack's store of choice and it was where he bought his pastries, liquor supply and country music CD's. Mills would class him as a hawk because of his adrenalin fuelled, driving nature, but sometimes he thought he detected just a touch of vulture there as well. On the job, Mack ran by scent not by sight, something like a bloodhound. He really lacked the finesse to progress above the Lieutenant rank but manpower was short, and as long as results were achieved, no one was about to criticise or find too much fault.

Unfortunately, the means, employed were not really scrutinised or even considered all that important. Not that Mack was stupid, he seemed to get the job done, but then he could have got the job done, handling 'fruit and veg' at Woolworths. Mack was part of a wave of dinosaur police officers that the Department would soon be required to drag, kicking and screaming into a new century and indications were that the inertia might be pretty substantial. The police department had a pyramidal hierarchy structure, with leadership filtering down from the top. The more cynical among the street smart, rank and file, often quoted that a dead fish always rots from the head and their observations appeared to show some merit.

Over the years, Mackenzie had enjoyed some modicum of success but failures had come along as well and he was generally considered 'adequate'. Solving a difficult crime was a fairly nebulous thing at the best of times; nobody was about to do a rewind and show how a better result might have been achieved by utilising different tactics. The Police schedule was always a busy one and at this stage there were still no 'management experts' at Parker Centre.

## Leah's Place

Mina's mother had gone out to take her sister Margaret, to the hospital where she was scheduled to have an operation to remove cataracts. Mina had lost her father in an accident on their farm in Oklahoma, when she was thirteen, but fortunately he had left the family well provided for and after moving to LA, Mina and her mother had initially lived with Aunty Margaret before getting their own place. Mina had two elder brothers who still ran the farm quite successfully, and were able to contribute to their mother's welfare when required. Mrs Jenkins had never remarried and was now a totally independent woman, and some of this had certainly been an influence on her daughter.

It had been a relaxing day for the girls. After returning from the mall, Mina hung out at Leah's place and ended up staying for a slap-up dinner thrown together by Leah and Brad. They ate in front of TV and talked quietly. Brad was doing the set lists and making final arrangements for the debut of his band *'Moment of Truth'* at a fairly sizeable club and badly wanted the girls to be there for moral support. "Yes, why not," Mina said, "we'll try hard to be there. It sounds like fun." Soon after, she decided that she had better be going home. She wanted to be there when her mother returned.

"Sleep in tomorrow morning," Leah said, "don't dare ring before 10:00 a.m. but we'll have lunch. Caitlin might be free too. OK?"

"Yes, OK!"

# Tuesday
## Lieutenant's Office

"Find the girls," roared Mackenzie to a couple of his officers who had just watched the media circus on TV. Adam had fronted for work as usual and was seated in the briefing room. He stood up, "No, not you, Mills, the others can handle it. Look son, your father called me. I believe you were trying to help out but we are being crucified right now. There's nothing on the surveillance cameras. The Italians saw nothing; no witnesses have come forward and the damned media is pushing the police brutality thing."

There was no doubt, Mackenzie had an 'us' and 'them' relationship with the general public, and certainly with the media. "Opus is no choir boy, let me tell you," he stated banally, "Two drug busts, half a dozen cases of assault and battery and unlawfully dealing with a minor; a traffic record as long as your arm. That's what we know about. Maybe you did the city a favour, but you understand, we have to weather this storm…" The telephone interrupted him as he drew a breath to continue. "Yes, what is it?"

## Chief Medical Examiner's Office

"Chief, the cops are calling this a suicide," Kelvin said slowly, with some surprise as he entered Mills' office, still reading the pages of a thin police report.

"When did the police report come in?" Mills asked.

"I just came back from the building site with Warren and it was here," Kelvin said.

Mills snorted, "Hmmm."

"Chief, it's not mentioned in the report about the workers renovating the building." Kelvin said. "They erected a safety net around the outside of the building on the eighth-floor level; that's where Warren and the cops recovered the body. It would have prevented the death if it was a suicide jump."

"Really!" Mills scanned the report carefully.

"So, the deceased jumped off a building, not realising there was a safety net below him?" Mills questioned. "He didn't even bother to look down?"

"That's what they must figure, Chief."

"But the cause of death was a shotgun blast?"

"That's correct, Chief."

"Jesus, are we on Candid Camera or something? We'd better take another look. This one could get pretty ugly."

Dr Mills was an outstanding Chief Medical Examiner, but he needed all the facts. So far, this case made no sense at all. As for the deceased, it again proved that regardless of the circumstances, if your time is up, you can't out-bargain the Angel of Death. Mills blinked twice as he recalled the hundreds of bodies that passed through his department and wondered if there was a precedent for this case. With Kelvin, he took the stairs to the morgue area and set up the body for examination.

"I don't know why Mack would call it a suicide," Mills said slowly, "...look there, you can see where the deceased sustained severe injuries, but it appears that was some time prior to his death. Some ribs are 'green stick' broken here and the colouration would suggest earlier bruising. Wouldn't it be reasonable to assume he was tortured and then shot and thrown off the building?"

"I asked the same thing when the body came in, Chief," Kelvin stated, as if it would score him brownie points, "it seems the cops found his shoes and jacket, on the top of the building, with no traces of blood."

Mills nodded, "And that makes it a suicide?"

"Not really!" Warren chimed in. He was working at his desk nearby, "I talked to a building worker at the site, who recalled seeing him standing there on the roof by himself, Chief," short pause while Mills nodded. "The guy then moved around to work on the other side of the building and didn't give him another thought."

"He didn't consider anything was suspicious? He didn't hear a shot or see anything more of him?"

"It seems the building workers were making a lot of noise with jackhammers. Maybe the police think the deceased jumped and was then shot," Kelvin added.

"Who the hell shoots someone in the act of committing suicide? First of all, it's kind of unnecessary and secondly, I like to think suicide should be, well, sort of…private!"

Mills looked further at the body pondering if maybe it was easier for the cops to sweep this one under the carpet by calling it suicide. Kelvin, adjusted his black framed glasses, puffed out his chicken chest and went on, "…If the deceased jumped from the roof above the tenth floor, it would have been a certain suicide attempt. It could have been successful, except for the net. As you say, it seems reasonable to assume that he would have looked down before he jumped, and therefore, he must have noticed the net below."

"One would think so!" Mills added, "It's only hypothetical anyway, because the shotgun blast was the cause of death, so either way it's a homicide!" Mills paused, rubbing his forehead, considering the implications…"Mack will be on this one for a while," he predicted, shaking his head. Kelvin and Warren both had the good sense to leave it alone. With nothing in the tank, they just smiled knowingly. After a thorough examination and copious notes, Dr Mills returned to his office and phoned Mackenzie.

## Lieutenant Mackenzie's Office

"What the hell are you telling me, Don?" he exclaimed. Immediately, Mack yelled for a detective, "What's this I'm hearing about a safety net around the building?"

"Yes sir, there are workers renovating some of the building's cladding." the detective said, "They have a safety net erected around the outside of the building on the eighth-floor level; that's where we recovered the body. It should have prevented the death of the deceased, if he jumped."

"Good God!" mouthed the Lieutenant almost silently, slowly building in volume, "There's nothing about that in the report," he was tapping the document, "and that's not a good thing to leave out, sonny! When will you people start making accurate reports? You screw up like this again and your ass is grass; you understand?"

Firmly stuck in the 70s. No one actually said that stuff anymore but regardless of the vocabulary, the scorn in his voice could have been gainfully used to strip varnish from the archaic windowsills of the old Police building.

Mack's sarcastic outbursts no longer served to intimidate his staff detectives, like they once did, but they certainly didn't motivate or endear them either. He hesitated a moment to regain control, then quieter, "Bring me the pictures, will you? We all look like morons when stuff like this happens. Son of a bitch!"

"It was all the way around the building," the detective explained, needlessly pointing to the photograph of the body, "a suicide wouldn't have been successful with the net in place."

Mack's attention was returned to the phone he had temporarily forgotten. "You're right Don; we'll get the pictures over to you in a minute. Anything else for us?"

"The head wounds came from square-on at fairly close range, 2 or 3 metres," Dr Mills stated. "The penetration of the shotgun pellets, leads us to believe that the trajectory was square-on to the body, or in other words, most likely close to horizontal. For example, he couldn't have been shot from the ground. Mack, I must say I don't much like…"

"Right Don; I'm on it." Mackenzie cut him off abruptly, hanging up the phone.

The Lieutenant delivered a broadside to his available detectives bringing them up to speed with developments. "Get in there and talk to everyone in the building…Concentrate above the net, particularly on the eighth, ninth and tenth floor. Move!"

## Find the Girls

Adam left the precinct. He suddenly realised, he had nowhere to go and nothing to do. His life was on hold. He walked aimlessly around the city, occasionally looking in a shop window but mainly just walking, walking, walking. *You're a detective*, he thought, *come on brain…they were attractive, well-dressed, modern girls. It happened on the weekend. How would you go about finding them? They drove a distinctive restored Mustang, they might be regular customers at the Café, but the Italians claimed they didn't know them. There could be a credit card receipt or the altercation might have been captured on a security camera. Mack would be checking that out.*

Adam needed to be doing something, but what could he do? The girls could work in fashion, but then they could be secretaries or schoolteachers or personal trainers. Perhaps they were just visiting the city and actually hailed from far out in the northern suburbs barbeque belt but then they could be tourists from Maine. They might work in hospitality or…Who was he kidding, they could be plumbers or advertising execs or they might have just joined the Army. He didn't know where to start.

Adam was no geek, but right through school, he'd never been really hip or cool, spending most of his time training or studying, working towards his future. Even now he was more interested in his studies, martial arts and its peaceful philosophy than in partying and raging. He had to admit it, he had never really had much success at finding girls.

## Opening Night

"Leah! I have to go with my mum to visit my aunt in hospital, but I'll be back by 7:30 or 8:00 p.m." Mina said into her chic, Parisian cell phone.

"Brad is on at 8:30 p.m. so that should be perfect," Leah responded happily.

The girls actually met up just after 7:30 p.m. "Is your aunt, OK?" Leah asked.

"Yes, she's fine, just had dual cataract surgery, and needs a night in hospital, for supervised recovery. It was all very dramatic."

"I only met her once," Leah said, "she is a dear but she sure likes to know what's going on, all the questions, Jesus!"

"…and she just won't listen. She thinks I fly airliners," Mina said sighing, pretty well summing up the situation with Aunt Margaret. Leah still had her older brother's Mustang, and they drove to the club where Brad was debuting with his band.

"Really, 'Moment of Truth' totally rock, and Brad is actually quite talented," Leah exclaimed, more in surprise than in support it seemed. He had not long ago been the noisy, pesky little brother and old habits die hard, even though she still fondly recalled doing 'life guard' duty on his baths, when he was just a toddler.

They reached the entrance and noted the huge 'MoT' logo that was stylised as a coloured tattoo across the subdued image of a woman's breast. Well, you couldn't miss it…and the central 'O' was imaginative. Quite a nice piece of artwork, actually. Way cool for the fans at least. 'Moment of Truth' banners were on display everywhere, featuring the same tattooed artwork. "He designed the posters, worked out all the stage show and lighting and everything. He can really sing and plays a pretty mean bass. Some friends have seen his rehearsals and say his band is destined for stardom."

The girls bought drinks, and sat at a table overlooking the stage as patrons filed into the club. Mina noticed that just a moment later, Leah was effectively scoping the scene, seeking out the available talent. 'Spot the Spunk' it's called. *She just can't help herself*, thought Mina, never suspecting that Leah was actually searching with Mina in mind. Leah must have realised that her friend's taste in guys was vastly different to her own but apparently, it never occurred to her, how unlikely it would be for Mina to discover the man of her dreams at this rowdy suburban club. Nevertheless, in her mind, the talent search was at least partially for Mina. That's what friends are for.

Despite the financial crisis, or perhaps because of it, the club was noisy and well patronised for a Tuesday night and the crowd seemed jovial and happy with life in general. Maybe they just needed a quiet drink and a bit of entertainment to escape life for a while. Mina and Leah were sipping their drinks, engrossed in the different atmosphere and anticipating the show. Suddenly all the lights in the packed room flickered and went out causing some mild concern and a few gasps.

Apart from a few exit signs, the place was pitch black and a bit scary. Then the sirens started. Rising and falling. Loud! Very loud! They were reminiscent of British World War II air raid sirens, piercing and persistent. Suddenly, they heard the sounds of approaching aircraft, becoming louder and louder. On came the searchlights, combing the black ceiling trying to pinpoint the marauding enemy bombers. It was so real most people had trouble believing the deep-throated sounds came from the giant PA speakers and horn loaded 'W' Bins.

Then the ack-ack guns opened up and the thunderous noise in the darkness was mind numbing. A moment later, bombs were falling around them; the only light on stage, came from the pinpoint spots searching the 'skies'. Meanwhile, 'explosions' shook the room and took the crowd into another realm. It was like a London air raid during the 'Blitz'. The noise was deafening and you could cut the atmosphere with a knife. The girls could smell smoke and saw it curling and wafting in the path of the searchlights. Along with most of the audience, they visualised the city in rubble.

The bombers droned on and as the noise began to subside, out of the darkness and cacophony of sound, penetrated a powerful, clean, bass guitar riff. With pinpoint accuracy all the spotlights, cued to perfection, converged together, illuminating the ceiling and then as one, dropped to the smoky stage. The stage lit up as the rest of the band came in on the bass riff, and Brad, looking very cocky, wild hair shining, stepped up to the microphone and opened his mouth to sing, *"He...just threw out all of his old clothes..."*

Mina was blown away; she had never been to a rock concert or seen an opening number like this, and Brad kicked serious butt. No one would forget this performance for a while. He was really good and this was rock star stuff. Although it was incredibly loud, Mina was really enjoying it all. Despite it being her brother, Leah was carried away by the song.

"I love this bit," she shouted and sang along, *"The drinks are cheap, and vinyl's cool, what do you think of my new shoes..."* The crowd loved it too and many people rose up to dance. *"They...try to get up to dance, but they're all wearing spray on pants..."* Leah didn't know any more words, but Brad sang on, *"They, go to all the same clubs, where everyone takes all the same drugs and talks about how they're so fucked up..."*[2]

## Lectures

This evening, Adam found it hard to concentrate on the psychology lecture, which was part of his study curriculum at California State University. Most times, he loved psychology, getting inside the criminal mind and all that stuff. He enjoyed the logical progression of solving a case by classic detection methods, sort of like doing a giant jigsaw puzzle, adding pieces until a lucid picture formed. Even the boring Law precedents didn't trouble him too much. He was in fact, well suited to his job with an investigative mind, a disciplined demeanour and a steady temperament.

Adam also had a deep compassion for people and an acute sense of justice, but right now, his headspace was totally occupied with a million other thoughts. His future had looked so rosy and now he was an outcast, a maverick bull, separated from the herd, alienated over this stupid incident. He just couldn't accept any wrongdoing on his part. He was the same person for goodness's sake. Couldn't they see that? What would have happened if he had not stepped in? Did they think of that? Two guiltless girls would have been badly assaulted, perhaps scarred for life, maybe even killed. This was madness.

## Medical Examiner's Report

"What do we have now?" Dr Mills asked his subordinate.

"He was a user, Chief…mainly coke. As you pointed out, he was injured before he was killed. His clothes are sharp but cheap. Nothing in his pockets, no wallet or credit cards. No ID. No mobile phone or car keys, no piercings or tattoos. No identifying marks; hopeless, smudgy, partial fingerprints and no trace of any dental records."

Mills had a problem and thought about it for a bit. "Do you think he could have been tortured and then pushed?" Mills was fully aware that Kelvin could not possibly know this from the evidence before him. He was just flying a kite.

"Quite possibly, Chief, but we know drugs were involved so it could have been a 'Thrill Kill' or something like that. I mean, shooting someone in the act of suicide is pretty 'way out'."

"You can say that again!"

"If a drug ring was involved, maybe he was beaten up, pushed off the top of the building and then shot as an example…sending a clear message to others in the organization," Kelvin suggested thoughtfully.

"That would likely keep them in line!" Mills replied slowly with some cynicism.

"I've checked and checked…He's definitely not among the current list of missing persons we have, so he may be a loner and more than likely, doesn't come from a conventional family situation."

"Thanks for that, Kelvin. You must be tired; you go home now." Kelvin gathered his things. "Oh! Before you go, the clothing and stuff that came with the body?"

"Right over there, Chief."

"Is that all of it?"

"As far as I know Chief, that's all that came in."

"OK. You go; I'll stay and have another look."

Dr Mills pulled on a white gown and gloves and systematically checked every inch of the body, muttering medical terms to himself as he went. He checked several things against Kelvin's work but could find no real discrepancies. He made a few notes then looked closely at the '666'. It was as Kelvin had stated, marker pen. No pen had been found at the scene or in the pockets, so he must have written it on his forehead beforehand. Not the sort of thing you'd usually wear down the street. It was possible that this could indicate something weird, like some sort of satanic, sacrifice ritual.

He proceeded to give the victim's clothing a cursory look. Nothing there, but as he folded the trousers to replace them, he noted a slight bulge in the fold. He lifted the garment and again searched the pocket. There appeared to be nothing in it, until his probing fingers located a small thin piece of yellow paper, somehow caught in the top of the pocket cavity. It appeared to be a self-adhesive 'post-it note', stuck to the upper pocket wall. The Police had likely checked all the pockets and missed it. The fancy cut of the sharp clothing made it possible to insert a hand and entirely miss the small sheet lodged there. Mills unfolded it and gasped. "My God!" he said aloud.

"Mack, it's Don." Mack was still in his office, "I located something in the John Doe's pocket."

"What…what have you got, Don?"

"Well, it's a scrappy note, I guess you could call it a suicide note of sorts, but there's no name and it is signed with a '666' for a signature. It doesn't help much, just musing about how despondent he was and how much he hated everybody. Maybe you can make something of it."

"And our trained experts missed it," Mack yelled sarcastically, "I'll have someone's ass in the morning."

"No, Mack, it was adhered to the pocket wall. It was damned hard to spot."

"You found it!"

"Mack…anyone could have missed it. I'm on my way home now, so I'll drop it off."

"OK!" Mackenzie hung up without even saying thanks.

Don Mills held the phone for a while deep in thought. He dialled another number, calling his wife Sarah, to say he was about finished for the day and would be heading home soon. "I'll leave a message for Adam to drop in for some supper on his way home from lectures. He's taking this hard and needs our support, Sarah."

"It's hard on all of us Donald," she said sincerely, "I told Renee on the phone today, and she is just stunned." Sarah was referring to their daughter, currently working on her PhD in Hawaii.

# Wednesday
## Breakfast Time

When Don Mills came down for breakfast, his wife had just turned off the TV set. She shook her head, silently dismissing what had been on the news and looked despondent. "Oh Donald, this is all so unfair. Adam looked dreadful; it's taking a terrible toll on him." Dr Mills sat deep in conversation with his wife throughout his breakfast. Sarah poured him another coffee and one for herself.

"The media have judged him guilty until we can prove he's innocent, but it seems there's so little we can do," she added. "They are just looking for a scapegoat and some sensational mileage. Now they're asking why Adam, with all his training, couldn't just restrain him. Adam told us how it was. This person wasn't about to be restrained. He hit one of the girls and was about to punch the other and then he attacked Adam with a chair, doesn't that count for anything?"

"I'll talk with Mack this morning," Mills stated, "maybe he can call this Ronald Opus character in and have another talk with him. Maybe he can get the truth out of him and get the charges dropped. God, Mack should have talked to the media immediately and put a stop to this madness. We need the media to alert the two girls to come forward, they could easily clear Adam."

"He is so caring and gentle," Sarah added. "If only they all knew that."

## City of Angels

It had been a hectic break. Mina and Leah both had an early breakfast with their families, said their goodbyes and left together in a taxi for the journey to LAX and ultimately, Europe. They had thoroughly enjoyed their time at home except for the stupid episode at the coffee shop. From the taxicab, they looked out at the LA skyline. "I don't know," Leah said, "just 18 months ago LA was my city. I knew my way around this one city in the world. I could have worked here forever and never known another place."

"I guess that is pretty parochial when you think about it," Mina added.

"I can now navigate my way around New York, Paris, Munich, Frankfurt, Dusseldorf, Hamburg, Copenhagen, Kuala Lumpur, Singapore and even Sydney to some extent. We've been to Dubai, Cairo, Melbourne, Johannesburg, Capetown, Athens and Rome, but we still come home to LA." She paused for a moment after rattling off the list. "Are you aware Mina, its full name is **'El Pueblo de Nuestra Senora la Reina de los Angeles de Porciuncula'**? It took me weeks to learn to say that. It means, 'The Town of Our Lady, the Queen of the Angels of the Little Portion'."

"What's the 'little portion'?" Mina asked with some surprise.

"Don't know! It's something to do with the little bit of land, originally allocated for a church mission or something. That little portion for the mission became a town and eventually all this...," Leah indicated the expanse of the city.

"Fascinating!" Was Mina being facetious?

"It's the 'City of Angels', where dreams come true," went Leah, "...aren't you glad you live here?"

Mina nodded slightly, still thinking about it, while not really committing herself.

**Morning Briefing**

Mackenzie took a long sip of his regulation issue, Police coffee, vile, black stuff that would keep an African bushman awake in Tsetse fly country, the victim of acute sleeping sickness. This particular brew might be more effective if he could throw it at people. He always believed in a solid briefing before work started each morning. He would map out where the detectives were on each case, where they were going and exactly what needed to be done. From there, he would allocate his available manpower where it was most required.

At times, he appeared to be something of a micro-managing control freak; however, this system had worked well enough and gave all the detectives an idea of what else was happening in the precinct and on several occasions, the cross pollination had yielded surprisingly good results.

Mackenzie was on edge this morning and his inner stress was evident as he plucked the spirals of his notebook with the exuberance of a shred guitarist...It may have been the caffeine charge or perhaps it was Don's words that caused this apprehension. Far from 'having someone's ass' for the perceived incompetence of the body search, Mackenzie took the time to emphasise the importance of the note that the Chief Medical Officer had found.

He suggested some vital scenarios where it could have cracked the case. If it had been signed with a discernible name, it could have led to identifying the body. They would try this morning to lift prints off the paper. If it was found to be a genuine suicide note, that could rule out ritual murder and pinpoint suicide so it possibly could be of paramount significance. For once, Mack explained the importance of every piece of evidence in a case like this. His tactics were a welcome change and served to reinforce in his people the need to be thorough in their investigations.

He recapped to a few red faces, about the missing details from the original report concerning the safety net and how incompetent it had made them look, undermining confidence in their investigation and how it reflected badly on the entire police force. It reflected badly on them as detectives, on him as their Lieutenant, and on the Department as a whole. No one believed, however, that Mackenzie had turned over a new leaf with any permanence. By tomorrow, they figured they would again see his usual sarcastic, bulldozing style. He wouldn't change; unfortunately, he had the fickle temperament of a leopard and even displayed the liver spots on the back of his hands.

**The District Attorney**

"We are bringing Dr Hannaway, up from San Diego tonight," the robotic voice of the DA said on the phone.

"There's no need for that John; I'm managing fine," Dr Mills said.

"I know you are, Don, but we'll borrow him for a few weeks anyway. You have plenty on your plate and I'm sure you could use some help on this one. Look, I know Hannaway's a bit crusty, but he cuts through the bullshit and gets the job done and that's what we need here."

"OK, if you think that's best, John," the Senior Medical Officer said. He suspected it was because Adam could be facing charges and it irked him just a little. He hated subterfuge and would feel better if it had been brought out in the open. Don had met Barry Hannaway a few times and he was a fellow Rotarian and not a bad guy, but he really didn't need him.

What could Hannaway do? How he ever left the remote back-blocks of Australia and gained medical qualifications, seemed to be an ambiguity to everyone. Mills could picture him as a rather good country veterinarian but how he became a Medical Examiner was one of life's mysteries.

Mills had overheard someone at a Rotary meeting ask Hannaway what he was doing in America. "Oh, just having a look around," he had responded. It must be a pretty serious 'look', he reflected, because at last count he had been here almost five years. Why was the DA so intent on getting Hannaway involved? It seemed somewhat strange. Maybe it was political, he ventured. Oh well! Play the game.

## LA to Europe

It was all business on the Lufthansa flight back to Europe. Mina and Leah certainly looked professional in their stylish uniforms, demonstrating the safety features of the aircraft and looking to the comfort of their passengers. They had been through extensive training in Europe, and they did it so well.

"I'd like to give him more than Jack Daniels," Leah whispered, indicating a smartly dressed young man in Business Class, to whom she had just delivered a drink.

"You're an alley cat, Leah," it sounded stern, but Mina was smiling and shaking her head.

She moved to answer the Hostess call button further down the aisle. "Could you please watch my little girl while I go to the bathroom?" a young mother asked quietly.

"Certainly," Mina said. It wasn't busy right then and she could spare a minute or two and the little girl was just so cute. "What's your name sweetie," Mina asked.

"Typhanie." She answered showing her Disneyland nametag with the unusual spelling. She was wearing it as a brooch and seemed extremely proud of it.

"That's a pretty name, what are you reading there, Typhanie?"

"It's Cinderella, and Momma didn't finish it."

"OK; would you like to finish it now?"

"Yes…please." She was delightful.

Mina became quite involved as she read the last few pages to the little girl. Leah came past just as Mina drew to a close, "…and then Cinderella and the handsome prince lived happily ever after." Mina was cuddling the little girl who was delighted with the story and all the attention. Leah took in the scene and whispered, "God, I hope so, Mina."

## The Mills Home

Don Mills arrived home in his late model Volvo Station Wagon. He lived in a magnificent home in the LA hills in an upmarket, leafy neighbourhood. He greeted his wife, and pulled a bottle of superb Petaluma white wine from the refrigerator and poured her a glass and one for himself. He paused as a newsflash came on the TV in his living room.

*"In LA today, police detective, Adam Mills was stood down, pending investigation of police brutality allegations. Mills, who won a bronze medal in Martial Arts at the Atlanta Olympic Games, was not acting in an official capacity at the time of the incident and police sources say they are seeking witnesses who can help with their enquiries. The victim…"*

Mills turned off the set as he noticed the tears welling in his wife's eyes and moved to comfort her. Sarah Mills was usually robust and incredibly strong, but not surprisingly, this media performance got under her skin. The whole thing was so non-sensical and unjust.

## Adam's Apartment

After watching the same broadcast, Adam turned off the TV in his apartment and looked miserable. Usually a careful eater, on this occasion he was in a daze of bewilderment at how his life had suddenly been put on hold. He hadn't felt hungry all day and now he picked up what looked very much like a stainless steel dog bowl, poured in an entire packet of cereal, added the contents of a carton of milk and slumped down on his couch to devour this meal. It was after dinnertime and a more balanced repast was probably far more appropriate, but he just didn't care.

He was usually a disciplined young man and never indulged in self-pity but this was something he couldn't fight. These charges were like a flitting ghost that was deliberately taunting him from the shadows. Adam was a winner; he loved martial arts and would face up to any opponent and take his chances. Pit his strengths and weaknesses against an adversaries abilities, man to man. If this thing was animate, he could fight it face on; if it would just show itself like a martial arts opponent, he could deal with that, win or lose, but this situation was not animate at all.

It was chipping away at his confidence, it was ruining his reputation and it was destroying his soul. Adam tried to calculate precisely what it was, that he had done wrong, to deserve this punishment. He tried to relax and meditate but it just wouldn't work; he couldn't focus at all. "Come on," he yelled at his reflection in a small mirror featured on his china cabinet, "lift your game, get a grip on yourself. Get the lead out of your boots." Right there in his lounge room, Adam performed a flying martial arts kick at the air, perhaps in a subliminal attempt to kick his own backside. Instead of the usual kihop cry, he yelled, "The Pity Train just got derailed at the corner of Suck it up and Move on."

Epic fail at motivation, the despondent feeling remained.

The phone rang. It was a journalist looking for a comment about the case. It didn't matter much what he said. No one seemed to care. They would print what they liked anyway. "Talk to Lieutenant Mackenzie," he said mechanically and hung up. *Lieutenant Mackenzie*, he thought, *what was he doing to help?* None of the heavy lifting, anyway.

## Hamburg

"Come on Mina, we have time to hit the gym," Leah said playfully, "I'm badass with a great ass." *She was in a sweat already*, Mina thought, *thinking about tall blonde Germans lifting weights.* They found the gym and had a solid workout, a sauna, a spa and did a few laps of the small lunge pool. It was some time later, after they had left the showers, that Leah added, "Look lively girlfriend, Hamburg back to Paris. This is a dream run and there could be some eye candy on this flight."

## Police Central

Mackenzie actually felt a bit guilty; this new case had plainly rattled him. He was making fairly slow progress and there had been mistakes. Everything about it was so weird. He knew he should be supporting his man, Adam Mills, or at least putting some damage control procedures in place to protect Mills, as well as the Department. He could have talked to the media and explained that Adam was a good guy who had been teaching young students at the Police Youth Club in his own time on the weekend, and had only been trying to prevent some innocent girls from being assaulted at a café next door.

The thug had attacked him with a chair. He should have appealed to them; come on guys, he cares about people; he was doing voluntary work at the Youth Club when the incident occurred. This is the USA bronze medal winner from the Olympics. Mackenzie could have asked them to support their local police, all that kind of stuff. He really should be making every effort to shore up his staff, especially someone as diligent as Adam. Why hadn't he done that? Somehow, he just resented the whole…the phone rang, interrupting his thoughts.

"Mackenzie," he shouted into the phone, then listened with his eyes darting backwards and forwards across the room.

"Kirkpatrick here sir. We've checked the entire building. No one saw a damn thing, sir. The building worker has nothing to add, he just saw the jumper standing on the roof. He didn't know him and none of the tenants have a clue on the identity of the deceased. No one heard a shot; no one owns a shotgun…dead ends everywhere."

"Keep on it," Mackenzie yelled and slammed the receiver down. "Bastards!" he breathed apparently not referring to his own crew, probably meaning the residents of the apartment block, although it could have been aimed at the populous in general or at least the media who had recently occupied his thoughts. He yelled for his assistant Briggs, to get together a meeting of all his available detectives. He entered the briefing room scratching at the eczema that plagued him around his abdomen.

"…then there's the safety net on the eighth floor to consider," a young female detective was discussing. Mackenzie dropped into his leather chair as things went quiet in the room.

"That usually makes no difference, if the deceased jumped intending to commit suicide," he aimed at the detective. "Even when the cause of death is not what he intended, it is still defined as committing suicide." Mack rubbed his ruddy face and gave his trousers a bit of a hitch, "But Christ, maybe not when he's blown away by a God-damned shot gun. He left his shoes and jacket and a suicide note of sorts, so we believe he jumped and was then taken out with a shotgun. Either way that could make it a homicide."

"So…what do we have? Fact, we definitely know that a shotgun was fired at that apartment block. Someone who was in that building is likely going down for murder. Somebody knows something. Question them over and over. Start checking if the deceased abandoned a vehicle nearby. Check the missing person's lists again. Rip the place apart. Find them."

"Goulden!"

"Sir?"

"Look at this close up photo from the coroner's office. What do you make of the '666' on his forehead; are we dealing with some Satanic Cult or something?"

"I'm not sure sir."

"Follow it up, will you?"

Goulden shrugged and hesitated…"Yes…Sir!"

He paused a moment, sucking in air, murmuring to himself, "Now how the hell am I supposed to go about that?"

## Text Message

Adam came out of his lecture and switched his cell phone off 'silent'. He read the text from his dad and nodded. He moved to the campus car park, jumped in his small RV and headed for his parents' home to join them for a light supper.

"Don't worry Champ," Dr Mills said, "we're getting on top of it. Everything will be OK." It was not entirely true. Dr Mills was becoming frustrated that actually nothing was coming together. In fact, they weren't making much progress at all, but he would grasp at any straw to assist Adam out of this ridiculous situation.

## Thursday
## Barry Hannaway

Next morning at 9:00 a.m. Dr Mills reflected yet again on the strange anomaly of Dr Barry Hannaway. The Australian was already in the office, silently reading the typed report in his hand, as he moved towards Mills' office. He wore R M Williams ivory moleskins held up by a mahogany, plaited kangaroo hide belt, complete with a pocketknife pouch. Added to this was a blue stockman's shirt with double breast, patch pockets and a nicely polished pair of square-toed William's dress boots, also in a rich mahogany colour. He was a big, pleasant faced man in his early forties, but the quiet voice that came out of him was just remarkable. It was delivered through thin lips in a lazy Australian drawl and was really quite disarming. I guess he's a dove, ventured Mills to himself; a quiet, unassuming, Australian dove.

"Barry, welcome to Central Forensic…" Mills started, offering his hand.

"This bozo draws '666' on his forehead then jumps off a bloody building. OK, that's suicide, plain and simple. No one's arguing whether or not he should be awarded a Darwin medal for removing himself from the human gene pool. He even left us his jacket and his sneakers; bloody considerate of him. Vinnies might be ever so grateful. Oh! He also left a note, but the silly bloody cops couldn't find it, until it was shoved under their noses."

"Now I am asked to believe, that some unknown citizen couldn't wait half a bloody minute to see him splattered all over the footpath, so they blew his bloody head off with a shotgun. Where I come from that's called murder! Then by some mystical twist of fate, it turns out there's a bloody safety net strung up around the building, so the suicide would not have been successful. Regardless of all this, we are left with a homicide, but nobody saw anything and nobody knows anything and we can't even identify who the silly wombat was. Now we are asked to decide whether the jump would have killed him but the smart money would have to be on the shotgun. Am I missing something?"

"It's a weird case," Mills agreed, raising his eyebrows and silently applauding the Australian's concise appraisal.

"What the hell am I doing here, Don? Stuck around like a singed Bandicoot on a burnt out ridge. They couldn't even wait for Monday. You've done everything that needs to be done. Your report is spot on. You've told them he might have been tortured and ritually sacrificed. Christ, he might have been pushed, but that's for the cops, not for us. You've given them what they need. I guess the cops will stuff around a lot, yell and scream a bit, then it will all be over and I can go home."

"The DA wanted you here, Barry. It might be political."

"Righto mate, it's not for me to argue. If anyone wants me, I'll be in my lovely little office here, sitting on my dot, checking out the view and making bloody kookaburra noises."

# Paris

Mina and Leah were having a late lunch of baguettes and jamon, the lovely French ham, washed down with Perrier water, at a sidewalk table within sight of the Eiffel Tower. "It's such a lovely icon," Mina muttered, looking at the tower through the fading afternoon light, "We'll have to climb it when we have the time." Accordion music filtered through from somewhere inside the kitchen. Mina started giggling and broke into peals of laughter.

"Come on, share," Leah begged.

"I was just thinking of Brad's silly joke," Mina whispered, pointing to a Frenchman eating escargot. "Buuuuurp!" She did it with the same rising inflexion that Brad had used, and they had their arms around each other laughing. This was the good part of the job, a rare stopover in Paris, where they embraced the excitement of the city and talked about so many things.

"He has a crush on you, Mina."

"Who does?"

"Brad does. He even wrote a song for you."

"Really? Really? God, I had no idea."

"Mum says his band is going great at the club and they are preparing to cut a demo for some record company."

Mina found that when you flew with someone like Leah there were no secrets. "Wow! He is really talented and I think he's destined to be a star. His band totally rocks and his original songs are amazing."

"Even if he gets to be a mega star, I'll still know about his grubby room. My God, all those fossilised pizza crusts and the sweet aroma of fermenting socks."

Mina laughed, "It was a fun night, wasn't it?"

"Yes, I was actually surprised how much I enjoyed it all."

"His stage show was awesome, when the lights went out and the sirens started, I thought it was real…I don't know…a fire or something."

"So did most of the crowd."

"He's only sixteen, isn't he?" Mina asked amazed.

"Sixteen and a life support system for a raging bunch of hormones."

"Speaking of hormones, which we weren't…" Yet again, they discussed in detail, the amazing hero with the sparkling eyes, whom they knew only as Adam. It had all happened so fast, Mina could recall very little detail about the entire incident, but the look of those beautiful steel blue eyes was something that just might stay with her forever.

It seemed to be indelibly etched in her memory. He seemed so nice and gentle. Well, he'd been gentle with them; not too gentle with the creep. He was obviously well able to handle himself, but still so sincere and nice. Why couldn't she attract someone like that?

## Guardian Angel

Mina always carried a small crystal angel in her bag. When she was a little girl, she won a painted wooden angel in a writing competition. She had carried it everywhere. It got her through a tough time when she was in hospital with inflamed tonsils. It comforted her when the family cat disappeared and they thought it had been run over and of course she embraced it during the tough time of her dad's accident. The wooden angel knew every secret and every fear of her childhood. The paint was chipped and the wings had broken off before it was finally lost, many years ago.

When Mina saw the beautiful crystal angel sparkling in the down lights of a jeweller's shop window in Hamburg, she had been overcome with nostalgia as she rushed in and bought it. This figurine had become more of a talisman than a lucky charm and represented her belief in a real Guardian Angel. She would put it on the bedside table of her hotel rooms and make sure it knew how she was doing each day.

That night, she told her Guardian Angel all about Adam, and intimated how nice it would be if she could attract someone special like that. She couldn't begin to identify what it was about Adam that appealed to her, but he was even showing up in her dreams. This was really quite silly since she only met him for a moment, but she just couldn't help it.

### Visit of Condolence

Adam's apartment; he was in an old dobok, mechanically running through some Tae Kwon Do, poomsae training patterns. His heart wasn't in it, but he needed to be doing something and kept at it. A news broadcast came on the TV playing in the background and Adam paused to watch. It was the case his dad was working on.

*"In central Los Angles today, there was a bizarre turn of events when a suicide attempt turned into a murder investigation. Police revealed that a man who apparently jumped from a building yesterday was killed instantly by a shotgun blast as he fell. Police have not ruled out that a satanic cult or a drug ring could be involved, and it may have been a ritual killing. The body has not yet been identified."*

"Here it comes…" breathed Adam. The broadcast went on:

*"Still in central LA Police are seeking two well-dressed young women who apparently witnessed a fight that involved Police Detective, Olympian and Martial Arts instructor, Adam Mills. The victim Ronald Opus, who was knocked unconscious in the fight, is claiming 'Police Brutality' and states that the fight was over a girl…"*

Displaying amazing balance and coordination, Adam executed a perfect slow motion side kick at the button to switch off the set with his toe.

Knock, knock, knock. He didn't want visitors right now. *Please go away and leave me alone; just let me wallow in peace*, Adam thought as he walked over and slowly opened the door. There stood a pint sized African-American girl from his beginner's class with her younger brother.

"Sir, we need you back at the club…reeeal bad," she began, bobbing her head as she spoke. Adam wasn't ready for this at all. In any other circumstance it would be almost comical, except for the intense sincerity of the two children.

"Lila isn't it," he said gently. She nodded, "A…an…and this is LeRoy."

Adam invited them in, sat them down on stools at his breakfast bar and served them healthy bran muffins and apple juice, which they attacked with obvious relish. It was amazing that as their instructor he was so totally confident at the Club, yet here, in this 'one on one' situation, he was completely at a loss. Lila was nervous too. She hesitated, plainly uneasy in her role as a spokesperson for the younger students, "Sir, we believe in you and we need you back."

"Thank-you Lila, but I'm in a bit of trouble right now." He felt uncomfortable.

"Trouble's, nuthin' new for us," the child answered. Her brother nodded emphatically, his mouth full of muffin, indicating that in his seven years he'd seen more than his share, "…but you got to rise above it," he added still chewing. "You taught us zat, Sir. You taught me that my name LeRoy means 'the King', that is way cool. We need you sir." God, he sounded like Gary Coleman. (What choo talkin' about Willis).

"You gotta rise above it," his sister echoed embarking on a monologue about all that had happened at the club in his absence. Adam was stunned…the students had become the teacher. They trusted and believed in him…in him, Adam Mills.

"OK…Thank-you for coming, Lila and you too LeRoy. I'll try to get back there s-so-soon," Adam stuttered, choking up inside as Lila continued to look at him in the same disarming way that his grade-one schoolteacher had. When it came to that look, women were all sisters; they somehow learn their moves at an early age. Lila had come for a commitment and 'soon' wouldn't cut it. "I'll try to be there for Tuesday's training," Adam heard himself say. As they left, he assumed the 'ready' stance, snapped his sleeves down and then bowed deeply at the closing door.

Respect!

## Forensic—Medical Examiner's Office

Barry Hannaway was in his temporary office carefully reading every word of the John Doe file, circling bits with a red pen. Mills glanced at his Rolex…after 6:00 p.m. he walked to Hannaway's door with a bottle of single malt scotch and two crystal glasses. "Drink Barry?"

"I never heard of anyone choking on one, mate."

Mills poured generously into each glass.

"Thank you, Don, this is really civilised." Hannaway was appreciative.

"What's a kookaburra, Barry?" Mills asked.

"What...oh, a kookaburra; it's a beautiful brown and white bird with a strong beak, that eats grubs and lizards and things. It has a call that sounds like laughter. Kook, kook, kook, kook, ka, ka, ka, ka, ka, ka, kook, kook, kook, ka, ka, ka, ka, ka." He thought a moment, "A kookaburra would likely piss itself laughing at this silly bloody case." He tapped the file on the desk with the back of his huge hand.

Mills raised his eyebrows, even if he agreed with him, he certainly wasn't about to wind up the irreverent Hannaway. There seemed very little to say about this so he just remained silent. It was pretty apparent that Hannaway didn't want to be there...No! Actually, that wasn't right at all, now that he considered it. Hannaway was laconic and irreverent but it was the subterfuge and secrecy that got under his skin. Everything out on the table, nothing hidden; that was the big Australian's way.

Hannaway sipped his drink with obvious appreciation. Finally, Mills voiced his thoughts, "Look Barry, the building worker saw the deceased standing, looking out from the roof with no one near him. The shotgun blast hit him on the side of his face at close range so he would have had to turn around if he was blasted off the roof by the shotgun pellets. Mackenzie seems to think he jumped and was then shot. The trajectory of the pellets is almost horizontal, which actually supports that. Can you think of anything we can do to ascertain if he was pushed or if he actually jumped? It seems stupid, but I guess what I'm asking is, can we ascertain whether he was blown away while on the roof, or after he jumped."

"You're really asking the million-dollar question, was it suicide or murder. Is there any way we can be sure? You know the answer to that Don, the cops will ask silly bloody questions like, 'Was he feeling despondent or depressed lately'; that's if they ever find out who the stuffing hell, he was. The suicide note doesn't really mean a thing." He stood up for no apparent reason and paused while Mills topped up his drink. He doesn't have much respect for the cops, thought Mills, I wonder if there's something in his background.

Many Aussies came from colonial stock, British convicts, a lot of Irish. Maybe that caused them to still resent symbols of authority. It seemed Hannaway also subscribed to some additional egalitarian philosophy. He appeared to resent authority but maybe it was just that he genuinely viewed everyone as equal and reacted against those who set themselves a peg higher. He was an unusual man.

Hannaway sat back down. Maybe he'd just been stretching. He tapped the photo of the partly obliterated 666 on the victim's forehead.

"Don, I don't go in for too much of this Satanic-Voodoo stuff but back in the Territory there's a place called Kakadu National Park and right next to it, Arnhem Land…a huge Aboriginal Reserve." He took another sip of the mellow scotch and grinned appreciatively. "Right in the North of Australia, 110,000 square miles of un-spoiled strange and mystifying country…white fellas don't go there…it's rugged and beautiful country…The Aboriginal culture is intrinsically linked to the land, and it's an ancient land. They have very serious taboos and if one is broken, the tribal chief sentences the culprit to death and they bloody well mean it, mate." Another sip.

"They make this carved, pointed, ceremonial bone with a human hair rope knotted onto it. If they point the bloody thing at a tribal member and chant these weird songs, in time the poor bastard drops dead. I was sent to a place called Oenpelli to pick up this poor coot of the Manilakarr people…I don't know what the hell he'd done, probably knocked up some black sheila or something…" Here Hannaway paused toying with his glass, remembering the eerie, beautiful scenery and the haunting didgeridoos that played in the background.

"'Me bin sung; me bin sung!' this poor bloke croaked out, as if that explained everything. He was in a bad way and couldn't eat. I carried him to a swag I'd laid out in the back of my vehicle. I tried to pour some water over his face and in his mouth but couldn't do much for him. I was in a Tojo 4X4 and I gave that poor truck heaps to get him to Darwin Hospital. They fed him intravenously…but despite all their efforts, he died just a couple of days later, poor bastard…there's stuff we just don't understand, Don."

As if suddenly remembering what his monologue had been about, Hannaway leaned over and touched Mills' shoulder and said quietly, "What do you make of this '666' stuff?"

"It's from the Bible," Mills said sincerely, "the Book of Revelation says the Mark of the Beast is '666'…six hundred, three score and six." Here he sighed and seemed to think deeply, debating whether to go on. He appeared to make a decision and continued, "It's very much misunderstood. Most folks react to it without thinking and say it is occult, mysterious…devilish. That's not strictly true; the Beast is really a bad English translation of the Hebrew word 'Golem' and that involves a very specific, ancient mysterious ritual. The Christians took the Bible from the original Jewish Tanakh but even the clergy don't have a clue what it all means. So much is allegory…"

He sipped his drink. "When a Jewish Cabbalist receives the secret of the Holy Name of God, it's called a 'tetragrammaton'; that's the actual unpronounceable, sacred name of God that is shortened to YHWH. The Tetragrammaton represents a 216-letter name made up of 72 Hebrew triplets devised from a code contained in the Book of Exodus. The ancient Jewish 'Book of Splendour' called the 'Zohar' describes this code and how to arrive at this sacred name."[3]

"Now in the New Testament Book of Revelation, it describes the creation of a 'Golem' which is what the Cabbalist uses to test his ability to pronounce this name correctly. In this procedure, an image of a man is made out of clay. The word TRUTH in Hebrew (ahmeh-t) is written on the clay forehead of the image. The Cabbalist then chants the seventy-two intonations of the 'Holy Name' over the clay image. If the sounds are correct, down to the last nuance, then the image supposedly comes to life."

"Bloody Hell," Hannaway was listening intently, not moving a muscle as Mills went on, "The soulless beast is then destroyed by rubbing away a Hebrew character, which changes the word TRUTH into DEATH. The image of the Golem then reverts back to clay."[4]

"Today, we assume that this is just mythical, nonsensical, ancient Jewish folklore, but actually I'm not entirely sure. The Cabbalists are versed in esoteric magic and we really have no way of proving if this is possible or not. They claim their initiation ceremony into Kabbalah involves actually creating a Golem. If you Google the words, 'Golem of Prague' you can read about a famous Golem created in that City in the 16th century by a local Rabbi and allowed to continue living there. Its remains are supposedly still stored in a Church attic with the stairs removed. Today, they have the thing on post cards and T-shirts, promoting Prague. I don't think they fully understand what they are promoting. There's a lot of mystery involved with the Golem and the Tetragrammaton."

"A tetragrammaton," Hannaway said, experimenting with the word, keeping a dead straight face. "I'd like to walk into the Noonamah Pub, chuck a ten spot on the bar and say, 'give us a double tetragrammaton will ya'?" Slight smile. "Johnno would likely have a fit." He got serious again, "A tetragrammaton?"

"Yes, 'tetragrammaton' is from the Greek and simply means 'four letters' and plainly its usage is not restricted to the Hebrew. Actually, in a great number of languages, the divine name of their deity is expressed in four letters. We find the Egyptian—**Amon**, **Aten** and **Isis**, the Sumerian—**ENKI**, the Greek—**Zeus**, the Latin—**Deus**, the Spanish—**Dios**, the Scandinavian—**Odin**, the German—**Gott**, the English—**Lord** and even the thunder God—**Thor**, to name a few."

"Now it is interesting that in Revelation 13 it states that, 'the number of the name of the image of the Golem shall be '666'.' This is the number of 'the beast', but it is not some satanic and sinister mystery as is often claimed; it is a direct statement of one of the principles of the forty-two laws of the Jewish Kabbalah. This principle is called 'Gematria' where letters represent numbers. It bears thinking about, that this Cabbalistic procedure is so closely related to the creation of Adam…the creation of mankind, out of clay."[5] He threw down the rest of his drink quickly, as if to put out a fire burning in his chest. Perhaps he was thinking of how he had named his own son Adam.

"You've boggled me, mate," Hannaway said quietly.

"That's the real answer, Barry, but it probably has very little bearing today. The reality is that most people…even most Christians, have never heard of a Golem and this is exacerbated by the inane translation to 'beast' in the Christian Bible. They just think the '666' symbol is evil and satanic. People fear the unknown. Kids unwittingly use it as an occult symbol of rebellion."

# Friday
## Helping Adam

Mack Mackenzie had arrived at the Parker Centre early with a buzzing headache. He dropped a couple of aspirin, updated a few entries in the file, checking things out and making a few alterations as he went. He seemed on edge and somewhat frustrated as he worked. Finally, he grabbed his coat and headed out of the building with a purpose. He walked past the Police Youth club and sat down for a cappuccino at the Italian kerbside coffee shop that was just opening. It was not busy and the staff hadn't yet arrived, so the Italian owner served him personally.

"What's your name?"

"I am Carlo."

"Who helps you here, Carlo."

"Maria, my wife, she be here soon. We have other girl Carmella, sometimes help."

"Have a coffee with me, Carlo," Mack demanded of the owner.

The chubby, little Italian had work to do but hastened to comply. He could see 'cop' written all over Mackenzie. Mack was not usually this subtle, but he slowly explained how one of his men had been involved in an altercation at their establishment on the previous Sunday morning and he wanted Carlo to tell him all about it. He gave his stomach a scratch, then flashed his badge in an intimidating manner.

"Police already talk to me; I see nothing. Maria tell them, she see nothing," insisted Carlo. A stony stare from Mack. "We tell them over and over. We not know them, we not have credit card receipt…we not see them before. We see nothing…"

"Are you both blind then?" Mack asked sarcastically, "Tell me what you saw, now." Raised voice.

"I serve coffee and muffin to girls; molto bellissimo, but I not see any fighting." Mack looked at him with a threatening stare.

"I see broken chairs and knocked over table, broken cup and plate. Maria call ambulance for man who is hurt."

"Did the girls come here often?"

"I think it is first time," Carlo lied.

"Did you know the man who was hurt?"

"No!" Carlos exclaimed, a bit too forcefully.

"Tell me about the fight."

"I not see any fight. It happen quick, I not see nothing."

"Would a visit from the Health Department improve your memory?"

"Please sir, I not see nothing."

It was hopeless. Either it had happened so fast he genuinely missed it or he was scared stiff. Adam had said it was over very quickly.

"The hurt man, Ronald Opus, did he come here often?"

"I not see him before, Sir." Mack didn't exactly believe him, but he was getting nowhere. "Call me if the girls come in again," he said without much hope, flipping a Police card to Carlo. Maybe Opus had something on the Italian, maybe not, but this was not going anywhere. Carlo was not about to recall anything and Mack was wasting his time with this line of questioning.

Back at the office there were a few things he wanted to check out. He phoned Ron Opus. It went to message bank. Mack checked the mobile number Ronald Opus had left when he filed the complaint. Right number, but it went to message bank again. Bloody hell! Mack left a message for Opus to contact him urgently regarding his statement of complaint.

**The Fugitives**

Blissfully unaware that half the LAPD were looking for them, Mina and Leah were busy serving meals and drinks to a full flight of passengers en route to Switzerland. They had not done a Zurich flight before but had loved Berne and were looking forward to the evening off to look around.

"I caught up with Claire at the terminal. You want to hear what she told me?" Leah said when they got a break, "That steward called Helmut, from Frankfurt, got suspended."

"Goodness, what did he do?" Mina asked.

"Well, you know he was always a bit of a chauvinist."

"Yes, he thinks women should know their place."

"Well they were on a long haul and Claire says a woman in Business Class was nursing a baby and didn't want to change it herself, so she got Claire to do it for her, while she knocked down a few drinks. She had a container of disposable nappies. A couple of hours later, she asked another flight attendant if she would change her baby for her. She just sat there drinking. A while later she asked Helmut if he would change her baby, so he did."

"Helmut did?" Mina looked astonished.

"Yeeeeah! He took it down the back and 'borrowed' a black baby from some African lady and took it back to the Business Class lady. 'OK Ma'am, I've changed it,' he says, offering her the black baby. The tipsy woman totally freaked and complained to the captain. The passengers saw the whole thing and Claire nearly wet herself laughing."

"You've got to be joking!"

"I'm not!"

"You're joking?"

"Pinky swear, I'm not. If I was joking, I'd say, a horse walks into a bar; the bartender says, 'why the long face'?"

Mina smiled. "Leah, be serious."

"True story!"

# Teen Challenge

The sign said *'Teen Challenge—please walk right in'* and Detective Goulden did just that. He introduced himself to a likable young man in a temporary office. On his desk was a plaque that read:

**'All that is necessary for evil to triumph, is for good men to do nothing.'**

*Fitting*, he thought.

Coming straight to the point, Goulden explained the situation, showed the young man the photograph and asked about the '666' on the victim's forehead and questioned what it could mean.

"Well Detective, in common street vernacular, '666', the Mark of the Beast is satanic. That is not quite scriptural or strictly correct, but it's likely the perception, not the truth that stands here. It would be a fairly dramatic statement to write '666' on your forehead before jumping off a building and this could possibly link the deceased to a satanic movement, but not necessarily."

"Would it be possible that a satanic group coerced the deceased to suicide and then murdered or 'sacrificed' him as he fell?"

"Well, it's pretty bizarre, but of course it is possible. We all remember Jim Jones and the Kool-Aid thing."

"Do you think it's likely?"

"We must be cautioned here Detective, because a number of young people are rebellious and seeking shock value. There are some who draw Swastikas as graffiti, but that doesn't make them NAZIS." He thought a moment. "Writing '666' on your forehead isn't much removed from drawing a swastika there. It could be equally well linked to 'Heavy Metal' music or just open rebellion. On the other hand, it could be a genuine cult related statement. We are certainly aware that there are satanic movements operating in this city!"

"How would you know the difference?"

"You wouldn't, without additional information…without knowing the background of the deceased. Look, there's no doubt that satanic rituals are being acted out in LA and we even hear of human sacrifices and weird rituals in cemeteries at night but to what extent they are operating, simply cannot be ascertained. The perpetrators are not going to advertise it, are they?"

"What would be your take on such a suicide…?" Goulden indicated the photograph.

"Look it may be drug related and have nothing whatever to do with any cult. This is pretty heavy stuff and I would only be guessing; I suggest you talk to Professor Manteit at Pacific States University. He is an authority on cults." Detective Goulden received directions to find Professor Manteit, thanked the young man, then walked to his car. Soon after, he was driving towards PSU, only about three miles away.

## Detective Greaves

There was excitement in the delivery, "Sir, it's Greaves, we've got something in the apartment block, I think you should come right over…and Sir…we might need a search warrant."

This is what Mack had been waiting for. "I'm on my way." He did nothing about the warrant. Greaves was waiting outside the brownstone.

"Sir, a few people on the ninth floor thought they might have heard a shot, but the building workers were making a lot of noise and they put it down to them. They'd all been interviewed before and were getting a bit jumpy. When I was enquiring about the shot, a scruffy old guy appeared to be getting more than just agitated. His wife looked pretty nervous as well. I asked about a shotgun and he denied owning one, but I thought I saw her nod and then wince. I believe he's got a gun in there and I believe she's scared stiff."

"Right, separate them; you and Briggs take him in for questioning, cuff him if you have to; I'll talk to her and search the place. Call me when you've interviewed him." Mack hesitated, "Good work, Greaves."

## Professor Manteit

Meanwhile, Detective Goulden found Professor Manteit, introduced himself and stated why he was there. The professor was considerably younger than he expected and sported long hair and a Led Zeppelin T-shirt. Not what he'd expected at all. Goulden decided that he actually looked more like a rock band's roadie, than a professor, but it turned out he was extremely astute and really knew his stuff. The detective outlined the situation and showed him the photograph, then asked about satanic cults.

This was the Professor's favourite 'hobby horse' and he was only too happy to answer questions. He searched for the best way to explain. "Stories of satanic cults, of satanic paedophilia and ritual abuse of humans mostly involving children, are coming to light with fairly staggering frequency, particularly in

North America, but also right across the world. A few prosecutions are gaining media attention and possibly as a result, psychologists are encountering some pretty strange rumours."

"There are reports of 'recovered repressed memory', where, years after a ritual supposedly took place, the victim recalls the event. Psychologists have come to believe that patients of 'multiple personality disorder' in many cases may have been interfered with as children. These things have only really been investigated since the early 1980s when such allegations of ritual abuse began to surface."

He paused apparently recalling his studies of these earlier days…"In the 80s the number of alleged cases began to grow in epidemic proportions. Hundreds of victims were alleging that thousands of offenders were abusing and even murdering multitudes of people as part of organised satanic cults, but Detective, there was little or no corroborative evidence. The very reason many 'experts' cite for believing these allegations, is that many victims were involved, who never met each other with all reporting almost identical events. Actually, this should be the primary reason to question, at least, some aspects of these allegations." Detective Goulden was hearing more than he had planned for.

"A percentage of the reported memories must certainly be real; however, no one knows where the actual figure lies and no benefit can be derived from making premature estimates."

"How do we locate these groups?"

"You won't! These involved cults are entrenched, they're secret, highly organised and supposedly devoted to Satan worship, human and animal sacrifice, sado-masochistic ritual sex, child abuse and other crimes which are committed during ceremonies involving pentagrams, black robes, chanting, satanic theology, candles, goblets, daggers, and other paraphernalia. If what we believe about them is true, they are very high-level operations. They have their own networks and are pretty much untouchable." Goulden just watched the professors face for a minute, lost in his own thoughts and wondering what he could tell Mack. He snapped back to reality.

"So, getting back to our jumper with '666' on his forehead?"

"Well, you need to know what sort of person he was, who he associated with, what were his beliefs concerning religion, track his movements and so forth."

"No professor, in this case, we are working backwards. We are in the dark. He was just someone unknown, with '666' on his forehead; as for the other things, we don't even know his name. I was hoping you might give us some direction."

"Forget it Detective, if drugs were involved it is more likely that the jumper was making a statement, shock value—you know 'Highway to Hell' stuff. You're also wondering if it was a ritual killing, if he was part of a cult, if he was pushed off the building, if he was driven to suicide and if he was shot as a message to others. That's a lot of 'ifs'. I certainly wish you luck Detective, but you're not going to find it easy getting to the people involved in satanic practices in order to gain answers to those questions. Even if you do locate these groups, it could be a total waste of time. If they were involved, no one is going to talk about it."

## Central—Interview Room

"For Christ's sake, their name is Opus!" Mackenzie roared, "They're the parents of Ron Opus who put in the complaint about Adam Mills." Mack had returned from interviewing Maggie Opus and brought with him the double-barrelled shotgun wrapped in a cloth. He shook his head as if to clear it. "You should have at least got their name." Mack calmed down. "It looks like we finally have a breakthrough. Mrs Opus says her husband was threatening her with the shotgun when it accidently went off." Mack paused while rubbing his face. "So…how's the hillbilly doing?" he glared at Briggs and Greaves, the two detectives who had brought Clive in.

Clive Opus had not been co-operative at his first interview, but they had gleaned enough to be reasonably sure that he had no knowledge of the jumper. He assured them, he had not intentionally fired the weapon at anyone, but if that was true, it stretched coincidence to an almost unbelievable level.

Mack had told them on the phone that he thought a bit of softening up in the cells would be a good idea anyway. Now Clive Opus, still sporting his dirty singlet, was brought back into the interview room to face a fairly intimidating Lieutenant Mackenzie, who was holding out his shotgun, with two used shells in the breach. His arrogant demeanour had certainly undergone a fairly dramatic change after an hour in the cells, coupled to the threat of a murder charge.

The psychology of seeing the Lieutenant brandishing his shotgun further emphasised his predicament. He suddenly realised that Maggie had no reason to bail him out and there was no lawyer waiting for him to call. He became a paragon of virtue and co-operation.

"Never done anything wrong in me life," he pleaded in his whining nasal drawl, "an' I didn't know the gun wa' loaded," he repeated for the tenth time.

"Who was the person you shot at?" questioned Mack.

"I didn't shoot at nobody…didn't know the gun wa' loaded."

"Why do you keep a shotgun in your apartment, Mr Opus?"

"Owned it back in Arkansas," he whined, "and never got round to selling it."

In reality, he liked the sense of power it gave him and had no intention of ever selling it.

"When did you last fire it?"

"Prob'ly more'n eight years back."

"Where do you keep your ammunition?"

"Got no ammo left." That seemed right. His wife didn't know if he had shotgun shells or not. Mack had found the gun in the bedroom closet, but despite a thorough search, he found no ammunition in the apartment.

"How did it fire both barrels then?"

"Somebody else must have loaded it," he whined, "I got no ammo."

"Come on Mr Opus, who would come into your apartment, load your shotgun and leave?"

"I dunno."

"Of course, you know. Come on, who?"

"I dunno."

"Well did you load it?"

"NO!"

"Did your wife load it?"

"Course not."

"Well, somebody loaded it…WHO?"

"I guess it musta been me son Ron!"

"Why would he do that?"

"I dunno!"

"You do know! Why would Ron load your shotgun?"

"Maybe, so's I'd shoot the ole lady."

"Now why would he do that?"

"Cos he waz fightin' wi' her. He woulda used me to get at her."

"He must have known you threatened her regularly then!"

"Nuh! First time ever."

"That's a lie Mr Opus. Your wife said it happens with monotonous regularity. It wouldn't make any sense to load the shotgun to get back at her, if he wasn't aware that you threatened her regularly. You're lying to me and you can go back in the cells."

"I mighta done it once or twice before."

"I think we'll put you back in the cells until your memory improves."

"Orrite, I threatened her pretty reg'lar; but she asked for it."

"So, you pulled out the gun, to threaten your wife when it suited you?"

"Yeah. I had ta keep the bitch in line."

"And you thought the gun wasn't loaded?"

"Yeah! I got the shock of me life when it went orf…I never shot at nobody."

"OK so where does your son Ronald live?"

"He lives with us at home, but he stays away a bit."

"Where does he stay?"

"I dunno."

"Yes, you do. Where?"

"He has a mate called Flynn; I think he stays with him."

"Where does Flynn live?"

"I dunno."

"I've been trying to contact your son. Where is he?"

"I dunno."

"Yes, you do. Where is your son now Mr Opus?"

"I dunno. E's likely with Flynn."

"Take him back to the cells; I'll have more questions later."

"Hang on, you said I could go."

"You're dreaming Mr Opus, back in the cells. You could still be charged with murder."

"But I never shot at nobody." Clive was whining almost hysterically.

Mackenzie left the interview room and urged his detectives to get on the case, pushing them onward like a pack of huskies. Mush! Mush!

Dr Mills was waiting to see him.

## Central—Mack's Office

"I'd like to go through this case with you," Mills said, quite reasonably, "to understand why your report calls it suicide."

"OK, hit me," Mack said, somewhat arrogantly, not looking at Doctor Mills who had remained patiently seated while Mackenzie was in the interview room. "Start at the beginning and tell me where we are going with this God-damned case."

"OK, Mack." The doctor quickly outlined how the body of the deceased was viewed by his medical examiner who concluded that instantaneous death had resulted from the shotgun blast to the head. "The deceased had left his joggers and jacket on the roof of a ten story apartment block and had a note in his pocket when he apparently jumped from the roof with the intention of committing suicide."

"Suicide!" Mackenzie exclaimed, looking pleased about it and counting it on his first finger.

"By an amazing twist of fate, either before or after he jumped, a shotgun blast killed him instantly," continued the doctor with some trepidation.

"Homicide!" Mackenzie barked, reluctantly snapping back the second finger that had just finished probing an itch on his left side.

"It would seem that the deceased was not aware that building workers had installed a safety net at the eighth floor level, which ordinarily would have rendered the suicide unsuccessful," Mills continued.

Mack's wriggling third finger got a reprieve for the moment.

"Ordinarily, if a person sets out to commit suicide and ultimately succeeds," the doctor explained, "even when the actual mechanism that causes his death, might not be what he intended, it is still defined as committing suicide."

"Correct," Mack agreed, "So accordingly, it's a suicide."

Ever the diplomat, Mills rubbed his tired eyes and chose his words carefully, "The cause of death was the double shotgun blast so regardless of whether the deceased was shot on the way to what would be considered 'certain death', except for the existence of the safety net, it caused our medical examiner to believe it was a homicide."

"I can understand that," Mack agreed.

"What now?" Dr Mills asked.

"Well…" Mackenzie said, "…in a ninth floor apartment, we located a hillbilly couple who had been arguing. The slob regularly threatened his wife with a shotgun. He apparently thought the gun was not loaded. For dramatic effect, he drew back the hammers and then as he swung the gun away, pulled both triggers. According to the wife, he was shocked as hell when it went off. He missed her and caused the instant death of the jumper." Mackenzie spent a few seconds considering the astronomical odds. "One in a million chance!"

"That's just too weird," Mills said shaking his head, "more like one in a billion…but if it's right, I believe it rules out a ritual killing. All the '666' stuff was just a red herring."

"It would seem so." Mack agreed softening a little as his defensive attitude subsided, "By the letter of the law, if someone plans to kill person 'A', but instead accidently kills person 'B', then he is responsible for the murder of person 'B'. So we just might have to look at homicide," Mack emphasised it by tapping the appropriate finger.

"That's what we were thinking, however, that's not always the case either," Dr Mills added, "Barry Hannaway, gave a talk at the AAFS about a case in Darwin, Australia, where an assailant saw someone he didn't much care for, in an open air cinema, of all places. He pulled out an equaliser and bang! He missed the person he wanted and took out a Chinese cook. I don't know of any other existing precedents but with no motive, that one was assessed as an accidental shooting."

"Well," Mackenzie said, moving his shoulders, but not voicing his thoughts on that case, "when confronted with a murder charge, this hillbilly, was adamant that he believed the shot gun was not loaded. His wife, somewhat reluctantly, backed him up on it and we found no cartridges in their apartment. He claims he doesn't know the deceased, hence, it appears there was no premeditation or intent to murder. It seems that it was a regular occurrence for this creep to threaten his wife with an unloaded gun. She told me he had pulled the same trick a few times in the previous couple of weeks, but hadn't actually pulled the triggers on those occasions."

"Therefore, we can't determine at what point the gun was loaded. Since they both claim, it was a threat and he had no real intention of killing her, the homicide of the jumper must be classed as an accidental death. With no motive or premeditation, it can't really be murder and since the evidence suggests the victim jumped, we have to list it as suicide." Here the third finger was finally snapped forward to accentuate the point. Don Mills pondered this situation. Little did these men know that more was to come that would require the fourth finger.

# Chapter 3
# Aussie Philosophy

**Saturday**
**More Coffee?**

After consulting a sheet to confirm the address, Barry Hannaway had an early breakfast in his hotel restaurant, skipped coffee and went out presumably for a stroll. A few blocks later, he stopped at the sidewalk coffee shop of Carlo and Maria, who were just opening. In his usual, friendly manner, he ordered a large black coffee in a mug and slowly sipped it without sugar. From behind the counter, Carlo was taking clandestine peeks at the big man, his every instinct telling him that despite Hannaway's friendly demeanour, this could be trouble.

"OK," Hannaway said to Carlo at last, with a big grin, "I have a little problem I want you to fix for me, mate. We can do this the easy way or the hard way; what do you reckon, sunshine?" Another grin.

"Not understand you," said Carlo.

"Course you do mate," Hannaway said with a smile, "You lied to the Lieutenant, but you won't lie to me." He smiled again in a disarming manner.

"What you want from us?" Carlo asked, not unreasonably, "Maria and I we see nothing. We tell the Police we see nothing."

Hannaway smiled again, "Let me explain something then. Two girls came here for a coffee last week. There are about half a million places they could get coffee, but they came here. Within about five minutes, one Ronald Opus turns up and wants to beat the living snot out of them. You see my problem now?"

"Not understand," exclaimed an animated Carlo.

"Yes you do matey, because it's as plain as an ugly sheila. The girls came here often and you were the bloody cockatoo." Here Carlo genuinely didn't understand, but Barry Hannaway made it plainer. "You were to call this mongrel, Ron Opus, when the girls turned up here, and you did that didn't you, Carlo?"

"NO!" It was shouted.

"Yes!" it was Maria who answered quietly from the counter. "Carlo, don't be stupid, he is the Police…he knows."

"So what did he have on you mate?" The sardonic smile again. "Were you peddling dope for him, from this place here?"

"No!" Maria exclaimed, "Sir, we just work hard and mind own business. This man Ron cause us trouble. I think he meet people here and sell his drugs. We are not involved. Carlo he call him, like you say, otherwise he cause us more trouble."

"Thank you Maria." Barry said politely indicating that he believed her, "Now that wasn't too hard, was it?" The thin smile again.

"Now, what about the fight?"

"We not see fight, sir," Maria said, "We hear on TV, man in fight is young detective. We know young detective fight with Ron Opus, but is very quick. We tell truth, we not see it."

"You were out checking for signs of rain; am I right?"

"Not understanding, sir."

"You guessed what was coming and you didn't want to see it, hey?"

"We not see fight," Maria said with absolute finality.

"So you heard breaking cups and tables knocked over and didn't even bother to take a bit of a squiz; is that what you're saying?"

"We not see fight," Maria said again.

"What do you know about the girls?"

"We not know them. They were beautiful girls…nice clothes."

"Do you know their names or where they work?"

"No sir!"

She seemed quite genuine. He pulled out one of his business cards, underlined his cell phone number and said, "If they come in again…call me. If this drongo, Opus gives you any grief at all, even if he turns up here and asks questions, you call me OK?"

Maria nodded. As Barry walked away, Carlo turned to Maria, "What is 'drongo'?"

Maria slapped him on the shoulder, "You Carlo…you are drongo!"[6]

## Paris Hotel

"Are we going down to dinner?" Mina asked.

"Nuh, I ate too many croissants, I feel like a fat pig, and I'm too tired to look for the gym," Leah claimed. She was working on a broken nail.

"I'm not hungry either," Mina said gently. "Want to have a swim?"

"Nooo! Jesus no! It's cold and my feet are too sore."

Silence for a while. "I wonder if we are sent here to fix up the mistakes we made in a former life," Mina added dreamily, falling on the bed and contemplating Leah, framed between her big toes, "I wish I understood more about spiritual things. Every denomination claims they alone know the right way and all others are wrong and likely evil. There's just so much to know and no guarantee you are ever on the right path."

"Mmmm," Leah let out a big breath looking at the ceiling. "I like the Buddhist notion; you're only here for a short time, so keep yourself amused and don't muck up anybody else's life."

"God, I wish everyone would subscribe to that philosophy." Mina said seriously, "Half the global population is put here with the express purpose of mucking up my life."

"Yeah right! The male half," Leah chimed in, laughing.

"Even on the flights, I get hit on by the creepiest ones," Mina added.

"I get hit on too," Leah said, "…and a few of them…well, not so creepy." This was accompanied by a hand gesture that made it funny.

"Like in Hamburg!" it was a statement not a question and they both laughed.

"My lips are sealed," Leah added with a plum in her mouth.

"I used to believe I had a Guardian Angel watching over me," Mina said gently, fingering the crystal figurine she carried. She turned it in her hand reflecting the light and thought a moment before blurting out, "My God Leah, you've certainly given your Guardian Angel some serious work to do, on this trip! You might be seeking your knight in shining armour, but you're sure leaving a long trail of frogs."

"I can't help it if I'm irresistible to men," Leah stated, raising her eyebrows and they both laughed. "Maybe you should work for Customs, where you could get well paid to strip search a few of them. You'd be a natural!"

"That's got possibilities," Leah confessed, "but…Nuh! Only the creepy ones carry drugs and stuff."

They both smiled at their own thoughts. Mina reflected the reading light with the crystal angel, forming rainbows on the wall and soon got quiet and serious again, "I really think she's abandoned me…" Silence…"My life is pretty good right now, but you watch, I'll find another loser and off I'll go again. It's like I just can't help attracting them."

"Hey maybe you could try Pizza delivery guys, at least you'd know they had a job and a car…and pizza." laughed Leah.

"Do I have a tattoo on my forehead saying 'Lame ducks welcome'?"

"No, it's not you, Mina…it's not your fault. We all want to be loved and needed. Remember when you were a little girl, did you think you were really a princess and a handsome prince would eventually find you and rescue you."

"Yes! YES!" Mina almost screamed it out. "I watched 'Pretty Woman', like, a hundred times." The big grin on her face is what Leah had been looking for.

"That was my dream! That was my…Do I really need rescuing? Maybe I do." Mina thought a moment. Adam had rescued her; so, was that really the attraction?

"Your dream is real, Pina Colada," Leah whispered dramatically, reverting to the pet name she reserved for Mina, "…dreams come true when the time is right."

"Not soon enough, girlfriend," Mina said placing her crystal angel gently on the bedside table and playfully throwing a pillow at Leah. "Nowhere near soon enough."

# Sunday
# Dinner Guest

Barry Hannaway had been invited to the Mills residence for dinner and despite his unique vocabulary and strange ways, he would prove to be a very amiable guest. Mills had warned his wife to be ready for the quiet, humorous delivery, but she was somewhat surprised at the charming charisma of the man. She found his humour and quiet sincerity, delightfully refreshing.

"What part of Australia are you from Barry?" Sarah Mills asked politely as she poured him a beer.

"From the top end, Sarah," he replied, "We call it the Northern Territory. Born and bred there, but I've lived all over."

"I've always wanted to visit Australia, haven't I, Donald?"

Mills nodded. Adam arrived and his father escorted him in. Introductions and pleasantries were exchanged and Barry shook Adam's hand firmly before going on.

"God's own country it is, Sarah. It's a wide, cruel and beautiful land. I came from the family station called 'Laurel Downs'. It always amused me that the one poor scraggly Laurel tree, presumably planted by my great-grandfather, never imagined it would be immortalised on the station nameplate above the front gate. It's right in the middle of nowhere, about 140 miles north-west of Alice Springs on the Tanami track between the Alice and Rabbit Flat; out where the crows fly backwards to keep the dust out of their eyes."

"Who would name a place, 'Rabbit Flat'?" Sarah asked sincerely.

"Well, it's not a bad little spot. It became quite famous back in the mid-80s when the population doubled overnight," Barry was smiling.

"Was there a gold rush or something?" Adam asked.

"Nothing like that," Barry said chuckling, "Rabbit Flat had a population of just two humans and a hell of a lot of rabbits. Young Jack Dawson and his lovely wife Sandy ran the pub, service station, local store and Post Office…until she had twins." He laughed out loud as he remembered. "Tell, you what; you can visit a monstrous great meteorite crater out that way, near Wolfe Creek. They reckon it's about the biggest meteorite crater in the world."

"You didn't want to stay on the property," Don asked, wondering if that wouldn't have better suited the big Aussie.

"No way, mate. It doesn't matter how tough you are, how hard you work, how smart you are; if it doesn't rain you are effectively stuffed. I cried UNCLE, fairly early on. I wasn't about to pit my wits against Mother Nature. She's a lot bigger than I am…it was no contest."

There was silence for a moment as he reflected on his childhood. "I saw what it did to my folks, sitting around waiting for rain. The old timers don't know any different; they can't understand it, but a lot of the younger generation blokes feel the same way I do. It broke my dad's heart when my brother and I didn't take on the property but every day I thank God we didn't. For a while there, we were about as popular as tripe lasagne, but he finally got over it, even if he didn't really understand. Actually, out there now, they're trying to have it classed as 'child abuse' to leave a property to your kids."

Many Australian bushmen have mastered the art of 'pulling your leg', which means telling a funny or ridiculous story with a straight face, pretending to be deadly serious as if every part was completely true. An entertaining Australian bushman can tell a crimson lie with more fluency than the average person can tell the truth casually and Barry was from this mould. "I don't often miss the place," he said sincerely, "I only ever recall dust and dry spells. The droughts were so severe that the old folk considered themselves lucky when they could put water in their tea again." Nobody believed him as he went on with his story, but he was certainly good company.

"Here Barry, can I pour you another beer," Sarah asked.

"Well, a man's not a camel and there could be a dry spell coming, thank-you Sarah," came the reply. He continued his monologue. "In the dry seasons, the birds would come in looking for water and a feed. The biggest flock of galahs I ever saw was on our place in the late 1980s when the drought broke. They were startled by a loud thunderclap and took flight. The spread of wings was so thick that not a drop of rain hit the parched ground for nearly half an hour. My young cousin was about 8 years old at the time and had never seen rain before and promptly fainted at the sight. Dad had to throw two shovelfuls of dust over him to bring him round." They all laughed; he was very funny.

"What's a galah, Barry?" Don asked.

"Well mate, it's a pink and grey bird, a sort of parrot. We also have bigger white parrots called cockatoos that make a hell of a screeching noise when they're disturbed and they both love to have a go at a decent grain crop."

"And do these birds cause a lot of damage to the crops?"

"Too right, Don, they can strip a paddock bare in a few days. One time on Laurel Downs, the galahs and cockatoos had been giving the harvest a bit of a caning. The old man had sworn at them until he looked like depleting his profane vocabulary and I can confirm, it was fairly extensive. Could he swear? His proficiency had been aided and abetted by a lifetime of regular rehearsal and comprehensive performances. The sentence construction may have been a bit succinct but the mind pictures he created were certainly impressive and original."

Barry blinked a bit, "He'd thoroughly exhausted his sanguinary, physiological and biological threats and was starting to indulge in pointless repetition, when my brother Mick arrived. The boss asked Mick to see if he could do something about the blanky birds before he got really blanky-well stirred up and did something he would blanky regret. So, Mick located a large tree where they would roost each night and coated the limbs and branches with a strong batch of birdlime, a sort of glue. Well, it worked like a charm, and next morning thousands of birds were all firmly stuck to the tree. Mick was creeping up on them, when he trod on a twig from one of the fallen branches."

"It made a loud snapping noise like a shotgun going off and alarmed the flock. They all tried to take off at once and pulled the tree up by the roots. Within minutes, it was about half a mile high, with a slight lean to the left and heading south." There were some chuckles.

"So, do you shoot these birds or what?" Adam asked.

"Too many, mate," Barry stated sincerely, "You could shoot all day until you ran out of shells and never even put a dent in them. Some blokes have tried everything, but nothin' seems to help much."

Sarah moved them into the dining room and got them seated at the table. Barry got right back to his story and it became apparent that reminiscing about Australia was dear to his heart.

"My mother tried hard to vary the men's diet away from mutton every meal, and experimented with galahs since these birds were so plentiful. She got us boys to shoot a few and tried to roast them, boil them, grill them, fry them, marinade them and even bake them in a pie but they always came out too tough. You wouldn't feed them to a Jap on Anzac Day. She finally asked the old campaigner, Curly the shearer's cook, if he knew a recipe for galah."

"'Yer cun pick from two,' Curly said knowingly. 'The first one, ya place the galah and a large stone in a pot and boil it until the stone goes soft; then throw away the galah and eat the stone. The other way is to work on the galah with a hoof rasp from the farrier's shop and then make soup out of the shavings.'" More chuckles all around.

"So are we to understand, you just can't eat them at all," Sarah sighed with a cheeky smile.

"Well, I'm not here to say that exactly," Barry stated slowly. "Some of the tucker out-back is a bit rough, so we have to make allowances at times. A mate of mine claimed he was travelling in the west and came on a pub a bit after dark. Being pretty hungry he headed straight for the dining room. The only two items on the menu were stewed galah and stewed feral goat. Not wanting to chew on a tough old galah, he pointed to the goat."

"'Nah sorry! Goats off,' the waitress exclaimed, biting at her pencil, 'do ya want galah?'"

"'Look I don't want to be hard to get on with, but could I just order a couple of boiled eggs or something?'"

"She returned a bit later and plonked down a dozen boiled eggs."

"'Thanks a lot,' he said with some surprise, 'but I can't eat that many eggs.'"

"'Look love, if yer can't find a couple of good ones in that lot, sing out and I'll boil up another dozen!'"

"My mate reckons he was taken aback and felt the desperate need for a drink coming on, so forgetting his hunger for a bit, he headed for the bar, shaking his head, somewhat exasperated. Before he could even order a beer, a bloke plonked down a glass of dark, evil smelling spirit, put a gun to his head and yelled, 'Drink that!'"

"Not having any clue what was going on, he was fairly terrified and threw it down in a couple of gulps, grabbed his throat and exclaimed, 'My God, that's the worst tasting stuff I've ever drunk.'"

"'It's crook all right,' claimed the other bloke, 'but it's all we've got. Now you hold the gun on me while I have one.'"

The Mills family looked at each other and exploded with laughter at this crazy guest. Barry actually appeared to be serious without a hint of a smile as he reminisced some more.

"There was a woman back home called Prickly Pear Polly who was a notoriously plain woman with a foul temper. Don, I swear she was crankier than Mack, and come to think of it, she did look a bit like him, only uglier, if you could imagine it. They might even be related. She looked like a ladder with a dress on, and she had nagged three husbands to death. There were days a man took his life in his hands if he even opened his mouth near her. When she hit hard times after the death of her last husband, one of the local farmers called Alby, gave her a job as a scarecrow in an attempt to save his crop. A few days later, a neighbour asked him, 'Alby, how's Polly going? Is she scaring the cockatoos at all?'"

"'Good Lord, is she scaring 'em?' echoed Alby, 'I've got birds bringing back corn they stole six weeks ago.'" Hannaway was a naturally funny man with perfect comic timing and they all smiled at the silly story. There was a pause while Sarah Mills served up a rack of lamb topped with rosemary and mint jelly and a fine selection of roasted vegetables. "Message received!" Barry exclaimed, "Engage your laughing gear in more productive pursuits. Over and out! Shut up and eat."

"Is it always so dry out there?" Adam asked during the course.

"Well, no!" Barry said, scratching his chin and thinking deeply, "The last flood was so severe that all the local fish drowned and the dogs were kept busy herding the sheep into the upper branches of the taller trees." Adam shook his head; *this guy is hopeless*, he thought. *No hang on, it wasn't a 'guy' in Australia, it was a 'bloke'...This bloke is hopeless.*

"After the flood subsided," Barry went on, "the mud was a bit of a problem. Riding around the sheep one day, my brother Mick spied a decent looking Akubra hat lying on the ground and stooped to retrieve it. 'Hang on mate,' came an Aussie drawl from underneath, 'I've still got the chin strap on.' Mick strained harder on the hat with no luck, when the voice spoke again, 'It's no use mate, I carn't get me feet out of the bloody stirrups.'" They were loving this quiet Australian humour and encouraged Barry to go on.

"Would you like some more lamb, Barry," Sarah asked politely.

"No, I've done very well thank you Sarah. That was a beautiful roast; it reminds me a bit of home."

"Another beer then?" Sarah asked.

"I guess we might as well be drunk as how we are." Hannaway said philosophically, as he handed over his glass. He voiced his thanks and got right back to his storytelling.

Barry exaggerated the Australian wildlife, speaking of adventures with kangaroos, koalas and emus and told yet another colourful story about a different Australian indigenous species. "Now this next bit is quite serious and important to remember for those considering a visit to Australia," he started. Sarah automatically leaned forward to listen before she guessed that it would not be serious at all. Foreigners and city dwellers may not be aware of the very dangerous Australian 'Drop Bears'.

Hannaway's voice had dropped to a whisper.

"Drop Bears?" Adam questioned with some scepticism, "Do you mean Koala bears?"

"No mate, I kid you not, ferocious Drop Bears!" He looked around conspiratorially, as if he was about to divulge a deep dark secret and even the walls had ears, "Fair dinkum, mate, those things are well worth avoiding, and last year alone, at least four Pommie backpackers were taken by Australian Drop Bears." Sarah looked a little concerned and Don winked at her. "Even my brother Mick reckoned there was little chance of escaping the big ones if they landed on you. Now, at that time, I had the laziest dog in Australia, called Bluey, but he saved me once from a Drop Bear."

Here he looked around again gauging the reaction of his audience and reverted to his whisper, "I was able to avoid it but the Bear dropped on my unfortunate dog. Since there was no reaction at all, it must have assumed Bluey was already dead. With a stump-splitting oath, I pulled my knife and was on it. I only ever did it the once and the end result wasn't worth eating."

He paused for a moment, "Anyway, back to my lazy dog…when we went for the sheep, the moment I would whistle for Bluey to 'Get around behind!' the dog would freeze and was actually pronounced dead on more than one occasion, by station vets! One season, a plover made its nest in the hair on his back, and was able to raise the chicks before that dog bothered to shake itself!" They thought Barry was quite mad but this was actually turning out to be a fun night. Adam wished his sister Renee was here. She would love these funny bush yarns.

The others did get a chance to talk, but they all found the big Australian's conversation so funny; they urged him to go on. Thus encouraged, Barry finally told them about an escapade he had when he came face to face with a giant wild boar with huge tusks and a mean disposition. "He was coming straight at me," he recalled, "I fired the last bullet I had, but it didn't stop him. I ran a little way down the track 'til I reached a big tree. It had a good-sized branch about ten feet up. He was charging me at full tilt. I made a mighty jump for it…and missed!"

"Well, what happened then," Sarah asked excitedly.

"I caught it on the way back down, didn't I?" Hannaway explained thumping the table and bursting out laughing himself.

During sweets, Don finally brought up Adam's situation and Barry shared what he had discovered from the Italians. "Yeah," he said, "The drop-kick was peddling dope from their place. It was a set up. The proprietor phoned Ron Opus to report that the girls were there, on the Sunday morning. We'll get Mack on to it tomorrow. Opus could easily identify the girls and tell the truth about the fight with Adam, but he's not going to do that, is he? The media won't want to hear about it either; much more fun to scream 'Police Brutality'. The drug pushing drongo! You should have arrested the mongrel, Adam."

"I'm still studying," Adam said, "I can make an arrest, but it's a heap of drama. Anyway, my only thought was to get the girls away from him. I didn't realise he was hurt. He must have broken his ribs when he hit the edge of the gutter."

Sometime later when the meal was over, Barry thanked Sarah profusely. He was a very sociable person and seemed to be really enjoying himself immensely. Over coffee in the lounge room, he launched into yet another story.

"Worst accident I think I ever saw was on the old home property, about fifteen years back. At the time, three prospectors were checking out a stony ridge in the backcountry looking for indications. Word came down that there had been a terrible explosion when their dynamite safe blew up, burning them badly and spilling all their guts out."

"They couldn't wait for the Flying Doctor to get there, so a message was sent to my brother Mick who was dressing a few sheep for the cookhouse at the time. Mick had to act quickly; he wrapped the fresh sheep skins around the worst of the burns, inserted the sheep's guts and sewed each of these blokes up with a bag needle and twine."

"But you've got to be joking; surely they couldn't have lived!" Sarah asked dutifully as her husband and her son smiled accommodatingly.

"Course they lived," Barry said with sincerity, "at shearing time, we got a good clip off all three and if yer really wanna know, one lambed next spring."

Sarah cracked up. She found the Australian hilarious and had enjoyed his company enormously. He really brightened up the evening that would certainly have become melancholy if they had all dwelled on Adam's ordeal.

As Hannaway left, liberally thanking them yet again, he winked at Don and said gently, "Hope Adam is feeling a bit brighter."

"Well, I'll be darned," Mills said to his wife after Barry had gone, "…I think we've underestimated him, Sarah."

"Do you mean all the funny stories were for Adam's benefit?"

"Well, I think we saw the real Barry Hannaway…but he certainly did take Adam's mind off his problems for a while. Sarah, think about it, it would have been quite natural for us to spend the night discussing all the negatives relating to Adam's situation. Thanks to Barry, we didn't do that, instead he made us laugh."

"Yes, he certainly did that."

Sarah was amazed at the subtlety of the big irreverent Aussie. She had certainly underestimated him. You couldn't entertain him every night though. He would wear you out.

# Chapter 4
# Girls and Apples

**Monday**
**Forensic Building**

"Beaut night thanks Don, I appreciate you having me over," Hannaway greeted as he came in on Monday morning. "We enjoyed having you Barry, thanks for coming. Look, something is troubling me; sit down will you and give me your opinion." Mills had come in early and seemed quite preoccupied.

"Sure mate, what's up?"

"When Mack told us he found the old guy in the apartment block who fired the shotgun and his name was Clive Opus…well it just about floored me. He is the father of Ron Opus who put in the complaint about Adam."

"Some bloody coincidence, hey?"

"More than that Barry, it's positively weird."

"Sure, it is! So, what exactly is bothering you, mate."

"This is!" Don Mills laid two labelled photographs in front of him and waited for a reaction. Barry Hannaway read the labels and looked at the two photographs blankly for about fifteen or twenty seconds. Then understanding began to dawn. "Stone the bloody crows!" he breathed, barely audible. "Crikey, Don, is that possible? We'd better check it out."

Hannaway picked up the phone dialled Headquarters and asked for Lieutenant Mackenzie. He carefully described what Don had just showed him and suggested that Mack get Clive and Maggie Opus and bring them to Forensics to confirm his suspicions. "You'd better insist that their son Ron come as well, if he is at home," he suggested to Mack. Clive was still a person of interest, but had been released on bail. Mackenzie agreed he would send a car right away and then come right over to the forensic building, himself.

"I've brought the lady here to see you sir," a young detective from Mackenzie's office said a short time later. He was tall with a college haircut and jangled a set of car keys, "Just Mrs Opus, sir. The others weren't available."

"Give me a minute," Mackenzie said to Mills and Hannaway, "it might look like an ambush if we all try to question her. I'll handle it. Let's see what she can tell me." He used Hannaway's temporary office.

Twenty minutes later, Mackenzie returned in a daze. "Well I'll be damned, hung, drawn and quartered," he exclaimed as he returned to Mills' room and slumped in a chair. "You are absolutely right, Don. It looks like the damned jumper is her son, Ronald Opus."

He rubbed his face severely with his hands and then had a good scratch, his face contorting. "Damn!" he exploded. "It's taking coincidence too far. She says that Ron stayed away a lot and it just never occurred to them that it could be their son who had jumped from the roof of their apartment block. They didn't even consider he was missing."

The same tall detective took Mrs Opus down to the morgue where Kelvin and Warren asked her to formalise the identification of the John Doe. Maggie was totally stunned by the state of the body but after a thorough inspection had to admit it was indeed her son. A mother knows these things. They phoned through to Dr Mills soon after. "Chief, the deceased has been positively identified as Ronald Opus."

"Thanks Kelvin," the doctor said, still appearing shocked as he shared the information with Mack and Barry.

"Then it was his own father who shot him," Hannaway exclaimed shaking his head, still not wanting to believe it. "Give me a break Don! No, there's got to be more to this. That just can't be possible."

Mack looked as if he'd been sucking a lemon, "Jesus, Don, we have the file on Opus, it just never occurred to me to compare the photo there with your photos of the jumper. This is all so strange the way it twists and turns. For Chrissake, I feel like I left Kansas and wound up in the Land of Oz," the Lieutenant stated, "…and there's no God-damned yellow brick road to follow on this one."

Mills was thinking along different lines, "Dear God, the prior injuries that threw us, must have been sustained in the fight with Adam at the coffee shop." He exclaimed.

"Yeah mate," Hannaway sympathised. "Well I guess if the jumper has been positively identified, I better start tidying up our paperwork a bit before the DA and his mates come sniffing about."

After Hannaway left, Mills and Mackenzie sat thinking.

"Ever studied Jung?" Mills asked quietly when Mackenzie showed no indication of wanting to get back to his office.

"Rather study the form guide."

"Seriously…Carl Gustav Jung the great psychologist and philosopher didn't believe in coincidence and over time developed the idea of 'synchronicity'. He wrote an enlightening essay on the subject called, 'An Acausal Connecting Principle' which cited the existence of an active force behind coincidence. That's what we're seeing here." Mackenzie looked dubious as Don continued, "Jung even identified a certain sense of humour at times, behind many coincidences. This would seem to indicate the involvement of some form of 'Cosmic Joker'."

"Funny, God-damned joke," Mack stated bitterly.

"There are things out there beyond coincidence and a lot we don't understand. A fellow at my Rotary Club gave a talk about it. For example; three Englishmen were traveling on a train in Peru, I think it was in 1938, and found themselves the only occupants of their carriage. Introducing themselves and striking up a conversation, they discovered one was named Bingham, the second man was named Powell and the third couldn't believe it. He was Bingham-Powell. That's what we are up against here."

"Fanciful," Mack said.

"Our Rotary Club speaker gave heaps of examples and detailed the inherent sense of humour. He had the room in stitches at times because of the apparent 'Cosmic Joker' in some coincidences. According to Jung, coincidence can manifest as an active force that works in many ways. He mentioned an Irishman from Dublin called Tony Clancy and reported that he was born on the seventh day of the week, seventh day of the month, seventh month of the year, seventh year of the century."

"He had seven brothers but was also the seventh child of a seventh child; that makes seven, sevens. On his twenty-seventh birthday, he was at a racetrack and noted that the number seven horse in the seventh race was called 'Seventh Heaven'. In addition, it had a handicap of seven stone. That was too good an omen to miss so he bet seven shillings for a win, a lot of money back then."

"And did it win?"

"It actually finished seventh!"

They both laughed. "That'd be right!"

"Mack, ask yourself this…who jumps off the roof of a ten-story building only to be shot on the ninth? Nobody! Nobody does! It doesn't happen! Then there's the safety net on the eighth floor. Unbelievable! This entire Ron Opus thing, that's the Cosmic Joker."

Mack gave him a look as if his hat might be too tight, but at least this time he remembered to voice his gratitude, "Thanks for what you did here, Don," he said tapping the photos with the back of his hand. "You do good work." Don walked him to the door without comment.

"Thanks for letting me know what Mrs Opus had to say, Mack. I wonder where that leaves Adam. Please do what you can for him. The darned DA will be all over us now, you can take bets on that."

## Heathrow—London

It was drizzling rain and cold. The flight to Kuala Lumpur had been delayed and the girls were waiting in the Lufthansa crew lounge.

"What's happening Mina?" Leah asked returning with bottled water and noticing her sombre demeanour. There was a moment's hesitation.

"Well, the Italians call it, *'piena di...sentimenti'*—my mind is full of sentimental feelings. I've been trying to analyse myself," Mina said quite seriously.

"Go on…" Leah said, sipping water with some hesitation, wondering where this was going.

"Well, when my dad died, my brothers Todd and Matti decided to take on the farm. They actually run it very well and help my mum out a lot. I love them dearly, but when we're together at Christmas, I soon run out of things to say. They're both a fair bit older than I am but their thinking begins and ends with the Oklahoma farm. When we were flying out of LA, you mentioned how parochial we were a year ago, when that was our city…" She appeared to have been voicing her thoughts and now trailed off.

"So now we're citizens of the world." Leah prompted.

"No, no, that's not what I'm saying at all," Mina tried to focus her thoughts, "It's just that I was…sort of…brought up as an only child by my mother. For a while, I really missed my dad and everything, but now I hardly even remember him or recall what he was like. I hardly even know my brothers and I find them so hard to relate to."

"What's this all about, Mina?" Leah demanded quite forcefully.

"Well, my mother brought me up by herself in LA. She never remarried and I guess I just never learned how to interact with males."

"OK, I see where you are coming from, Mina, that's possibly true. Men are certainly strange cattle and there is a serious degree of difficulty here. Men are as dumb as a post when it comes to women and romance. Most of them think monogamy is a kind of wood, so as a result, I believe they should be like Kleenex tissues; strong, soft and disposable, but that's not you, and that's not what this is about, is it?" Leah projected herself as a cynical expert on the subject of relationships with men.

"Well, it goes back to what we were discussing in Hamburg…no wait, it was Paris. We were talking about the juvenile childhood fantasy, where a girl believes she is really a princess and one day a handsome prince will come to rescue her."

"Yeah, I remember that," Leah said slowly, still somewhat puzzled and softening a little.

"Well, it's about Adam," Mina hesitantly said. "I once saw Gluck's brilliant opera, *'Orfeo ed Euridice'*. In the tragic ending, the hero Orpheus loses his true love and you hear the acclaimed aria *'Che faro senza Euridice?'* This heart-wrenching aria became pivotal in the development of modern opera and is classed as the most perfect expression of a lover's longing. 'What will I do without Euridice?' I can't get it out of my head; here I am repeating, 'Che faro senza—Adam'?"

Mina hesitated and drew a deep breath. "Try to understand, Leah, I met him once, for just a minute and I went ga-ga over him. I am besotted with someone I don't even know; I went crazy over the illusion. He's even been in my dreams and I can still picture his beautiful eyes. I have to confess; I think that is pretty crazy. So now, I have to believe, it might be because he actually rescued me."

"Oh my God! Mina, I don't know how your mind works sometimes. You're taking this far too seriously. You can go all romantic, and quote from tragic operas, but look, for goodness's sake, we're flight attendants. We have the sort of job where we meet dozens of eligible guys, but apart from the time constraints and the geography, our lifestyle is simply not conducive to long term relationships."

"You are very pretty, but you're also intelligent, educated, cultured and particular. That is enough to make most guys run a mile. Being all those things and a flight attendant too, well that labels you 'High Maintenance' and most long-term guys are not going to bother." Leah looked philosophical for a minute and asked, "Look Mina, honestly, what do guys really look for?"

Mina blurted instantly, "Tiny bikini bottoms and huge bikini tops?"

There was a pause before Leah went on, almost dreamily, "True, true, but that's not where this is going. Didn't your mother tell you about girls and apples?"

"Girls and apples? No—tell me!"

"Well, girls are really like apples," Leah breathed, brushing an errant strand of blond hair behind her ear, "some over ripe ones actually drop off the tree and although they may be a little bit rotten, plenty of guys want to pick them up because it takes very little effort. On the lowest branches of the tree are the 'easy apples' and there is no shortage of guys who want them. As you go up the tree the apples get harder and harder to get. Right at the top of the tree are the sweetest and rosiest apples of all, but it takes a committed guy prepared to take the risk of falling and being hurt, to climb all the way to the top, to try for one of these."

"Meanwhile, the apples at the top begin to think there is something wrong with them but really, it's just that they are so special. There are not many guys who are prepared to be that selective. Those apples simply have to wait for that exceptional guy, who is different from the pack, and brave enough to make the climb. When that guy comes along, watch out Mina, because he will be someone really special. He'll recognise instantly that you are certainly worth it, because you are right at the very top of the tree." Mina became a bit teary as she hugged her friend.

"There's our call. Come on, we have to go."

# Tuesday
## Another Call from the DA

"We want you in the background on this one, Don. Better let Hannaway, handle it," the metallic, filtered voice of the DA came over the phone.

"I don't think there's much more to do, John," Mills stated blandly, "Now we finally have identification on the deceased."

"Well, if there is, let Hannaway handle it," he repeated. "Who would have believed the jumper was Ronald Opus? Look, with Adam involved, you're too close to this one Don. OK?" Finally, it was out in the open. "The media could make a circus of this."

"Yes sir, I understand," the Senior Medical Officer said tiredly. He really didn't understand at all.

## Duck Therapy

Adam had to be doing something. He had tried training at the gym and had, of course, attended his lectures and written his assignments. He had even caught up a bit on his studies. Right now, he should be cleaning his apartment but somehow, there was no motivation and he just couldn't be bothered. His father had called and Adam had taken it hard that Ron Opus had tried to commit suicide soon after their encounter. It was fairly apparent that Ron's problems revolved around alienation and money and were really nothing to do with Adam or the beating he took; nevertheless, Adam was a compassionate person and still took it hard.

He had to get out of this apartment before he went stir crazy. Grabbing some grapes and the remains of a loaf of bread he jogged across to the park nearby, and spent some time throwing grapes and bread to some repatriated ducks. He did it mechanically, lost in his thoughts. Whilst the noisy bombastic ducks at the front flapped and carried on trying to get more of the fare, he took pity on the smaller ducks and made sure that they got their share as well. Adam did some serious thinking as he broke off bread for his captive audience, until all the food was gone.

Somehow he felt better as he spent time watching them swimming about and noticed people strolling in the park and walking their dogs, sitting eating, laughing and relaxing. Adam knew he had to keep from moping and feeling sorry for himself. He looked at the shops and wandered around aimlessly until he realised he had turned up in front of the Youth Club. God! It had sort of slipped his mind but he had given a commitment to his young students. A training session was just about to commence. He had a dobok in his locker there. There was nothing to stop him, no excuses. What the hell. He took a deep breath and went inside to face his class.

## Kuala Lumpur

Several members of the flight crew were having a drink in one of the hotel rooms. Everyone was laughing and joking when Mina and Leah arrived.

"Listen," Mina said, "this is just priceless…" She collapsed in mirth and it seemed she might die laughing before she got the story out. Someone handed her a drink. Mina braced herself and began to tell the other hosties what had happened earlier that evening. "When we got in, we didn't have long to shop," she explained, "all the clothing we saw was in tiny Asian, size zeros. Many of the shops were closing and we couldn't find anything we liked, so Leah and I walked along quite a bit. We were about to give it away and get a taxi back to the hotel, when suddenly Leah found something interesting."

"Set in the ground level of this humungous hotel with Asian writing all over it, we saw this amazing shop with big racks of beautiful gowns each one with a price tag showing ridiculously cheap prices, like around fifteen or twenty dollars each." That caused a lot of murmuring from the girls.

"Some of them were really nice," she went on, "Leah started going through them, holding each one up against herself. A Malaysian shop assistant came out going, 'jibber, jibber, jibber' quite annoyed; 'just looking', Leah says; 'jibber, jibber, jibber'; 'I'm just looking', says Leah more firmly. Again; 'jibber, jibber, jibber'," she paused to gain maximum impact. "It was a Dry Cleaner's Shop!" Mina shrieked, collapsing helplessly on the bed kicking her feet in the air while the girls roared with laughter. *God, it was good to have her back*, thought Leah, still smiling about the embarrassing incident.

## Flynn

Lila and LeRoy were still grinning from ear to ear.

Adam had sweated it out and felt much better after fronting his class. When he finally returned to his apartment the phone was ringing. "Adam," he said picking it up, expecting another reporter. There was silence for a while then a sinister voice said. "You're going down…loser!"

"Who is this?" Adam asked.

"You're going down…loser!" the voice said again.

"And I suppose you're going to do it," Adam said with a trace of boredom. "Get off my phone you weirdo."

"I'll go when I'm ready, but remember something, you've upset Flynn and that's not smart behaviour, loser."

"And you're Flynn are you?" Adam asked.

"That's right and Ronnie Opus worked for me," the voice said. Adam bristled at that name as the sinister voice went on, "Where's the money?"

"What the hell are you talking about?"

"You attacked Ronnie and sucker punched him in front of his girlfriend," Flynn said, "You drove him to suicide. He was bringing me some money, it didn't arrive. Now where's my money?"

"Flynn are you listening carefully," Adam said, "I don't want to repeat myself. I don't know anything about your money, I don't want to know about it and I don't want to know anything about you. Be a nice fellow and just go crawl under a rock someplace will you?"

"Mistake loser. We'll meet soon," Flynn said, "…very soon."

"Well you've got some education coming then Flynn," Adam said forcefully, "you'll find out I'm no loser." He drew a deep breath and hung up.

# Wednesday
# Hannaway's Temporary Office

"Bloody Hell, Don, I still can't come to grips with it! Is Adam, OK?"

"No, he's not OK, Barry, and neither am I," Mills said quite aggressively.

Silence for a bit but then Dr Mills let it all out. "I feel so damn helpless. A father is supposed to protect his kids and yet here is Adam bearing this all alone. He didn't tell me about it at first, but now he's had some drug pusher called Flynn, hassling him by phone, looking for money that Ron Opus was supposedly carrying. Adam didn't take any money. This is getting way out of hand. Everyone seems to forget, he was just trying to help, for God's sake."

"Does anyone understand he prevented two girls from being badly assaulted? He stopped a felony for Christ's sake. He didn't ask for any thanks; it's his job and he takes it seriously. The damn media want to hang him out to dry. Ask yourself why! Why Barry? Because he rose a little bit taller? Because he worked a little bit harder? Because he gave a little bit extra? Because he cared a little bit more? So, now they're determined to cut him down…Damn, it's just not fair…If only I could do something."

"I'll tell you what, mate, you did plenty. You did well to find the bloody suicide note, you did well assessing the body detail. Your report to Mack is spot on, you did incredibly well with the photos. You've certainly done your share."

Hannaway thought a minute, "Don, you even picked the prior injuries. I've checked out the congruency with Adam's report, it's a direct match. Same trauma, bruising and lacerations to the face, but after the shotgun blast it was bloody hard to pick."

Dr Mills sighed, "Adam's report said he hit the bitumen on his face and that's what the evidence shows. Blood samples proved he was a user, but the lack of needle marks would indicate sniffing coke."

"I checked the elbow crease," Barry said. "As you know, sometimes they cover the needle marks with makeup, but not this time. He must have been fairly new at it."

"With the DA breathing down our necks, Barry, we have to be right up on our toes with this one," Mills stated.

"Stuff the DA," Hannaway said explosively, "No hang on, better not, he's an ugly bugger!" Apart from a slight movement at the corners of his mouth Mills gave no visible response. Hannaway certainly resented authority. He was silent for a bit apparently deep in thought, before his own feelings poured out with solid sincerity.

"Look, Don, my concern is for you and Adam. You're dead right, mate. I'm not a bit surprised that you're getting pissed off. I agree with you totally; what is all this bullshit? Look it's not for me to judge, but I know this bozo did drugs and was some kind of pusher. In my opinion, he was a total waste of oxygen and rations, a walking billboard for birth control. Adam prevented this creep from punching out two girls for God's sake. What the stuffing hell is going on here? Adam's now wearing a suspension when he should be wearing a medal."

"Someone's got the whole thing arse about. Mack's been about as useful as an ashtray on a motor bike. He's become so uptight about it, if you fed him coal, he'd shit out a diamond. He should be sorting this thing out, and all he's done is sit on his dot." A deep breath and a snort of derision. "Have you seen the bloody identikit he's done on the two female witnesses? They look like Joe the plumber and his mate. Since I'm here anyway I stayed back last night and busted my arse trying to find something that would clear Adam."

"Thanks for that Barry, but do you think I haven't done the same?"

"Course you have, mate. Mackenzie just had the mother confirm the note is in her son's handwriting so it seems to confirm it was a genuine suicide attempt, but it still seems a bit screwy to me. In the note, he was feeling very despondent and hated his mother. Now we know she cut off his money and I figure he must have needed it to pay off this Flynn, most likely for drugs or the proceeds from some crime. The problem is that the drop-kick blamed Adam for humiliating him in front of his girlfriend; now he's dead and that doesn't look too good…"

"Ex-girlfriend," Mills corrected mechanically, "The cops are looking for her along with her friend."

"Yeah, that seems strange too. It looks like they've taken a powder and can't be found on God's little green Earth," he exclaimed in his whisper, "but then these wall-eyed cops couldn't find their way out of a wet paper bag with a bloody exit sign. If they use Mack's stupid identikits, they'll likely bring in Siegfried and Roy."

## Two Hours Later

Hannaway took a call. He was summoned to Lieutenant Mackenzie's office urgently. Hannaway dropped the phone looking startled or at least as startled as the easy-going Aussie could look. "Well, stone the bloody crows and starve the blue tongued lizards," he whispered not seeming to notice that no one had a clue what he was on about. He called to Smyth, an administration assistant who had been seconded from downstairs, "Can you get Don Mills in here mate, he might not be on the bloody case, but we need him in on this one…Jesus!"

"What now Barry…?" Dr Mills said a few moments later.

"It's about the shotgun. I'll let the Lieutenant explain it," Hannaway whispered, "I'll go and line up a car." He was unusually silent, even for Hannaway.

"Clint Eastwood," Dr Mills breathed. Clint Eastwood! That's what Hannaway's whisper reminded him of. "Go ahead, make my day," he whispered to himself. He smiled and tried again with an Aussie accent, "Go ahead you flamin' pea brained drongo, make my bloody day, ya dopey dropkick." No that didn't quite work either, but the thinned lips and whispered delivery were pure Clint Eastwood.

## Central Headquarters

"What's with this bloody case?" Mackenzie complained borrowing an expletive from the Aussie. The fingers again—"First suicide, then homicide, next we thought it could be accidental death. Now this!" Mack rubbed his face briskly.

"Now what?" Mills asked impatiently.

"We questioned the father about who he thought may have loaded the shotgun and we made enquiries in the direction he indicated. We tried to check it out a few different ways, without much luck. Now our investigations have turned up a witness who saw the old couple's son, Ron Opus, purchasing shotgun shells prior to the shooting."

Hannaway smirked slightly, he didn't have a high regard for the police investigations. He doubted there was much 'investigating' done at all, it was likely just dumb luck that they had stumbled onto something.

"You—have—got—to—be—joking!" Mills said, jerking his words out.

"Seems Opus was supplying dope," Mackenzie explained, "and he purchased the shells in front of a young pusher he was trying to impress." Mack launched into a lengthy explanation of how the pusher had been done by narcotics and under solid questioning, had blabbed it all out.

"When Mrs Opus cut off her son's financial support; knowing the propensity of his father to threaten her regularly with the shotgun, Ron Opus got the hair-brained idea to secretly load it, planning for his father to shoot his mother. He likely figured his father would go down for the murder and with his mother dead, he would then inherit the money." Mack rubbed his face again, "So by the letter of the law, the son who loaded the gun with a definite premeditated plan, would actually be guilty of the murder of the deceased, even though he had not actually pulled the trigger. So we're back to murder," stated Mackenzie, finally snapping back that fourth finger.

"Then he murdered him-bloody-self," Hannaway opined, "…which is actually called suicide."

He was right and Mackenzie had to use his thumb, "Murder-Suicide, I don't know," he wailed.

"Buggered if I know, either," Hannaway added.

"Where does this leave Adam," Mills asked abruptly.

"We're working on that," Mackenzie said, "but we are dealing with the three wise monkeys here. No one saw anything; no one heard anything and no one will say anything. We can't take any shortcuts. We've got to find the girls to confirm Adam's story. We've put out an APB, but we don't have much to go on. Two well-dressed girls in their twenties driving a restored dark green Mustang, it's not enough."

## About Flynn

"Before I go Mack, there are a few things you mentioned that I want to know a bit more about," Mills stated, "Adam had a call from a sinister character calling himself Flynn. He claimed that Ron Opus worked for him and was bringing him money. Opus never arrived, so Flynn didn't get his money and he thinks Adam took it. It seems Opus was desperately trying to get money from his mother, and even planned her death because she wouldn't give him any more. I don't think he had the money. It's even possible he was trying to get money from the girls he tried to assault."

"Jesus," Mack said, "Clive Opus said that his son sometimes stayed with Flynn. If it's the druggie, Billy Flynn, we've got real problems."

"Bad?" Mills asked quietly.

"You could say that; we've been looking for him for quite a while. Drugs and assault, yeah, a bad one. He's also got a few thugs in his gang. One is a psycho Iranian and he's really bad news."

"Oh, Christ!"

# Thursday
## Forensic Science Building

It was early. Wearing grim expressions, Don and Barry were consulting legal books. There was no known precedent; cases this weird weren't to be found in the textbooks. Barry outlined it on the White Board in Don's office:

- Opus jumped after writing a note—Suicide
- Cause of death—Shotgun blast—Homicide
- Shooter believed gun was not loaded—Accidental death
- It was Ron Opus who loaded shotgun—Premeditated Murder
- Ron Opus became the victim—Suicide or Murder?

"It doesn't make a whole lot of sense in this case," Mills stated, "but the law says fairly clearly that if the deceased jumped intending to commit suicide, even when the cause of death is not what he intended, it is still defined as committing suicide. Just possibly he did know the safety net was in place and was just putting on a show, so his mother would feel sorry for him and cough up the money he needed. But either way we are left with 'suicide'."

"Actually," Hannaway stated as he absently outlined the question mark on the whiteboard, making it bigger, "Opus jumped with the intention of committing suicide, sure, but he is also guilty of the premeditated, attempted murder of his mother even though it didn't come off. He is also guilty of setting a 'mantrap' causing the accidental shooting of himself."

"Barry, it's your call," Mills dialled and passed him the phone, "See what the DA wants to do."

Barry talked on the phone for some time, and slowly walked the DA through the list on the whiteboard and added Don's take on it, and then his own. "He's gonna think about it and get back to us," Hannaway said, "but he's leaning your way—suicide. He doesn't want to convene a jury because it's a technicality and they wouldn't have a clue either." He paused a while with a slight chuckle. Barry saw the funny side of everything, "It's really a bit like waiting for the electronic referee in the Bunker at the footy."

Mills looked up, "The manner of death was a shotgun blast, the cause of death…I don't know…two senior medical examiners and a DA and we can't even ascertain the cause of death. What a weird case!"

## Rotary Luncheon

Dr Mills was a long term Rotarian and had been awarded a Paul Harris fellowship for his service to the community. He attended the weekly Rotary luncheon at the City Plaza and sat with his old friend Carl Winter, a prominent downtown Attorney, who was actually Adam's godfather. After hearing the story of the pressure they had been under, Carl said, "For heaven's sake man, you're too close to this. Take Adam and go fishing. That's an order my friend, no correspondence will be entered into."

It was thus agreed and Mills accepted Carl's kind offer to use his cabin, beside the lake at Emerald Springs, so he and Adam could get away for the weekend. "You are more than welcome Don, just drop in tomorrow and I'll have the keys for you and instructions for the generator and pump. I'll give you a map to make sure you locate it. OK? You'll find it peaceful and relaxing for sure. Just what you both need."

## Friday
## Sydney—Australia

Sydney was fresh and clean after an early morning shower and the brilliant sunshine had returned. The people were friendly and the flight crew loved the hotel they had been allocated. It was quite charming, set back in a leafy street, just a nice walking distance from boutique shops and restaurants.

"Isn't this an amazing place," Leah exclaimed, "the harbour is beautiful, and the Opera House is incredible."

"Claire said we'd love it," Mina said smiling, "I was looking forward to coming here, the weather is just amazing. We have to see Darling Harbour and I hope that sometime, we can return to Australia and see the Gold Coast and the Great Barrier Reef as well."

"Did Claire tell you about her funny experience with the four Xs in Brisbane," Leah said.

"No, what…?"

"Well you know how all the sex shops in LA have three Xs on them?"

"Well I'm not a regular customer, but I have noticed…yes."

"Well Claire had an overnight stop in Brisbane and told me about it. We do a pit stop there on the way back but we don't have an overnight this time. When she was in the taxi going to her hotel in Brisbane, she noticed four Xs on signs painted up everywhere. As they approached the City Centre through Fortitude Valley she saw about fifty of these four X signs. She really thought it must be 'sin city' and asked a guy at the hotel."

"He just cracked up laughing at her. The more she asked about it, the more he laughed. She couldn't understand it at all. It turns out their local beer is called Fourex and the four red Xs are the logo featured on advertising signs as well as displayed on restaurants, clubs and hotels, where they serve that beer. The Australian guy thought Claire was very funny."

The girls caught a cab to Taronga Park Zoo to see kangaroos, koalas and emus for the first time and were awed by the magnificent view of the city across the harbour. They then enjoyed an afternoon swim at Bondi and later, a sunset cruise on the magnificent Sydney Harbour ending at The Rocks. Mina had heard about Darling Harbour and they had a look at all the activity there before grabbing a bite to eat and heading back to the hotel, plainly exhausted. They had done well but really needed more time to look around and reluctantly flew out of Sydney early next morning.

## Winter's Office

Maggie Opus had put up with more than enough. With the death of her son, she was running out of reasons for staying with the reprobate, Clive. Finally she plucked up the courage to consult an attorney to assess her situation. There was one listed in the Yellow Pages only walking distance away.

"Bass fishing!" Mills had told his son on the phone, "A little break in the wild…just what we both need." Adam had been a little hesitant at first but had soon agreed. *Great!* thought Mills as he walked the two blocks to Winter's office.

He entered the reception area and gave his name, Winter's personal assistant was expecting him, "I have the stuff here for you Dr Mills or you can wait a bit if you'd like. Mr Winter is with a new client right now; I'll interrupt him if you want."

"No, I won't bother him, thank-you."

Little did Mills know that he had missed meeting Mrs Opus by less than thirty seconds.

# Chapter 5
# Seeking Tranquillity

**Saturday**
**Bass Fishing**

They lost sight of the panorama for a bit.

The bush track was firmly defined but had thick encroaching trees on both sides and led right up to the cabin, set on a rise overlooking the sparkling lake and the first view from this vantage point was simply breathtaking. It was so peaceful, the perfect place to get away from it all. Both father and son were immediately captivated by the beauty and tranquillity.

A craggy mountain, as old as time, stood majestically in the background and the scenery was simply spectacular. Mist was still rising from the lake as Adam and his dad ate brunch in the open air, from the box of supplies Sarah Mills had packed for them. At first, it was hard to realise what was so different, then it hit them, there were none of the sounds of the city. No traffic noises, no sirens, no jackhammers, no voices or music. Instead they heard only the sounds of Nature, birdcalls, the gurgling stream and the occasional fish jumping, with a background of chirping crickets.

They had opted for an early start and the morning drive up had been easy and enjoyable. The track into the cabin was rough, but Mills had brought his 4X4 RV and the robust vehicle had handled the off-road track with ease. Nearer the cabin they had spotted deer and jackrabbits. Carl Winter was a dedicated fisherman and had no interest in hunting game. As a result, various species of wildlife roamed free around this little sanctuary.

"Those must be the actual 'Emerald Springs' at the far end there; it looks like they feed water into the lake," Don Mills said to his son. It was well named with the lake a deep emerald green. Water spilled over into a gurgling stream that disappeared into the undergrowth down the gully behind the cabin. After laying out their things, Adam checked the gas water heater and lit the pilot light. He started the generator and primed the water pump while his father checked on the fishing boat.

The boat engine started first pull of the rope and Mills was impressed. Carl Winter was an organised man and his property was beautifully maintained. The cabin was clean and tidy despite not being used for a while. It was well equipped with everything they could ever want. Fishing gear, bedding, a library of books, magazines, a telescope, crockery, cutlery, barbecue facilities, gas heating and even a well-stocked bar; it was all there. Sheepskins and colourful rugs adorned the floors and the walls were panelled with diagonally laid, light coloured timber. Still, comfortable as it was, they hadn't come to sit in the cabin.

"Tally-ho! Let's get at them, Champ," the senior Mills said as he carried their fishing rods and tackle to the boat.

"Got one," Adam cried soon after, and almost immediately his father's line also began to sing. The largemouth bass were ravenous and it was almost too easy catching them. They fished for some time, enjoying themselves immensely. The serenity of the lake was amazing and the sound of cicadas and birdcalls filled the air. Adam was looking around in wonder at the tranquil scenery rubbing his tired eyes.

The gentle rocking of the boat had a lulling effect and next thing Adam was sound asleep. No doubt he had been under enormous stress and had not been sleeping well, and as a result, had finally relaxed with the country air and succumbed to total exhaustion. His father continued to fish quietly, enjoying the surroundings as Adam napped. Dr Mills released a lot of fish and only kept the best of his catch before heading to shore.

As the glorious sunset faded at the end of the wonderfully relaxing day, Mills wrapped two fresh fish in foil with a little oil and garlic and cooked them in the coals of an outside fire. Served with the salad that Sarah had packed, this was a feast for a king and some added lime juice brought out the magnificent flavour of the fresh fish. Adam agreed, he had never before tasted such delightful seafood and eating in the open air under the stars was invigorating.

They talked of many things. Adam was a son to be proud of and Don Mills, ever the family man, told his son straight out how much he loved him and cared for him and would do whatever it took to help him through this hard time. He was aware of the pain Adam was enduring and took the opportunity of assuring him of his undying support. This trial would soon be over and the pendulum would swing back the other way. Adam was choked up.

This trip was exactly the medicine he needed at this time. He had a wonderful family and he was grateful for such an understanding and caring father, whose support never faltered. After the meal, they enjoyed a beer together under the brilliant moon that had risen while they ate.

"Dad, do you know the roughest part? I'll try to explain it because I really want you to understand. At the games, the Koreans and Japanese were the firm favourites but I was totally focused; I was disciplined; I had done the work and I…I…I was ready to give it my best shot." Adam became quite emotional with his sincerity, "The thing I didn't count on was the crowd. They were truly amazing. Not just cheering and clapping and screaming, urging me on, but a kind of patriotism manifested like a solid cloud from within their ranks and enveloped me; they actually loved me. It's hard to comprehend, but I could feel them actually projecting love towards me. Dad, I could feel it…like a spiritual experience and I never focused clearer. I gave my all for them, my own countrymen and women; my friends. It was an unforgettable experience."

With misty eyes Adam went on, "Now, that's all changed. I'm the same person with the same mentality, the same values, the same ethics, but now through a stupid, misunderstood situation, that's all changed. I tried to do what was right…to protect a couple of decent girls from a madman, who was moving in to assault them. I believe I did the right thing and am still worthy of that same love, but the media is telling those people that I am not, that I'm the public enemy…that I'm a bully. Police brutality they called it. What if I had been a postman or a mechanic? With each report on TV…I could feel the people pulling back that pride…and sort of…taking back their love…"

He trailed off and Don took his son in his arms and just hugged him. "I understand exactly what you're saying, Adam and don't worry, it will end soon. Let's get some sleep now, son. Tomorrow will be a new day. Things will work out. We'll beat this together. Hang in there, Champ!"

## Sunday
## Reducing Stress

Next morning they awoke just after daybreak, to the cacophony of birdcalls around the cabin. With the thick canopy of trees, it took a while for the sun to penetrate through to their haven by the lake. They had both slept well in the comfortable cabin and could feel all the stress of the past weeks ebbing away. "Bacon and eggs on toast, with grilled tomato slices, then a walk before fishing. How does that sound, Adam?"

"Sounds perfect to me, Dad," Adam said grinning openly for the first time in a week or more. They chatted and enjoyed their day in the idyllic location. Their walk led to a waterfall and they tasted the fresh clean water before heading back to fish for more bass on the glorious lake. Adam could not recall ever feeling so close to his father and talking so openly about things in his life.

They paused to enjoy a sandwich for lunch and continued fishing and chatting into the day, just enjoying the natural surroundings. As late afternoon approached they iced down some of the days catch with the dry ice they had brought in a polystyrene cooler, in order to take it home. They cleaned up the boat and the cabin and packed their things into the RV. They had really enjoyed the break. Oh well, back to the rat race now.

For many miles, they discussed how wonderful the trip had turned out and how successful the fishing had been.

"All too often, we get caught up in our work and our family activities and forget to take the time to recharge the batteries," Dr Mills said thoughtfully, "Try to remember this, Adam, no man ever looked back from the grave and said, 'I wish I had spent more time at the office.'"

"Sure, Dad, you're so right."

"One day you'll have a wife and children and you will need to remember to get away sometimes with the ones you love and enjoy the things that are really important."

"Nothing on the horizon at present," Adam said wistfully.

"It will happen," predicted the older Mills.

## About Flynn

It was on the drive home that Don Mills finally broached the subject of Billy Flynn. He stuck to the facts with no elaboration or speculation, but warned Adam to take a lot of care.

"Flynn has been wanted for quite some time, along with some of his thugs, and Mack says they are a bad bunch," he told Adam, "Mack has posted an APB on Flynn and his gang and is trying hard to bring them in, but you must be careful, Adam. Tomorrow, I will have our locksmith put dead locks on your apartment door and fit window locks as well. OK? Take this seriously son. These are not nice people."

"OK Dad, I'll take care…and thanks. I appreciate your support."

# Chapter 6
# It's All Happening

**Monday**
**Returning the Keys**

It had been an enjoyable break. Adam seemed much more relaxed and Dr Mills himself, felt refreshed. He phoned Carl and thanked him profusely, emphasising how much they had enjoyed the use of his place and explaining that Adam was doing much better. "I'll get the keys back this morning," he promised, however, that was not to be. Mills was almost immediately called downstairs to assist Kelvin and Warren with a new case. A young female found dead in the Botanical Gardens from a suspected drug overdose with indications of bruises on her throat that suggested they may have been forced on her.

"I need a stroll," Hannaway said, "let me drop the stuff back for you."

"Thanks Barry," Mills said with genuine gratitude, "I'd appreciate it."

Barry Hannaway walked jauntily along the LA pavement wearing his Akubra and not looking too far out of place, even though, strolling behind a mob of sheep somewhere in the middle of the Northern Territory may have appeared more fitting. He easily found the address Don had given him, dropped off the keys, thanked Winter's assistant on behalf of Don Mills, told her she was a 'bonza sheila', and turned to leave. Just then he heard the warm female voice.

"Thank you for sorting that out so quickly for me Mr Winter, you've helped a lot and I certainly appreciate it."

"Glad I could assist you Mrs Opus," answered a male voice that Hannaway took to be Winter's. With mention of the name Opus, he pricked up his ears like a blue heeler at feeding time.

**Coffee with a Stranger**

When Maggie Opus eventually came out of the building, she looked up with a start when she heard her name called in a quiet Australian drawl.

"Excuse me, Mrs Opus; I'm Barry Hannaway and I need to talk with you. Could I buy you a cup of coffee, ma'am. It's pretty important." The stranger indicated a nearby coffee shop. He was a big man, but there was nothing threatening about him. He appeared quite charming and Maggie agreed easily. Hannaway explained who he was as they walked to an outdoor table where he ordered for them.

Over coffee and dainty little butterfly cakes, which looked slightly ridiculous in his huge fist, he commiserated with her for the loss of her son and the tough time she had been through. He wasn't patronising or condescending and he really seemed to understand. Then gently and slowly he outlined the whole story. Emphasis was made of the involvement of his colleague's son and just how badly it was affecting Adam.

She appreciated his honesty and respected the fact that he was entirely non-judgmental in his assessment, particularly concerning her late son. In his own way, he was very kind and considerate, and the way he spoke of Adam, projected his genuine concern. She had been a parent, she understood.

They chatted on like old friends for some considerable time and Barry even told her a little about Australia, mostly funny with a fair bit of exaggeration. Then he explained how he needed to find the female witnesses to confirm precisely what had happened. For some reason, they had not come forward to assist the police.

"Dr Hannaway," she started, reading it from the card he had given her.

"Barry," he corrected, "although at home I'm mostly called Bazza."

She laughed, "I wouldn't feel right referring to you as 'Bazza', but anyway Barry, I'll help all I can and you must call me Maggie." She took in a deep breath and appeared to be thinking hard. "I wonder…my son had a girlfriend for a short time; I only met her briefly. I was with Ronnie once when he picked her up from the airport and she was in her stewardess uniform. If you think it could be the same girl who was at the coffee shop, her name is Mina. She is a lovely local girl and she and her friend were hostesses with an overseas airline."

"That would explain so much," Hannaway said thoughtfully, "they might be out of the country and not even know we are looking for them."

"Mina and the other air hostess, were from LA," she went on, "I can't remember her friend's name and I'm not sure which airline it was, but it was from somewhere overseas and they both looked really smart in dark tailored uniforms with pretty yellow scarfs and I seem to recall a gold badge on them."

They finished their refreshments. "That could be a big help Maggie. I am grateful. Look we are all really sorry to hear about your son. Please call me if I can be of help in any way." With a pen Barry underlined his cell phone number on his business card, still out on the table in front of her.

"I'm planning on leaving soon," she told him, "I have a widowed sister in San Diego who wants me to come and stay with her, once I've tidied up things here."

"I'll be going back to San Diego as well, when I finish here, Maggie, so stay in touch and when you are ready to move, let me know so I can help you with your things, OK?"

"I would appreciate that very much. Thank-you so much Barry, you are a kind young man."

"I don't know about the young part, Maggie, but I appreciate the thought," he was chuckling to himself, "Can I get you a taxi?"

"Oh no, I'm only walking distance away," she said indicating the direction. "Thank-you for the coffee and the chat, Barry. I enjoyed it and I appreciate your support." Maggie had loved just talking to a decent, friendly human being for a change and although she was still mourning her son's death, her spirits had soared and the future appeared just a bit brighter. If Barry could help with her move, that would be a real load off her mind.

Hannaway used his cell phone to call an old acquaintance from his Rotary Club back in San Diego. He finished the call and immediately tried to contact Don Mills. He was still busy, tied up with the autopsy downstairs.

"Look Smyth, get him out of there will you? Use gunpowder if you have to; just get him to meet me at Mack's office right away. It concerns the girls who can clear Adam." Hannaway had a spring in his step as he walked to the Parker Centre and into Lieutenant Mackenzie's office.

A panting Mills arrived a moment later from the other direction; he had certainly made good time. Mills had a look of, 'what the hell now…?' but he remained silent. He listened carefully as Hannaway told of his conversation with Mrs Opus at the coffee shop and outlined the possibility of why the girls had not come forward.

"She gave me a good indication of who the dark-haired girl might be. She is possibly a flight stewardess called Mina, working out of Europe, most likely with Lufthansa." The friend he had phoned was in the airline business and had assured him that Lufthansa recruited American Flight attendants and they wore a yellow scarf with a gold badge as part of their dark dress uniform.

"Why didn't she tell that to the cops…" Mackenzie roared. Barry felt a bit protective towards Maggie Opus and was not about to take any nonsense from Mackenzie. "Maybe you didn't ask…" he suggested more gruffly than Mack or Don would have expected; then almost inaudibly, "or maybe you just didn't take the time to listen!"

A very relieved Don Mills was actually thinking something along the same lines with a newfound deeper respect for Barry Hannaway; in his own quiet way he certainly got results. Mack wilted under the scathing gaze of Barry Hannaway. He looked more and more like a blundering keystone cop, particularly in his dealings with people. The corners of Don's mouth moved with an involuntary action as he watched the pecking order sort itself out.

He remained silent and acquiescent, simply looking agreeable but all the while deciding that it would be a grave mistake to underestimate the quiet Australian. If it really came to serious blows, he was prepared to bet Hannaway would take Mack in a single gulp, spitting out nothing but skin, hair and bone fragments.

On this occasion, Mack was smart enough to let it rest. He made some frantic phone calls and realised he was being shown up pretty badly by the irreverent Australian and the polite Don Mills.

"I wish we had known this sooner," he said, apparently his way of admitting that he could have been a bit more supportive of Adam and certainly engaged a bit more effort in trying to clear him. Now that things appeared to be coming to fruition, Mack realised he had made some bad choices and had certainly been pretty rough on Adam with his lack of compassion and support.

"So…let's talk to this girl now and get Adam cleared," Mills said visibly eager to move with this new development.

"OK, I'm on it, Don!" It was too much for him to say thank-you to Barry, or that he was sorry to Don.

"Thanks Barry," Mills said sincerely on the way out, "I am indebted to you."

"No mate, it was just dumb luck, really."

Mills knew it wasn't, Hannaway was a rough diamond, and a lot sharper than people realised. He could teach Mackenzie quite a lot about dealing with people. Dr Mills used Hannaway's cell phone to call his wife and then Adam, to say they'd had a breakthrough and were in the process of locating the girls. Both parties sounded very relieved.

## Lufthansa Flight Home

Ironically, at that moment, the girls were on a flight to LA. Both were serving passengers and as Mina bent over to unclip a passenger's tray, the reading light glinted for a moment on the Lufthansa badge pinned to the yellow scarf knotted loosely at her throat.

"Hey trolley dolly, get us another beer will you, love!" He was not only ignorant; he was fat, ugly and obnoxious. Mina was so stung with surprise she just dropped the can on his tray and moved on. "A 'trolley dolly' he called me," Mina whispered pointing him out to Leah, "…the Neanderthal jerk."

"Do you want me to snot him for you?" Leah whispered holding up her fist.

"No, better not," Mina said, "I'll just spit in his coffee and pretend its cream."

"Remember to shake the shit out of his next beer before you deliver it, the drunken, retard!"

Despite their conversation, the girls had been fairly efficiently serving passengers in the cabin. Right about then, the Captain beckoned them to the stainless steel galley area.

"Oh Jesus! Someone overheard us," Leah said, "we're gone!"

Relief flooded through the two flight attendants as the Captain explained that he had just been contacted by the LA Police on the radio. They would be waiting to see the girls at LAX concerning an incident in LA two weeks ago. They were hoping that the girls could help with their investigations.

"What have you young ladies been up to?" he asked. They both looked horrified and innocent at the same time, causing the Captain to laugh out loud.

"No idea," Leah said.

The Captain continued to smile at their startled faces, "The Lieutenant said you were witnesses only and not in any trouble. You head straight off when we land. The other girls will fill in. No, actually, I'd better get clear and come with you."

"It has to be about the fight with Ron," Mina exclaimed. "Oh my God, this is wild!" The Captain took his responsibilities very seriously and cared for the welfare of his passengers and crew, above all else. He insisted that he should accompany them to the interview and stay until he was satisfied all was well. They thanked him and were genuinely touched by his concern. He returned to the cockpit. "Je...sus, I thought we were really gone that time," Leah giggled soon after.

## Police Cruiser

They met at the Lufthansa counter at LAX and it all seemed a bit intriguing and dramatic. The detectives spoke with the Captain and explained that the girls were required to make a written statement at Central and identify someone from a line up. The senior one called Sam, said he would then arrange a ride home for them. He gave the Lufthansa pilot his card. The Captain was satisfied and entrusted the girls into his care.

The peak hour traffic was over, long ago, and the trip to LA Central was fairly quick and easy. The girls thought it was a classic situation to be riding in a police cruiser instead of the usual taxicab. "Hey! Put the siren on," Leah begged.

"Can't do that Ma'am," the older detective said, while the young one chuckled. Before long, they were at Central and were escorted to an interview room to make statements about the incident at the sidewalk café. They explained to the detectives that they had been out of the country and had no idea about all the drama over Ronald Opus. They were also totally unaware of the problems their absence had caused Adam.

## Mills Residence

"He's here with me now," Dr Mills said into the ornate phone in his lounge room, "Yes, I'll put him on." Mack had called Dr Mills at home to advise that the girls had been located and would soon be in a cruiser, with his detectives, on their way to the Parker Centre to give their evidence and make a statement.

"We have got to be there Dad," Adam said, "...the Lieutenant wants them to formally identify me from a line up, so nothing can be contested later on."

His father nodded, thinking this was actually, unnecessary. He knew the strain Adam had been under but sensed his growing excitement and hoped the stupid mess would finally be resolved. The police vehicle had made good time and when Adam and his father arrived, the girls were already entering the interview room. All Adam saw was a flash of two curvaceous young flight attendants in their dark uniforms, but it certainly was a good look. Dr Mills noted the yellow scarves and sighed with relief.

## Police HQ

"Police brutality!" Mina shrieked, "Is Adam a policeman?"

"He's a detective in the California State University, criminology study program, Ma'am," Sam who had driven the cruiser, answered.

"He also teaches martial arts at the Police Youth Club in a voluntary capacity," the younger detective stated. Mina nodded to Leah, they had seen his martial arts expertise in action.

"Well Detective, let me tell you something new, Adam should get a medal for stopping that low-life creep from beating us up." She said it quite sternly with a lot of conviction.

"That's right officer, he should," Leah added, then together the girls started to pour out exactly what had transpired and accurately describe the part that Adam had played.

They were hushed up and separated to make statements and both girls were truly shocked about Ron Opus' report and that he was now deceased. So much had happened in the time they had been away. Finally, their statements were dictated, typed up, signed and witnessed. The detectives were impressed by the girl's integrity and sincerity and had no doubt that Adam would now be fully exonerated, without too much trouble.

## Clearing Adam

It seemed that Mack distrusted the media and with a thoroughness bordering on paranoia, had arranged to have Adam paraded with four citizens and another detective, on the identification stage. The girls picked him immediately and coupled with their statements, this meant Adam was now pretty much in the clear. Mackenzie, however, was adamant that protocol must be observed and considered it unacceptable for the girls to meet and converse with Adam or for Don Mills to drive them home, when he offered. Mack turned to Adam, "I'll handle the Media. Until this dies down, do your university work and take the rest of this week off, see you Monday."

Mina and Leah left the precinct with the same two detectives. "God! He looked so scrummy," Mina exclaimed to Leah in whispered tones as they waited for transport, "…and did you see those sparkling eyes."

"There's other advantages as well," Leah said, "He's a police detective, right?" With a conspiratorial wink, "that means he carries his own handcuffs."

This resulted in a severe whack on the arm and a glare from Mina, causing Leah to break up with laughter.

The slap didn't supress her mirth at all and she was doing that stuff with her eyebrows again…"Look out if you ever burn his dinner, he might fire a few rounds into the ceiling then arrest you for arson. You eat your Brussel Sprouts, or he'll hold a gun on you. Forget his birthday and he'll use his karate to kick your face in. Fun times ahead for you, Mina McAdam." Another slap.

After a few comforting words, Dr Mills dropped Adam at his own apartment then continued home feeling thankful it was finally over. Adam was relieved at being cleared, but a little disappointed that there were no apologies and he had not been allowed to talk with the girls. He felt no elation…he didn't really feel anything. He hadn't even been told their names and he didn't know where they lived.

He understood the rules, but he thought in this case an exception could have been made. It wasn't as if he was a criminal or anything. Actually, the Department owed him, big time. For goodness sake, he had been hounded and disbelieved for a couple of weeks, then with no apology or explanation, they were now forced to see that his version of events was exactly what happened. No one seemed to care too much.

Sitting in the back of the cruiser, Mina was disappointed too. She threw caution to the wind and spoke to the younger of the two detectives. "Excuse me detective; do you work with Adam?"

"Sure do," the young guy said, "but I'm not on the same shift at present."

"Could you give him something, please."

Leah nodded, impressed at her friends ingenuity and determination. Mina wrote on the back of a shopping docket, 'Mina' and added her cell phone number…

### Adam's Apartment

Adam was restless. He had been cleared but it was…well it was like an anti-climax. He should be elated but somehow he was still out of sorts. He was feeling just a bit disgruntled with the way he had been treated and was actually re-assessing his future within the whole system, when his thoughts were interrupted by the jangling of the phone.

"Adam," he said.

"Hey Adam, it's Joel here. Sam and I drove the girls home and the brunette called Mina gave me a note for you. I'm not sure when I'll be on duty with you again, so I figured I'd phone it through. OK man?"

"Thanks Joel, what have you got?"

"Well…just Mina and a phone number…that's it, you got a pen? Adam…she's a honey, you don't need any more than that, you can trust me on this one man…"

Mina answered her cell phone, "Hello, Mina."

"Mina this is Adam, I can't thank you enough for…"

"No way, Adam, I'm the one should be thanking you." Oh God, she couldn't believe it, she was finally talking to him. She took a deep breath. "Leah and I are just about to have a shower and change, then we're going for something to eat, would you care to join us…" She sounded so cool, so thoroughly together.

"Sure!" Adam said, "…absolutely!" He surely would like that.

Mina told him about Lo Stivale.

## TV News Broadcast

*'Detective Adam Mills was this evening, cleared of all charges when two…'* Damned media vultures thought Dr Mills, introducing the very worst bird species in his categorisation. He watched the nonsensical report, his disgust mounting. No apologies were offered, he noticed, and no retractions were made for all their previous accusations and innuendo.

They operated with total immunity. No sign of any embarrassment for what they had dumped on his son; no regret for what they had put the young man through. They'd had their mileage so now it was all love and light. Chew him up and spit him out…they just didn't care. God damned heartless vultures! He hugged his wife, hoping it was finally over.

## Meeting Adam

"Sometimes I think Jack is about as deep as a souvenir teaspoon," Leah said, "but he's a sweetie and doesn't give me any drama. I actually like him a lot." They arrived at Lo Stivale, the small Italian restaurant where the girls often ate when they were home. They loved the convivial atmosphere and the food was good and quite reasonably priced. The Italian chef did an ossa bucco that was to die for, but it was a very rich and heavy meal and they weren't up for that tonight.

Right on cue, Jack arrived and saw the girls were having a quiet drink before dinner. The first thing you noticed was his hair, almost shoulder length and parted down the middle, glossy and a deep burgundy and he bore a striking resemblance to the singer Jackson Browne in his younger days. Jack was a casual, easy-going guy with a tall, well-proportioned physique and dark features.

He seemed smart enough but apparently lacked direction. Jack just didn't seem to care about anything, and it was this apathy that Leah mistook for a lack of perspicacity. It was a shame to see even traces of disillusionment in one so young, but in reality Jack was a survivor. He was not yet a full-blown cynic and it was probable that with maturity, he would 'find himself' and move on to great success, whatever direction that may take. Right now though Jack was just cruising. 'Emotionally constipated', he called it. He just didn't give a shit.

The girls commenced sharing with him all that had happened. It was a lengthy tale and about the time they got to the end, Mina saw Adam arrive.

"Be cool," Leah whispered realising how important this was to her friend and sensing that she was really nervous. "Here quick," she said as she virtually poured a glass of wine down Mina's throat, giggling all the while.

It started as a fairly formal greeting as Adam came in. "Hello, I'm Adam," he stated unnecessarily. *Oh God, look at those beautiful eyes*, thought Mina. She kept it together fairly well as she took in his tall, muscular frame and his striking chiselled features.

"I'm Mina, this is Leah and her friend Jack." There was something else about Adam that Mina could not identify. It was a mysterious aura of regal confidence that set him apart from other guys she had met.

"Hey Mina, great contact," he complimented, "Joel rang your number straight through to me, but wow, you ladies certainly played hard to get for a while there." Adam wore a big grin, offering his hand. Mina took it, but actually leaned up and kissed him on the cheek, making Leah wonder if the wine dosage might have been just a bit excessive.

"Hi Leah! Hey Jack," he added leaning over and offering his hand.

"Hi Adam!" Leah responded, "We were out of the country, we just had no idea."

"I want to finally thank you Adam for stepping in to help us the way you did. You were amazing and we certainly appreciate it," Mina stated… "and we're really sorry about all the trouble you went through."

"Thank-you for finally showing up to clear me, that was certainly a relief." Adam stated with genuine gratitude, looking closely at Mina. Joel was right, she was gorgeous and she seemed so articulate and smart.

"We thought the Lieutenant was a bit unfair not allowing us to even say thank-you," Mina said. "We had no idea of all the things that happened while we were away."

"Guys, time out," Adam said with some authority, using his hands to form the 'T' sign, "I think it might be better if we don't go on talking about all the drama and Ron Opus and everything…so can we please have no post mortems, if you don't mind. I'm really over it all right now. Can we relax and just have some fun?"

"Great," Leah said.

"You're right. I think that's a good idea," Mina said.

"I'll vote for you," Jack said who really couldn't care either way, "let me get you a drink, Adam." Jack had been 'briefed' by Leah and was to be on his best behaviour.

It turned out really well; in fact it was wonderful, four people with good reason to be happy, just enjoying each other's company and having fun. In no time, they were eating and drinking, talking and joking. There was no desire to go dancing or raging, this little restaurant was like an Italian trattoria with the focus on good food, wine and conversation. It was perfect for the occasion and they all relaxed and enjoyed themselves immensely.

"Back when Mina first moved to LA and showed up at St Catherine's we became BFF's," Leah said. "She was a country girl and like a breath of fresh air in that stuffy place. Everyone else was so snooty and up themselves," she continued with total sincerity. "It was such a select, elitist school, full of skanks and even their imaginary friends were mean bitches."

Mina cracked up at the thought as the others laughed out loud. Amidst all the laughing and joking and fun conversation, Jack held up his hands, "I've got to tell you about a contractor my dad has in his business. He's called Doug Turner and he's a pretty good guy. Doug lives on a small acreage block a bit out of town and has a huge shed where he keeps all the equipment, like his truck, a trench digger, a couple of concrete saws and a bobcat loader and stuff like that." Everyone was listening to Jack. "His house is on a hill and the shed is down a bit with a separate entrance off the roadway. Anyway, a few weeks back, he was woken about 2:00 a.m. thinking he heard a noise from down in the shed. Doug went quietly outside and, in the moonlight, saw four rough looking dudes in balaclavas, rifling through his shed. He didn't know if they were armed and wasn't about to take on the four of them so he quietly went back inside and phoned the police. The dispatch guy said he was sorry but they didn't have a car available and would send some cops out in the morning."

"What use would that be?" Adam said looking disgusted.

"Exactly what Doug thought, so he checked again and they were now carrying stuff out of his shed."

"What did he do?" Mina asked.

"Well, Doug was pretty mad, so he thought about it for a bit and then rang the cops back and said, 'Don't bother coming out in the morning, I just shot the four of them.'" Everyone gasped. "Within ten minutes, he had three car loads of police in his driveway."

"That sounds a bit like urban myth," Adam said laughing.

"Maybe it does, but I swear it happened. The burglars were apprehended but the cops put Doug up on some stupid charge like 'hampering Police in the execution of their duty'. When it went to court, the room was packed and all dad's men were there. The prosecuting attorney asked Doug why he had lied to the Police. Why had he phoned and stated that he had shot the four burglars, when in fact, he hadn't."

"'Why did the mongrels lie to me?' he responded. 'They said they didn't have a car available and they had three.' There was a total uproar in the court room…anyway, he got off." Everyone chuckled at the irony of the story.

Leah jumped in with a story and proved she didn't care much about being politically correct as she camped it up, "We had a funny thing happen on the airline. I wasn't there, but a hostie friend called Claire was on the flight and told us about it. She loves to gossip and tells great stories. She said it was a scream. She was working with a very 'out there' gay flight steward, who seemed to put everyone in a good mood as he served food and drinks."

"As the plane prepared to descend, they couldn't get the PA system to operate so the steward came swishing down the aisle screeching, 'We'll be landing at our destination in just a few minutes, so lovely people, if you could just put your seat backs forward and your trays up, that would be super.'" The others looked at each other. "On his trip back up the aisle, he noticed that a well-dressed and exotic looking young woman in First Class hadn't moved a muscle."

"'Perhaps you didn't hear me over those big noisy engines but I asked you to raise your trazy-poo, so the Captain can pitty-pat us on the ground.' She calmly turned her head and with a heavy accent, said condescendingly, 'In my country, I am a Princess and I take orders from no one, least of all a despicable little cretin like you.' Without missing a beat, the flight steward replied, 'Well, sweet-cheeks, in my country I'm called a Queen, so I totally outrank you. So...tray up, Bitch!'" They all howled with laughter, mostly at Leah's funny delivery.

"OK Mina's turn," Leah said a minute later.

"Well, this actually happened on a flight we were on. Leah will remember this. A Lufthansa employee called Geoffrey Gay boarded our flight here in LA with a free travel voucher to New York where he was taking his break. Soon after he sat down, someone else came and claimed he had the same seat allocation, so the flight attendant moved Geoffrey across to an empty seat and sat the new passenger there, until she could sort it out."

"The flight started to fill up and appeared to be fully booked. The rule on employee vouchers is that if a paying customer needs your seat, you have to surrender it and catch the next flight. So, when the aircraft became completely full, another flight attendant with a clipboard, went to the original seat of Geoffrey Gay and said to the passenger now sitting there, 'Excuse me, are you Gay?' The man was somewhat stunned, but he spluttered and said, 'Well...yes, actually I am!' The flight attendant said, 'I'm sorry, but you'll have to get off the plane.'"

"At this point Geoffrey Gay, who had been watching all this from his new seat, jumped up and said, 'Excuse me, I think you're making a mistake—I'm Gay!' Just then, another man sitting nearby stood up and said, 'Well, hell, I'm gay too! They can't throw us all off!'"

Everyone laughed, but Jack thought it was particularly hilarious and hooted with laughter. The mood remained jovial as their conversation covered a myriad of subjects. They were all enjoying themselves and Adam finally relaxed and began to feel the relief that had eluded him earlier.

"We were surprised to find you were a detective, Adam," Mina said.

"Sometimes it still surprises me too," Adam stated honestly.

"We never would have picked it," Leah said.

"Does anything funny ever happen to you on the job Adam," Jack asked.

"Well yeah," he said straight faced, "when the new Pope was visiting LA a while back, apparently, he told the driver of his limo that he always wanted to say he had driven in LA traffic. The driver wasn't about to question the authority of the Pope so he sat in the back and let the Pope behind the wheel of the limo. The Pope was having a ball and in no time was traveling between 70 and 75 mph in the high-powered Lincoln stretch."

"One of our LAPD rookie cops pulled them over. He radioed in to the Parker Centre, reporting a speeding limo, with a VIP inside it. A bit concerned, the chief asked: 'Who's in the limo, the mayor?' The rookie policeman told him: 'No sir, someone much more important than the mayor; I think it might be God!'"

"'What the hell are you on about,' our Lieutenant barked, 'don't be ridiculous……it can't be God.'"

"'I'll put it this way Sir,' the rookie said, 'I don't know who this guy is, but he's got the Pope for a chauffeur.'" The drinks helped considerably, but everyone laughed. It was that sort of evening.

"What about you Mina, did you always want to be a flight attendant?"

"Never," Mina said, "I just love the ballet. When I was a little girl, I wanted to be a ballerina. I started ballet training, but somehow, it just never happened."

"Really?" Adam said.

"When I hear the music, I feel the romance and get goose bumps." She went misty for a moment, "Flying is fun though, we have travelled to so many amazing places. It really is great. I love it."

"Mina, I was hoping to catch a movie at Central Plaza tomorrow, would you like to join me?"

"I'd…Yes, I think that would be nice. I'd love to Adam."

"That wasn't hard," Leah said on the quiet. She had been coaching Mina on what to say and what to do. "You hooked him; now reel him in!" Actually her student had forgotten all her advice when Adam arrived and had just followed her heart and it had worked out pretty well. It was decided that since Jack was dropping Leah off it was sensible for Mina to go with them. She kind of wished she could have gone with Adam, but it really wasn't practical. Still she had a date and Mina was very happy.

# Tuesday
## First Date

What a morning! Mina did her washing, spent time with her mother and aunt, caught up with some friends, heard all the gossip and answered all their questions about where she had been and what she had been doing. She had a myriad of phone calls from friends, then after lunch, washed her hair and worked out what she would wear. Thanks to her occupation, Mina had acquired a wardrobe of superb clothes from around the world and she carefully selected a dark red pantsuit and off-white blouse for her first date with Adam.

When finally ready, she looked stunning and appeared cool and confident. Nevertheless she explained to her mother that it was a bit like watching a swan gliding gracefully across the pond. It might look serene but you couldn't see how hard it was paddling underneath. Mina's mother kissed her daughter and sighed; somehow she sensed that this date was somehow special.

"Have a good time darling."

Adam arrived looking very suave and said a quick hello to Mina's mother, then they were off. He brought his small RV and they drove to the multi-cinema complex, talking all the way. He had chosen a rom-com and they laughed a lot and cuddled a bit and Mina hoped it would go on forever.

"What's your favourite food, Mina," Adam asked when the movie ended.

"Maccas with fries!" She exclaimed and Adam was seriously taken aback.

"Really?" He said in surprise, considering her healthy, trim figure.

"Kidding!" She said sweetly. "Oh goodness, I like a variety of foods. Leah and I have had some lovely food in Europe, and the French cuisine can be magnificent. I always love formal dining, but my favourite Asian food is Thai seafood."

"There's a Thai restaurant not far from here that's a bit of a favourite, will you take pot luck? I'm starved, how about you?"

"I'm a little hungry…yes, and Thai sounds great Adam."

Adam had chosen well. The food was sensational and Mina loved Adam's conversation and his company. He was unlike any guy she had ever known before. Quietly confident. No bragging or big noting, he was so open and honest and it was certainly a refreshing change. "Are you based in Germany?" he enquired.

"Well not really, but...yes sort of," Mina stumbled, "the Lufthansa head office is in Cologne but our crew mainly connects in Hamburg or Frankfurt. Leah and I fly all over, but we arrange our main stopovers to be here in LA."

"Is the German food nice?" Adam asked.

"Yes, it's really superb. A lot of people think it's all sausage and cabbage but that isn't true. I had a meal in Baden Baden near the Black Forest that was duckling stuffed with chestnuts and other seasoning, and on the side there was a large baked apple cored out and filled with stewed whole cherries. It was incredible."

"Sounds amazing."

"And I love Kartoffelfuffers," Mina said with a smile, noting the look on Adam's face, "...they are a German potato pancake with a piece of pineapple set in the top and a hot apple sauce poured all over them. Years ago, I had a friend called Chrissie who bought a bag of them, when crossing into the Communist side of Berlin at Checkpoint Charlie. They were all asked to get out of the minibus while the guards with German Shepherds searched inside. When she got back on board, the dog had eaten the Kartoffelfuffers she'd left in the packet on the seat. When she told the story it was so funny, we were cracked up laughing, because she went up to the guard saying, 'your dog ate my Kartoffelfuffers.'"

"The communist guards were pretty intimidating and didn't expect to be questioned by a young female. This big stern looking guard was saying 'Dog not eat Kartoffelfuffers' and she was saying, 'Look he's still licking his lips, he ate them,' and the guard repeated, 'Dog not eat Kartoffelfuffers,' it was hilarious the way she told it." Adam laughed. He loved being with Mina. She was so sincere, so genuine. So eloquent and funny.

"The detective called Sam who drove us to the Centre, said you are in the California State University, criminology study program. What does that involve, Adam?"

"Well, previously detectives were recruited from the Police ranks. Each candidate had to serve at least five years in uniform before becoming eligible for detective training. In Europe, it's done differently. Most detectives there are university graduates who join directly, without first serving as policemen. We argue that detectives do a completely different job and therefore require completely different training and abilities than uniformed officers." Mina nodded. "The opposing argument is that without previous service as a patrol officer, a detective cannot have a good enough command of standard police procedures. So, we are the guinea pigs in an experiment, to investigate introducing the European system into the US."

"And how's it working out?"

"There's just no comparison," Adam said seriously, "the pressures and requirements for a modern detective are light years away from those of a patrolman." He continued enjoying the tasty Thai cuisine, "Mind you, some of the uniform boys are very street smart. The biggest problem, we will have, is that the university guys have the head knowledge, but no 'street cred' particularly in places such as the Drug Squad. For that reason, we act as junior detectives, part time, while we do Uni." They ate in silence for a minute, "Now Mina, tell me all about yourself and how you took up flying."

Mina was not used to talking about herself, but this time it came so easily. She talked of her childhood in the country in Oklahoma, how her dad had been killed in an accident. She graphically described moving to LA to attend high school and meeting Leah. She told him about her love of classical music as well as some rock music, of the ballet and about her dreams. She told Adam about becoming a flight attendant and the places she had seen. She even told him about the incident at the Dry Cleaners in Kuala Lumpur. Adam laughed causing those wonderful blue eyes to sparkle. It was so natural and so enjoyable. "When did you last visit Sea World?" Adam asked suddenly.

"Adam, I haven't been in years, not since I was in school."

"Watching fish swimming around, is supposed to be soothing; will you come with me tomorrow?"

# Wednesday—Thursday
# Courting

Leah didn't see Mina again during the next two days. She went to Sea World and on to dinner with Adam, to a show, on a picnic at a stylish little boutique winery and they even went to the gym together. Something just clicked with these two and they enjoyed being together enormously. In a short time, they had become very fond of each other.

The breeze ruffled Mina's hair as she cantered back to the riding lodge. She reined up and admired the sleek bay mare as she whinnied, tossed her head and flicked her tail. She patted the mare's neck and rubbed around her ears. Adam stroked the mane of the black gelding he had ridden. Mina had carrots in her pocket and soon 'Bobbie' and 'Drifter' were munching contentedly.

"Adam that was so much fun," smiled Mina happily, "but I haven't ridden for years and I hope I'm not sore tomorrow." Adam and Mina led their horses back to the stables.

"I believe I will feel it tomorrow too," Adam said grinning, "but wasn't it great to get away from it all and see some wide open spaces?"

"I just loved all the green countryside and the wildflowers," Mina answered as she hugged him and paused to consider how many guys would think to take her out horse riding. She'd had her own cheeky little horse called 'Smurf' back in Oklahoma and had been a fairly proficient rider and it was so great to get back in the saddle. Mina thanked Adam sincerely for such a lovely time, but knew that duty called and she would have to fly back to Hamburg soon.

She told her mother about it. Mrs Jenkins smiled. Adam called to tell his mother why he had not dropped around. Sarah Mills smiled.

## Friday
### Déjà Vu

They were heading home and just on a whim dropped into Lo Stivale for a bite to eat. Jack and Leah were there when they arrived, enjoying a coffee.

"Hey Adam, Mina, How are you guys doing?"

"Never better, Jack," Adam answered, "How are you, man?"

"I'm great; Leah's good!" Jack said naturally.

"Just good?" Leah said forcefully, "Hello, I must have missed the exit to 'Fascinating and Fantastic'."

A smile from Adam and Mina, "I'll get you a coffee; have you eaten yet?"

"No we'll order in a minute, sit down and join the game."

"What game is that?"

"Leah and I are trying to recall ridiculous newspaper headlines. You will have trouble believing this, but honestly, a psychopath escaped from a mental institution in England, raped the laundry woman, stole her keys and escaped. The 'U.K. Sun' newspaper ran the story under the headline **'Nut Screws Washer and Bolts'**. That one is true. OK? We are in two teams and one person gives the headline and the other has to come up with the TV presenter's comments when they read the news headline."

Right on cue Leah jumped in with, "Hope the Cops **nailed** him."

Jack finished the explanation, "Then you get to sip your drink till it's your turn again. OK? But if either one misses their turn or can't think of anything, you have to forfeit and skoal."

"OK!" Adam said, "I can see we're going to need a lot of drinks. Actually, I've seen some of these on the net and they are really funny."

He returned with a tray and two drinks for each of them.

"You start Adam," Jack said.

**"Police Introduce Campaign to Cut Jaywalkers,"** Adam said remembering one he'd read.

"That should discourage them," Mina said.

**"Red Tape Holds Up New Bridge,"** Leah said.

"They've finally found something stronger than duct tape?" Jack added.

**"Experts Believe Something Went Wrong in Jet Crash,"** Mina said.

"Not really?" Adam added.

**"Panda Mating Fails; Veterinarian Takes Over,"** Jack said with a grin.

"What a guy!" Leah said. "Think of England," someone else said.

**"Miners Refuse to Work after Death,"** went Adam.

"If they did, it would rival the raising of Lazarus," Mina said.

**"War Outbreak Dims Hope for Peace,"** Leah said.

"I can see where it could have that effect!" went Jack with a wild crazy look.

**"Fireworks Burglar Forgot his Light,"** Mina said, getting the hang of it.

"I guess the Police had to let him off," laughed Adam and Jack snorted into his drink followed by a bit of coughing.

**"Tonight, 20 Dealers Anxious to Hear Car Talk,"** Jack said at last.

"What would a car know?" Leah asked.

**"Juvenile Court to Try Shooting Defendant,"** Adam said.

"Certainly, a quicker result than a fair trial!" Mina added.

**"If Strike Isn't Settled Quickly, Unions Say it May Last Awhile,"** went Leah.

"Ya think?" Jack said. His concerned look was quite silly.

**"Man, Recently Struck by Lightning, Now Faces Battery Charge,"** Mina said and everyone broke up.

"He likely is the battery charge!" Adam said, "But then…maybe his girlfriend just left him flat!" They all groaned.

**"Enfield Couple Slain; Detectives Suspect Homicide,"** Jack said having a shot at Adam.

"Just maybe, they're on to something!" went Leah.

**"New Obesity Study Looks for Larger Test Group,"** Adam said.

"You guys are out; you just aren't fat enough?" went Mina.

**"20 Year Friendship Ends at the Altar,"** Leah said.

"Forfeit," Jack said, skoaling his drink, "I know what to leave alone."

**"Children Find God in Chicago,"** Mina said.

"Who would ever think to look for him there?" Adam asked sincerely.

**"Country Girl Wins First Prize for Fat Cows,"** Jack said attracting a stare from Leah.

"Her boyfriend might be a Horse's Ass," Leah said pointedly.

**"Army General Flies Back to Front,"** Adam said quickly, to diffuse any aggression.

"The Air Force should give that a try," Mina said.

**"Astronaut Error Blamed for Gas in Spacecraft,"** Leah said smiling again.

"Maybe I should leave that one alone too," Jack said chuckling, "Oh well! It was a serious mistake eating all those Astro-beans!"

**"School Kids Make Nutritious Snacks,"** Mina said in turn.

"I wonder if they taste like chicken," Adam said.

**"High School Dropouts Cut in Half This Year,"** Jack said.

"Chain-saw Massacre all over again!" went Leah.

**"Ten Foot Doctors Sue Hospital,"** Adam said.

"For goodness's sake, give them what they want," Leah said out of turn, cracking up with laughter and thumping the table, "Will somebody please get me another drink?"

As their food arrived, Adam had an idea. "Look, this is a spur of the moment thing. My dad and I went to this beautiful place called Emerald Springs recently and stayed in a cabin there. It is the most beautiful place I have ever seen; I mean, this place is something special; the tranquillity can touch your soul. If you guys would like, I could try to get permission to go there again. I'd really love to share it with you."

Jack held back a wisecrack when he saw how serious Adam was about this. "It's really like a little piece of paradise with a serene lake, a little stream, great fishing and trail walks. It's really close to nature with birds and wildlife and you have got to see the sunsets and the stars at night. It's truly amazing."

Some discussion followed. Everyone agreed they would love to go there, before the girls had to fly out. Adam moved away from the group to get better reception and used his cell phone, "Dad, do you think it might be possible to use Mr Winter's cabin again, I would love to show Mina and her friends."

"You really like this girl, don't you Adam?" The old owl said wisely.

"Yes Dad, she is the most wonderful person I've ever known," Adam said realising he had never had a talk like this with his father before.

"I think she is…"

"I'll call Carl Winter right away and get back to you," promised the Doctor. What a difference a few days had made. Dr Mills looked at his wife and smiled.

# Chapter 7
# Emerald Springs

**Friday**
**A Fun Trip**

"Leah and Jack accounted for," Leah said the next morning as they piled in the larger 4X4 Adam had borrowed from his father.

"Mina and Adam are here," Mina said happily. Jack's two jet skis were mounted on a trailer behind and he was checking the tie-down straps. The girls had arranged the food and Adam and Jack organised drinks from a drive through. Adam had assured them that all the fishing gear they needed was already at the cabin, but he stopped for bait at a gas station he knew.

At a fruit shop next door, Adam also bought some ripe pineapples, a supply of limes, some fresh ginger and garlic. He wasn't particularly secretive but made no comment about his purchases. They were all looking forward to experiencing the destination that Adam was so passionate about.

Mina looked absolutely stunning, Leah thought as she saw how the relationship had developed over the past week. She was blooming and from all indications Adam was just as smitten. He had turned out to be the nicest guy ever and Mina seemed truly overjoyed with the way things were progressing.

They were soon underway. It was a pleasant drive from the city, with laughing and joking all the way. Leah told a funny story that supposedly happened on a flight she was on, "The Captain came on the PA and announced, 'Ladies and Gentlemen, this is your Captain speaking. Welcome to Lufthansa Flight Number LH-127, nonstop from Hamburg to New York. The weather at our destination looks clear and we can look forward to a smooth and enjoyable flight. Now please sit back, relax and…**OH, MY GOD!**'"

Silence followed, and after a minute, the Captain came back on the intercom and said, "'Ladies and Gentlemen, I am so sorry if I scared you there. While I was talking to you, the flight attendant tripped and accidentally spilled a cup of steaming hot coffee in my lap. You should see the front of my trousers!' A passenger yelled out: 'You should see the back of mine!'" Everyone laughed.

"I heard a story from one of the long-haul girls," Mina said, "On a Delta flight from Seattle to San Francisco, the plane was unexpectedly diverted to Sacramento along the way. A flight attendant explained over the P.A. that there would be an hour's delay, and if the passengers wanted to get off the aircraft, they would re-board in 50 minutes. Everybody got off except one lady who was blind. The flight attendant approached her and said, 'Ma'am, we are in Sacramento for almost an hour. Would you like me to assist you to disembark and stretch your legs?'"

"The blind lady replied, 'No thanks, I'll stay put, but I'm sure my dog would like a walk if you could arrange that.' The Captain came out of the cockpit and apparently knew the lady. 'Hi Kathy, I'll take your dog out for a walk on the grassy nature strip, you just take it easy.' All the people in the gate area came to a complete standstill when they looked up and saw their pilot still wearing his dark sunglasses, leave the plane holding the harness of a 'Seeing Eye' dog! Apparently, there were passengers trying to change planes, and others trying to change airlines!"

All four chuckled; they were in a jovial mood and spirits were high. This reminded Adam of a police dog story. "One of the dog handlers was telling me how he loves the simple honesty of children. He had just parked his Police van in front of the Parker Centre and was getting his equipment out of the back, when his dog, Jake, gave a couple of playful barks. A little boy on a scooter was staring at him as he went to lock down the grille on the canopy. 'Is that a dog you've got back there?' the youngster asked. 'It sure is,' answered the handler, thinking the little boy would be impressed with the Police dog. Puzzled, the boy looked at the cop, then towards the back of the van. Finally, he asked, 'What'd he do?'"

"That's so cute," Leah said.

"Since you're our only blonde, Leah, you must hear some good blonde jokes," Adam said.

"Hey yeah, come on share one with us," Jack pleaded.

"Well," Leah started, "A married couple was sound asleep when the phone rang at two o'clock in the morning. The very blonde wife, answered the phone rubbing her eyes, listened a moment and snapped, 'How the hell would I know, that's over a hundred miles from here!' and hung up."

"The husband asked, 'Who was that, honey?' The blonde answered, 'I don't know, some stupid woman wanting to know if the coast was clear.'" Adam and Jack both groaned. Guess you had to be there.

"Wait, I've got another one," Leah said, "A blonde was shopping and came across a shiny silver thermos. She was quite fascinated by it, so she picked it up and took it to the clerk to ask what it was. The clerk explained that it was a thermos…it kept hot things hot, and cold things cold. 'Wow', said the blonde, 'that's amazing…I'm going to buy it!' So, she bought the thermos and took it to work the next day. Her boss saw it on her desk. "I see you've brought along a new thermos," he said.

"Yes, it's really fantastic…it keeps hot things hot and cold things cold," she replied.

"So, what do you have in it today?" Her boss inquired.

"Well, I'm just trying it out with two popsicles and some hot soup."

More groaning from the guys!

"Come on Mina, help me out here," Leah said.

"Ummm…two priests decided to go to Hawaii for a holiday," Mina commenced. "They were determined to make this a totally relaxing vacation. They agreed not to wear anything that might identify them as clergy and get them roped into taking a service or handling a funeral or something. As soon as the plane landed, they headed for a store and bought some really outrageous shorts, wild Hawaiian shirts, sandals, sunglasses, etc."

"Then they went to the beach dressed in their 'tourist' garb. Sitting peacefully there on beach chairs, enjoying the sunshine and the ocean, was really pleasant, when a gorgeous, tanned, topless blonde in a thong bikini and Prada sun glasses came walking straight towards them. Try as they might, they couldn't help but stare."

"As the blonde passed them, she smiled and said 'Good morning, Father. Good morning, Father,' nodding and addressing each of them individually, she passed on by. They were both plainly stunned. 'How in the world could she possibly know we are priests?' asked one."

"The next day, they went back to the store and bought even more ridiculous Hawaiian shirts. Once again, in their wild new attire, they settled on the beach to enjoy the sunshine. After a while, the same gorgeous blonde, again topless, wearing a new yellow thong, came walking toward them with her assets swinging delightfully. Again, she nodded at each of them, 'Good morning, Father. Good morning, Father,' and started to walk on. One of the Priests couldn't stand it any longer and exclaimed, 'Just a minute, young lady.'"

"'Yes, Father?'"

"'You are right, we are priests, but how in the world did you pick it?'"

"The blonde lifted her designer sun glasses and replied, 'Father, it's me, Sister Mary-Kathleen.'"

It was not the usual blonde joke and caused some chuckles.

"Hey," Jack said, "Everyone think of an invention patented by a blonde." Jack apparently loved involving everyone in these games.

"Like the waterproof towel?" Adam asked.

"Right, you got it," Jack said, "…but I was thinking more of a helicopter ejector seat."

"Glow-in-the-dark sunglasses?" Leah asked.

"A dictionary index," Mina suggested.

"Inflatable dart boards," Adam said.

"Solar powered flashlights," Jack said.

"Submarine screen doors," Leah said.

"An instruction manual on how to read," Mina said.

"Pedal powered wheel chairs," Adam suggested.

"Powdered water might be good," Jack said.

"OK, I guess you just add water," Adam commented.

"Water proof tea bags," Leah said.

"A watermelon seed sorter," Mina suggested.

"What the hell do you do with a watermelon seed sorter?" Jack asked.

"Umm, you sort watermelon seeds," Mina and Leah said together.

"Zero proof alcohol," Adam said.

"Reusable ice cubes," Jack said.

"See through toilet tissue," Leah said.

"What?"…"Oh OK! Yuk!"

"Skinless bananas," Mina said.

"Do it yourself roadmap," Adam said.

"Motorcycle air conditioning," Jack said.

"The black hi-lighter," Leah said.

"The wooden barbecue," Mina said.

"The tricycle kickstand," Adam said.

"A cordless plumb line," Jack said. "Hang on don't they have them now."

"Touch activated grenades," Leah said.

"Umm, a glass hammer," Mina said.

"The battery-powered battery charger," Adam said.

"Fuchsia prunes," Jack said sincerely.

"I always wanted to say 'fuchsia prunes'. That would be a great name for a rock group; 'The Fuchsia Prunes'. Ladies and gentlemen, would you please make welcome, the Fuchsia Prunes! Clap, clap, clap, clap."

"I'm becoming quite worried about you," Leah stated looking at him with a stern look and feeling his forehead for temperature.

"Might as well be married to her," Jack complained. "Dear mother-in-law, please don't interfere in bringing up our children. I've lived with one of yours and you didn't do such a bang-up job." There was a stinging slap to his arm.

About then, Adam gave them a warning as they turned onto the gravel surface where a dilapidated sign covered in lichen, read 'Emerald Springs'.

"Pretty bumpy over the next bit," he said, "but at least it keeps the encyclopaedia salesmen away. Keep an eye on the jet-skis will you Jack?" He was right, it was bumpy, but the big 4X4 handled it with ease and there were no problems with the trailer. "Are we there yet; are we there yet," Leah chimed with a grin soon after.

Adam was thinking about something else and smiled to himself with a sort of mischievous complicity. He knew no one had really appreciated the beauty of Emerald Springs, that he had tried passionately to describe. They had been partly humouring him and were just a tad patronising, he thought. Now it was payback time and he almost chuckled aloud with anticipation. (A bit like that cartoon dog, Mutley, on TV. (Nuk, nuk, nuk, nuk!) Adam knew there was a really old, abandoned, tumbledown shack, just a bit further along that he had seen with his father.

"Just over this next rise a bit," he said at last, "You're going to love it." Soon they had topped the slope, "…there!…isn't it fantastic," he exclaimed slowing the vehicle and indicating the dilapidated, shack with most of its roof missing, sitting in an overgrown allotment that was anything but beautiful. The girls looked horrified.

"You have got to be joking!" Leah exclaimed.

"'Fraid not," Adam said, "It's a bit better inside."

The girls looked at each other, mouths open, but Jack twigged and started chuckling.

"Gotcha Dudes!" Adam said smiling. "Just kidding!" he said sweetly, mimicking Mina and thinking of the treat they had in store as he drove on a mile or two. "Now, get ready to be really blown away!" Adam was chuckling out loud a short time later as they rounded a curve and the incredible panorama across the valley came into view. It was a breath-taking scene with its mountain backdrop. After recent rain, everything was fresh and green and the scenery towards the cabin was even more magnificent than Adam had remembered.

The peace and tranquillity were a palpable thing; they became a part of you. The picturesque landscape was stunningly beautiful and each one of them was just awe struck.

"Look at this place!" Mina said in a hushed tone. "The Japanese have a word…Let's say you are crawling across the desert, dying of thirst and you crawl over a sand dune and see a beautiful oasis with cool water. They have a word that poets use to describe a scene that will draw an audible gasp from you. I can't remember the word, but anyway, this is it," she indicated the vista.

"An oasis in Japan?" Leah said mockingly.

"It was just an example, you twit. Japanese poets gasp at cherry blossoms or a plum tree branch or something," Mina responded.

"Or at fuchsia prunes," Jack said but he was smacked severely on the arm again. All four of them did audibly gasp soon after, as the 4X4 pulled up the rise to the cabin and they sighted the glorious elevated lake for the first time. They alighted from the vehicle and all just stood there transfixed, arms outstretched, taking in the ambience. Mina snuggled up to Adam, "This is unbelievable, just unbelievable. Thank-you for sharing such a special place." They had to actively draw themselves away in order to take their things inside. Jack was slowly twirling around and around with his arms out wide, trying to take it all in. Leah walked over looking furious and whacked Adam on the arm.

"That's for being a tricker," she said, "I believed you, back there at that feral hut." Delayed road rage.

## An Idyllic Place

While the girls explored the cabin, Adam and Jack saw to the pump, the generator and the gas water heater. Adam showed Jack the boat and he was suitably impressed. "Mr Winter who owns this place is actually my godfather," Adam said.

"He is a mad keen fisherman. Dad has gone out with him, deep sea fishing this weekend, that's partly how we got to use the cabin."

"Fabulous!" Jack said, "Man, this is really something! This place gives 'off the grid' a whole new meaning, hey?"

Leah was out with Mina's mobile phone taking a myriad of photos trying to capture the beauty of the scene. "I love this place…just think of all the new things we can do here?" stated Jack, plainly impressed, "I don't know…connect with Mother Earth, Study Nature, live off the land, fish, hunt, take up farming, reduce our carbon footprint, learn yoga, write a 'how to' book on stress relief. Man, I just love it all."

The girls prepared a light lunch of peppered pastrami and avocado on rye bread with glasses of freezing cold, apple juice to wash it down. They called the boys to lunch. Soon after they had eaten, they put on suitable footwear and took a circuitous walking trail that followed the gurgling stream flowing down the gully. It was a fairly easy hike with lush scenery and abundant wildlife. A myriad of wild vines climbed the trees everywhere and the fresh air was invigorating.

They saw delicate ferns that grew around the tree bases and magnificent orchids clinging to fallen logs. The happy chirping of birds accompanied their own quiet conversation. The four friends enjoyed it all and the exercise certainly felt good. They took their time on the return journey just enjoying the experience that was so much of a departure from their usual busy routine. When they finally arrived back at the cabin, Jack and Adam launched the boat and they all went for a joyride, stopping to look at the gurgling springs that fed the lake and gave the location its name.

Adam pointed out the fishing spots where he had the most success when fishing with his Dad and they just relished the experience of being together, in this tranquil place.

That evening they watched the sun go down, throwing out a mingled mass of yellow, red, pink and orange across the western skies and giving the few clouds a golden edging. Soon, the sun was in its death throes as the lake ripples sparkled. The sky continued coiling amber, red and gold, making the treetops appear to be on fire. Darkness fell quickly as Mina heated up beef stroganoff in a pot over the open fire. She had prepared it at home and included the cooked pasta in with the dish and when heated it made a tasty, satisfying meal.

Everyone ate their fill and after the boys cleared up the dinner things, they sat outside on logs around a blazing fire, sipping wine and nibbling on a cheese platter Leah had thought to prepare. The food had been superb and the wine ambrosial. They were relaxed at the close of a wonderful day, at peace among friends, contented just chatting and looking at the heavens.

## A Million Stars All Around

"Have you ever noticed," Jack said, "that in a situation like this, there is always someone in the group who rattles off, there's the Pleiades in Taurus, that one's Venus, that's Vega and over there is Altair."

"Not here," Adam said, "I haven't got a clue, mate."

"I don't think the ones who spruik that stuff have either," Jack said with a grin.

"A rose by any other name," Mina said philosophically, "they are all just beautiful no matter what they're individually called. It's just so peaceful and wonderful here under the stars." Mina continued dreamily, "A Swiss astrologer called Paracelsus claimed that God created the jewelled heavens for more than the sake of beauty; he gave them to us for interpretation, so that we may live a more productive life."

"Hang on, I don't see how that would work," Jack said, "What did Rod McKuen say…? 'Clouds are not the cheeks of angels, you know, they're only clouds.' Sorry…I thought it was stars…anyway it's the same thing. OK, the stars are nice but don't get too carried away, they're only stars. We can see them better because there is less air pollution and no lights out here."

"The reason doesn't matter; in the city we don't see all this," said Leah indicating the heavens, "Out here, it's not hard to believe the stars are actually watching us, you can kind of feel it."

"Maybe it's the angels." Mina said in quiet tones, "Do you believe in God, Adam?"

"Well not as an old man with a long beard up in the sky somewhere, keeping record of people's misdemeanours," Adam answered, smiling as he touched Mina's arm gently, "I view God more as the revered force behind Nature and I see that same power inherent within each one of us. My father's parents were Jewish and Dad is amazing, he is a very spiritual person and he knows so much about theology…Christianity and Islam as well as Judaism."

"He doesn't really follow any specific religion and he doesn't force his views on anybody…but he is so knowledgeable and has taught me heaps about doctrine and religious tolerance. I have read a lot about Eastern spiritualism and New Age stuff and although I am non-denominational, I have fairly specific views on spiritual things."

"That's interesting, and it seems topical since we feel so close to Nature here. It is just so peaceful," Mina said again, "it's hard to remember there is hardship and hunger and war and stuff like that out there," she appeared to generally indicate the rest of the world.

## Quiet Conversation

"Perhaps we make things more difficult than they need to be, by the way we view them," Jack stated candidly, "the fundamental law behind everything in the universe appears to be mostly plain and simple, no matter how abstruse or complex things are made out to be."

Leah was quite happy to tell you, she had chosen Jack for his body, not for his mind. On this occasion, she was surprised at the depth of his perception; perhaps she had underestimated him. "I read this amazing book," he continued, "that makes the claim that as modern science uncovers the interaction between creative intelligence and our levels of reality, the image we currently have of the universe, becomes more and more untenable. The probability that human consciousness and our complex universe could have come into existence, 'BANG', through random interactions of matter was compared to a tornado blowing through a junkyard and accidentally assembling a 747-jumbo jet."[7]

"I think I've flown in that one," laughed Leah.

Jack went on undeterred, "This scenario is then used to 'prove' there is a God managing this universe, but I can't agree with that conclusion at all. No one seems inclined to consider the probability of this, or more likely, the improbability." He hesitated thinking deeply, "Look, 'Intelligent Design' is always put up as proof of 'Creation by a God', but I believe that the designer himself has got to be at least as improbable as the 'Ultimate Boeing 747'."[8]

There were nods of agreement as they considered Jack's discourse.

"Leah sometimes laughs at me for mentioning my 'Guardian Angel'," Mina said, "I even carry her with me and some people view it as a good luck charm, but it's really not," she held up the tiny crystal figurine.

"Hang on," Jack interrupted, "Many Christians wear a cross around their neck on a chain and that is far weirder. If Jesus had been shot, would they wear an AK-47 around their neck?"

"They didn't have AK-47s back then," Leah said sweetly.

"You know what I mean," Jack said, "it's really quite bizarre wearing an instrument of torture and death, around your neck as a symbol of faith."

Mina got to finish what she was saying, "Look, whether we pray to a spiritual God or stand in awe of the vast expanses of Nature and the Universe, (which is very easy to do in a place like this), whether we worship within a mainstream religion or within a New Age concept, we must recognise that virtually all religions revolve around a dualistic system of Good versus Evil."

"We all hope and pray that Good overcomes Evil for the common good of Mankind…for the common good of all of us. I don't really care if guardian angels are specifically right or wrong. The concept of a special positive force that can assist me against the negative parts of my day, well…this just happens to suit me."

"That is quite profound," Adam said admiringly, looking misty eyed at the lovely girl next to him. "The Eastern religions work on pretty much the same principle. The yin and yang of the 'I Ching' convey that same truth to us and the concept is basically simple, which is exactly what Jack alluded to before."

"The E what?" Leah said, "The I Ching," Adam said drawing the circular logo on the ground to demonstrate. "Is that what it's called? I thought it was the yin and yang."

"Sure! The yin and yang make up the symbol called the I Ching which tells us: 'Within the greatest Good, lies the seed of the greatest Evil and within the greatest Evil, lies the seed of the greatest Good.' It's part of Korean, Tae Kwon Do philosophy as well."

"Its classic dualism then, just like Mina said," Jack interrupted, "Good versus Evil."

"Of course, it is," Adam went on, "…and it's certainly been around for a while. Plato wrote about a discussion between Socrates and his friend Crito. Socrates was apparently an adherent to a similar philosophy because Plato had him state something cynical like: 'I only wish…that people could engage in the greatest evil; for then I'd know they were also capable of the greatest good!'"[9]

"I wasn't aware that Plato wrote that," Jack said amazed. "Plato was Greek and that's really wild. I thought it was an Eastern symbol." He paused for a bit. "Is it hard for you, with your grandparents being Jewish, living in a primarily Christian country?"

"Not at all," Adam stated, "…I believe people today are certainly more accepting of religious investigation. My parents certainly are. It seems we're finally dispensing with the 'blind faith' thing. You see, like it or not, every religion on Earth has been fabricated and then modified over time. They all claim to have a monopoly on fundamental truth, but if this was entirely true, they would not need faith. Faith is a pivotal part of each and every religion. Faith is what makes religions work. Even in the Bible, Jesus said, '**come** as little children'…but he didn't say '**stay** as little children'."

"I believe the greatest honour we can give to any God is to diligently seek him but most religions don't encourage investigation and scrutiny. It is a known fact that religions thrive best in an uneducated environment. But what about you, Jack; how do you see it?"

Jack considered this for a moment, "When children hold to a religion, I would think, in most cases it is that of their parents, so geography is more likely to dictate one's religion rather than investigation and selection. However, I agree, kids today are becoming far more 'New Age' so I guess the effects of intolerance are likely diminishing a bit." He paused for a beat.

"Of course, the media associates Islam with terrorism which somewhat spoils the argument since this obviously creates discord. I have never discussed religion with my parents at all. What seems far more important to me, is living in harmony with others and with Nature; certainly, more important than the strict and irrational religion of my grandparents. I just don't think I could ever accept God and the devil as real live entities, who are watching us to record our good and evil deeds on their celestial scorecards. That is just juvenile and controlling."

"They don't have to be animate entities, Jack," Mina said quietly, "it's just a way of personifying the Good versus Evil thing again. In the Bible, God and the Devil are dualistic adversaries and hence, eternal enemies. They represent the opposites of good and evil."

Here Adam jumped in again, "That is precisely the difference I see with Eastern philosophy. The yin and yang are uniquely in **harmony** as opposed to the eternal **conflict** contained in other dualities. The theory of inherent evil is at the pinnacle of the T'ien-t'ai philosophy of perfect harmony in which all opposites are identified and harmonised. This then effectively erases the concept of good and evil, heaven and hell, 'nirvana' and 'klesa', Buddha and sentient beings, and so forth."

"Go on Adam, this is fascinating," Jack said.

"Yes, it is," Mina stated, while Leah nodded.

"Well, using Buddhism as an example, in this holistic view, there has to be a harmonious balance of good and evil. Inherent good is contained within all beings. This means that some degree of evil must be part of the Buddha, in order for good to be an integral part of the icchantika."

"Hang on Adam," Jack said, "what is the icchantika?" The others looked blank.

"Sorry guys," Adam said, "Icchantika are base and spiritually deluded beings, who according to some Mahāyāna texts, are lacking in Buddha-nature and would thus, normally also lack the potential to gain enlightenment. Other religions would brand them as infidels or sinners and write them off as being of no consequence, but not Buddhism. The theory affirms the icchantika's Buddha-hood and Buddha's humanity."[10]

"So, you see, to maintain the all-important harmony, an element of evil in the Buddha is essential, in order to generate feelings of compassion to view all fellow beings sympathetically, since he and they, then, have an identical human nature. In the Holy Book called the 'Vimalakirti Sutra' the Buddha actually spells it out: **'Because sentient beings are sick, I am also sick'.**"

"That's a bit too deep for me," Mina said.

"Mina, it's really not deep, it's a wonderful philosophy. It may all sound new and strange, but really, it's just an expanded Eastern version of the dualism you mentioned earlier," he explained. "Motivated by compassion, the Buddha **deliberately** takes on and manifests a degree of evil, in order to relate to the nature of his followers, particularly the sentient beings who commit evil, and a bridge is thus built between the Buddha and all sentient beings.[11] Because of this, spirituality doesn't then rely on perfection. It also means that within the spiritually void icchantika, the unenlightened now **have** the capacity to gain enlightenment, the unredeemable **can** now be redeemed and the unlovable **can** now be loved."

"Wow!" Leah said and Jack had his chin in his hands contemplating Adam in a new light and listening intently. Mina was doing the same.

"That is amazing when you put it like that," Mina stated with far more understanding than she had credited herself, "…in Christianity they would be branded as worthless sinners and outcasts and told they are destined for eternal damnation in Hell." She now sat silently considering if it was actually this peaceful spirituality Adam manifested, that made him so different, and attracted her so magnetically.

"You are exactly right Mina; my point is that no such bridge exists in Christianity, Judaism and Islam," Adam continued. "Instead, they have a doctrine that promotes a self-deprecating, miserable religion originally created for the austere, tent dwelling Jewish fraternity." Adam was on a roll and sold his point well, "People, our religion is meant to empower us! We are not fallen sinners in dire need of rescue!"

"Leah is!" Jack said playfully, getting a smile from Mina and a slap on the arm from Leah.

Adam continued unperturbed, "Women are not here to make restitution for the sin of Eve! Men are not crawling from the mire of original sin! The neurotic Church has promoted fear, guilt and inadequacy, mainly to ensure dependency on the clergy."

"The Catholic Church has a lot to answer for," Jack said seriously, "Raking in billions and claiming it operates on a mandate to help the poor."

Adam nodded, agreeing with him, "To call its scriptures the 'Word of God' is to legitimise all the bloodlust, the wrath, the bigotry and the hatred within its dogma. Accordingly, the denigration of mankind found in our Christian Bible is cast in a spirit of unworthiness, retribution and fear of punishment."

Adam sucked in the clean country air and let it out slowly, "In the Old Testament, YHWH demands the sacrifice of 'first-born' babies.[12] As a religious principle, this is totally abhorrent to me as he chooses to brutalise and debase the humans he supposedly created, for the inadequacies they display. This makes no sense at all. Why didn't he create them better if that is his problem? Can you visualise the arrogant, wrathful and bloodthirsty, Old Testament YHWH ever stating? **'Because my creations are sick, I am also sick.'** Somehow, I don't think so."

Adam was moved by this speech and unobtrusively went around and filled each glass, lightly resting his hand on each one's shoulder as he did so. It was a simple unconscious gesture of a gentle, spiritual man who genuinely cared for those around him. This had accentuated the pain his suspension had caused him. Mina understood and was moved deeply. She was sure she loved him and couldn't wait to spend the night in his arms.

## Sunday
### A Day Shared

Next morning they awakened to the chatter of the woodland birds chirping happily, punctuated by the sound of the approaching motor boat. Jack had left silently, more than an hour earlier and now returned with a catch of plump bass. They had talked late into the night and only Jack had stirred at such an early hour. Leah was actually stumbling out, not yet fully awake.

"I wasn't in a quest for 'beauty sleep'," she slurred, "I needed to hibernate!" It was mid-morning and by the time they had showered and dressed, the beautiful aroma of frying fish was coming from the outdoor fire, Jack had stoked up. "Jack, you're a keeper," sighed Leah joining him still in her PJ's, "This is simply wonderful, I was never one for camping," she confessed, "…but this is the nicest place ever. The cabin is incredible. It's like camping, resort-style and I just love the fresh air and the smell of that fish…Mmmmm."

Mina nodded, silently confirming those sentiments.

"What do you call fish with no eyes?" Jack asked with a grin. No one would hazard a guess. "Fsh." Jack totally cracked up at his own silly joke.

"No!" Leah said, rubbing her eyes, "on second thoughts, I'm throwing you back after that one."

"Dear mother-in-law…" Jack said and for self-preservation, left it unfinished. "Good morning sleepy head," he added kissing Leah's forehead.

"I like sleeping," Leah mumbled, "it's like being dead without the commitment."

"Bush walk!" Adam said decisively after breakfast, "It's a bit rough, you'll need solid footwear. I want to show you the waterfall that Dad and I found and if we are quiet we may see some wildlife up close."

"How wild," Leah asked seriously, with her smile giving her away, "like lions and tigers?"

"Like lots of birds and squirrels and perhaps a deer with a baby fawn," Adam replied. They set off in good spirits. The walk through the rain forest was interesting with beautiful ferns and wild flowers and when the friends finally got to the falls, they were in full flow from the recent rain. Sunlight penetrated the canopy of thick foliage in silver shafts. The crystal water cascaded down onto the rocks below and tiny rainbows appeared in the air like holograms. Some of the giant old trees appeared to have been growing there almost from the beginning of time, and it was humbling to consider the insignificant of a human generation in comparison.

"Hey," Jack said, "let's everyone share their pet hate." No drinking game this time.

"Well," Mina said, "I hate every form of child abuse." The others nodded.

"Religious intolerance," Adam said, "and it follows on from what Mina said…There are no Christian children or Moslem children or Jewish children. They are children of Christian, Moslem or Jewish parents. The little minds are taught to believe everything their parents say, so they are indoctrinated that their birth religion just happens to be the correct one, with all others wrong and likely evil. The belief that their school-yard squabbles are sufficient to send them to a fiery hell, just has to screw up tiny minds, along with the thought that a deceased friend or family member might be in permanent torment in Hell, because he once told a lie."

Mina jumped in again, "I actually heard a mother in a shopping centre screaming at a kid. 'Stop telling lies Peter, if you keep lying, Santa won't come to you.'"

"Double standard; she was actually lying herself," Adam said. "What's your pet hate, Jack?"

"I can't stand air hostesses who make sure you are firmly strapped in and then ask if there's anything you want." Some smiles, but daggers from Leah.

"I think my pet hate is men," she stated, "…and also wastage. Why does it take one million sperm to fertilise an egg? Partly because the male ones don't stop and ask for directions. What do men and sperm have in common? They both have a one-in-a-million chance of becoming a human being. What did God say after creating man? 'Hey, wait a minute, wait up, I can do better.'"

"Dear Mother-in-law…" Jack said rubbing his brow and wincing, as they all smiled. "I suppose after that, it's a bit too late now, to discuss the things we actually like."

About then Jack turned and presented Leah with a posy of wild flowers he had secretly gathered. "Are we good? Friends?" He asked gently.

"Is this meant to be a turn-on?" Leah snapped but a slight grin gave her away, "For future reference, do better."

"I really suck at this romance thing," Jack complained, "Could you grade me on effort?"

The canopy of foliage filtered out some of the light making this little grotto a haven away from the rest of the world. They removed their shoes and sat on the smooth rocks, relaxing in this serene, idyllic place, dangling their bare feet in the crystal waters. For some time, they just chatted quietly before deciding they should head back.

"Movement up ahead," Jack whispered as a deer with two fawns crossed the track not far in front of them. "That is quite unusual," he explained later. "It is very rare for this species to have twins and it is possible the doe adopted an orphan that lost its mother." The girls were enthralled. Being this close to nature had a huge impact on all of them and they happily embraced the special invigorating feeling.

The spiritual discussion out under the stars the previous evening was likely precipitated by the subtle call of Nature. Everything around them communicated itself in a cathartic, harmonious and altruistic way that bonded them together in the manner a shared exotic experience might. The city seemed light years away and they found the isolation captivating. It brought out noble feelings of compassion towards all kindred spirits. It was also the perfect setting for new love to blossom.

When they reached the cabin, the four friends changed into bathers and had a swim in the clear waters of Emerald Lake, to cool off. Time appeared to stand still as they frolicked in the sparkling waters, beating the heat and humidity. Later, Leah and Jack made sandwiches for lunch, while Adam and Mina lazed in the hammocks on the cabin verandah, talking quietly. Some time later, Adam asked, "Will we put the jet-skis in, or would you rather go fishing?"

"Let's do both," Jack replied, "You and Mina start on the skis and Leah and I will catch our dinner."

"I'd love to try jet-skiing," Mina said.

Possibly as a result of her ballet training, Mina had superb balance and she was a natural at Jet-skiing. She aced it and she and Adam played with the skis until the sun was getting lower in the west before bringing them back for Jack and Leah. They preferred to continue fishing for a bit, before they swapped over.

Adam was lighting a fire when Jack and Leah finally returned. "That is a superb fish Jack," Adam said admiringly.

"Leah caught it," Jack said, "I only helped land the monster."

"Oh my God, Leah!" Mina exclaimed, "Look at the size of it."

"I'll clean it as long as I don't have to cook it," Jack added, as he took a knife and commenced the task.

"My treat," Adam said, "I'll prove I'm domesticated."

"I'll do sweets," Mina said.

Jack and Leah had another run on the jet skis, while Adam and Mina got things ready for dinner. Towards dusk, Adam cut up two ripe pineapples and made a tropical sauce; he also put some long grain, wild rice on to boil. Mina looked a bit surprised at rice with fish but nothing was actually said. Staying with the tropical theme, she was cutting up more pineapple and banana into a bowl.

Adam took the huge fish and with a large serrated hunting knife made diagonal cuts an inch apart along the body. Into one cut he placed fresh sliced ginger and into the next, crushed garlic. Into the cavity of the fish went the pineapple cores. The whole fish was smeared with oil and lime juice, then wrapped in aluminium foil. Adam was placing it in the coals of the outside fire as Jack and Leah returned.

"That was brilliant fun," Leah exclaimed, wrapping a huge towel around herself. "Hey, just look at the beautiful sunset."

## Close to Nature

"Isn't it great to escape the rat race for a while," Jack exclaimed.

"Certainly is," Mina agreed.

"Rat race is right," Jack continued. "Back in LA, at times I feel like one of those white rats on the little treadmill things, running, running, running and getting precisely nowhere. I can picture those rats going at it for months on end but then one day the light comes on and they just say, 'stuff it, I'm going to go and do yoga with the cat.'"

The others just looked at each other while Leah silently shook her head, looking stern, but with a small movement at the corners of her mouth giving her away. "I never believed I could adore being so close to Nature like this!" she claimed, the surprise now showing on her face. "It's like the rest of the world has been nuked and we are the only ones left on the planet."

"Well," Adam said, "this might surprise you, but I am coming to believe that there is actually an active attraction of mankind to Nature. There is evidence that somehow, it calls us instinctively to itself. There are people studying the phenomenon that animals share a mysterious bond that is somehow in sympathy with Nature. It appears that their 'animal instinct' is some form of natural, psychic clairvoyance. If this can be shown to be true, then why not humans as well?"

"That's a bit bizarre, but it makes sense." Leah said, "Most people would find it a bit 'woo woo' though."

"Well not me," Adam exclaimed, "and I'll tell you why. There is one maverick American geologist who predicts earthquakes, volcanic eruptions and other natural disasters, with amazing accuracy, just by monitoring the 'lost pet' ads in various newspapers around the world. I'm not kidding, this is true. In the two weeks preceding a natural disaster, the number of missing pets rises almost exponentially and this is reflected in the many newspapers he subscribes to. It would seem the animals receive a mental forewarning and promptly leave the vicinity."

Adam checked his cooking before continuing, "...and honestly, this is not something new-fangled. Way back in 373 BCE, ancient historians actually documented that creatures, including rats, snakes, and weasels as well as household pets, were observed leaving the Greek city of Helice, just days before the place was devastated by an earthquake. It is also well documented that in February 1975, the residents of Haicheng in China were successfully evacuated just before a 7.3 magnitude earthquake hit the area."

"Authorities admitted that the decision to evacuate, was as a result of the strange behaviour of pets and other animals leaving the vicinity. Around 90,000 lives were probably saved as a result. In Liaoning China, animals are now monitored in Anshan Zoo in an organised study to aid the prediction of natural disasters. Far out, maybe, but we still have a lot to learn about these esoteric things."

Mina had joined them and was listening intently before adding, "I read that when the tsunami devastated Sri Lanka and parts of Thailand, on Boxing Day, 2004, there were no dead animals found in the devastation. It seems that they left all the areas that later became inundated. It was reported that many elephants and oxen had broken away in order to depart to a safer place."

"That's a WOW..." Leah was lost in thought for a minute standing mutely with her mouth open, "I've watched birds execute amazing synchronised manoeuvers and fish all dart away together without hitting each other and often wondered if that indicates that they somehow communicate with each other. I guess in some things, they are far more sensitive than humans."

Adam nodded for a bit. "After he apparently walked on the Moon, the astronaut, Edgar Mitchell, radically altered his worldview as he journeyed back from space. He claims he suddenly saw the Earth as a living organism: he realised we could explore a small part of our Galaxy but we had barely begun to probe the deepest mystery of the universe—the fact of consciousness itself and the workings of the human mind. He became convinced that this uncharted territory was the next frontier to explore, and that it contained possibilities we had hardly begun to imagine. Within two years of his expedition, Edgar Mitchell founded the 'Institute of Noetic Sciences' which is a branch of metaphysical philosophy concerned with the study of the human mind and intellect."

"Oh! Wow! That is so interesting." Jack said, "Do you think that in time a higher consciousness just may stop us killing each other and lead to World peace and enlightenment?"

"We can only hope." Adam breathed.

"Seriously, Adam, that should be our primary aim, it really should. If you can help pull that one off, you're the man…if you were Bongolese, you would be honoured with a ceremonial feast where you would be entitled to snort snuff from the dried scrotum of a goat."[13]

"You're crazy man," Adam re-joined smiling, "You sound like you've been sniffing something a bit wilder than snuff!"

## A Lovely Evening

"You know what's so great here." Mina observed thoughtfully some time later. "No TV and no phone reception. Just look how much conversation we've shared since we arrived and how much we can learn from each other."

"No self-opening glass doors," Jack said re-joining the group after securing the jet skis. He carried some greenery from the lakeshore. Jack had decided to contribute some decoration to the evening meal by laying out plates decorated with a variety of sweet smelling fern as a garnish. He did it like a bumbling gourmet chef, putting on a ridiculous, French accent, extolling the health benefits of this particular water plant as he arranged it on each plate.

His herbal expertise and knowledge had proved to be the preventative cure for everything from halitosis to warts, he claimed, with considerable alleviation of varicose veins as a side benefit. Jack was a natural comic entertainer and this caused more merriment in the camp.

"If there was TV we could see how the situations in Syria, Iraq and Afghanistan are going," Leah said facetiously.

"Don't get me started," Jack warned. "Even the most patriotic American would have trouble accepting that Osama bin Laden was responsible for the September 11th atrocities or that hi-jacked airliners actually brought down the Twin Towers. Nevertheless, aircraft supposedly piloted by kamikaze Saudi Arabian terrorists somehow justified the USA ripping into the Afghans and then invading Iraq. That is stupid. It's not logical in any way. It doesn't make any sense at all to me. At least seven of those Saudi Arabian terrorists named in the press as suicide pilots, whose photos adorned our newspapers, are still alive today; go figure."

"He's right," Leah said. "They told us in a training session that a flight attendant called Amy Sweeney, on AA Flight 11, had the presence of mind to call her airline and reveal the seat numbers of the hijackers who had seized the plane, so they could be identified from the seating plan. We can prove the official story is not true, because guess what; these supposed Arab 'terrorists' who were named, regardless of what names they might have used, are totally absent from the manifests."

"They don't show up on boarding videos and yet we are asked to believe that they took over the planes with cardboard box cutters and prevented eight different pilots of four aircraft from transmitting a four-digit hijacking code, on 'fly by wire' aircraft. Seriously, that is plainly impossible!"

Adam looked a bit lost, "Fly by wire?" He questioned.

Mina explained, "It's hi-tech airline security. Whenever 'fly by wire' aircraft are hijacked or an attempt is made by the perpetrators to fly an aircraft to an alternate destination, at the flick of a switch, the pilot or co-pilot transmits a code and control of the aircraft is automatically transferred to a federal ground facility, allowing the aircraft to be remotely landed at the nearest suitable airport. Of course, in this situation the controls of commercial airliners are instantly rendered inoperative and there is nothing the hijackers or the pilot can do to alter the situation. This is now standard procedure in most commercial airlines."[14]

"Amazing!" was all Adam could say, shaking his head considering the implications.

"Essentially, they are lying to us," Jack said sadly, "I personally viewed the film of the impact that punched a hole in the wall of the Pentagon. It was taken from a gas station security camera. I think it's still on the net. Several eyewitnesses claimed it was a missile and not an airliner that hit the wall and I must agree that this is plainly apparent in the security film. For a start, there was the relatively small hole through the brickwork; then we have the situation where the trauma plainly didn't resemble an aircraft crash site at all. In a crash where the aircraft is utterly destroyed, it would be normal to still see wing-tips, wheels, most of the tail and sundry bits of wreckage."

"The monstrous tail plane, the wings and at least some seats would have been left outside the wall even if there had been a massive fire, which there was not, in this case. Not even the remnants of the huge engines were visible at this site.

No wings hit the building and there was no indication of them burning up. There is no evidence that any aircraft was ever there at all."

"We are asked to believe this was an aircraft crash, with no wreckage. It was also a fairly major coincidence that the impact point at the Pentagon was miraculously, 'closed for renovations' at the time, with all staff moved to the other side of the building."

Mina enjoyed these evening discussions. She was an intelligent young woman and added something she had heard, "I just find it hard to believe that burning fuel from the airliners could generate sufficient heat to melt the structural steelwork and cause the eventual collapse of the Twin Towers. They were designed to withstand an aircraft impact. What about Building 7, it wasn't hit by anything, but it still came crashing down. Something doesn't gel here at all."

"You are on the right track," Jack said sincerely, "Eyewitnesses reported hearing explosions immediately prior to the collapse of each tower, which further serves to refute the official story. In addition, in the videos you can see little puffs of smoke called 'squibs', ejecting from alternate floors, which my father says, demonstrates obvious signs of controlled demolition."

"Do you really believe it was a demolition, Jack?" Adam asked, whilst packing hot coals around the fish.

"It's easy enough to prove with High School physics." Jack said, "I checked it out at length. Look, the World Trade Centre Towers were 1,300 feet tall and 208 feet wide. We can calculate that after initial acceleration of around 33 feet/second/second until terminal velocity of around 125 feet/second is attained; the building in a freefall situation, should take almost 12 seconds to hit the ground from the force of gravity—understand?"

They all nodded, but still looked a bit unsure.

"I'll make it simple," Jack said writing in the dirt with a stick and walking them through his calculations, *"If you dropped a brick from 1300 feet up."*

| | |
|---|---|
| First second it would fall | —33 feet |
| Second second | —66 feet |
| Third second | —99 feet |
| Fourth second | —125 feet |
| (Terminal velocity is reached) | |
| Fifth second | —125 feet |

| | |
|---|---|
| Sixth second | —125 feet |
| Seventh second | —125 feet |
| Eighth second | —125 feet |
| Ninth second | —125 feet |
| Tenth second | —125 feet |
| Eleventh second | —125 feet |
| Twelfth second | —<u>102 feet</u> |
| Total of | —1,300 feet |

Jack underlined it heavily with the stick. "Now watch a film clip of the fall of each building and with a stop watch, time the crash…just short of 8 seconds. It is simply not possible for 1300 feet tall buildings to crash to the ground, by gravity alone, in this timeframe. The 'pancake' effect of each successive floor's collapse would, of course, retard it much further still. Burning aircraft fuel won't do it either as Mina said."

"The only way an entire building can freefall at more than the velocity of gravity is with the aid of explosives which cause an enormous electromagnetic pulse. Such a pulse would also wipe computer discs and render mobile phones inoperative, which is precisely what happened. A massive C-4 plastic explosive blast, for example, would likely do this, so accordingly it becomes very difficult to entertain any other explanation."[15]

The fish was beginning to smell wonderful and Jack's nose twitched like a rabbit's making them all laugh. "Actually, subterfuge is even more evident because according to demolition experts, and my father is one of them, the 'pancake' effect of each successive floor, should retard the fall to something close to 96 seconds and yet somehow it took only 8."

"Your dad works in demolition?" Adam questioned.

"Yeah, so do I. Dad owns a demolition company and I work with him. Sorry, I should have explained that. Dad got very upset with the garbage on TV about the Twin Towers. He claims the electromagnetic pulse associated with the use of C-4 would create a sonic boom and as we saw, all the windows in the surrounding buildings were blown out. Demolition experts don't do it that way. We can drop a building without blowing windows out, using what we call 'micro-nukes'. The fact that the windows were blown out, confirms that a larger shockwave pulse was involved, such as occurs with C-4 Plastic." Adam, Mina and Leah were thoughtful.

"Another thing that confirms this scenario from a completely different perspective is that records are available of 'put options' purchased on the Wall Street stock market in the four days before the atrocity." Jack had certainly done his homework. "Put options are where you bet that a particular share price will fall, and a fortune can be made with a relatively small investment. In the few days preceding 9/11, thousands of times the normal scale of 'put option' investment was placed on airlines, insurance companies and companies with their head office in the Towers."

"Literally, thousands of times what is normal was invested on these specific shares…so apparently somebody had to know what was planned…and this is proved conclusively by this record amount of mass insider trading." Jack shook his head sadly, "The evidence is readily available, but things are actively hushed up. Seriously, no one wants to know, or they simply don't want to open that particular Pandora's Box. US citizen heads are firmly in the sand. America is still napping, worrying about its weight, watching Judge Judy or the wrestling or hanging out at the mall. The bus will be over the cliff before the passengers wake up."

"Wow! It's a scary thought when you can't even trust your own government," Mina said sincerely.

"The implications of all that stuff are pretty staggering." Adam said.

Jack thought the conversation was getting a bit heavy, "The implications will be a lot more staggering if I don't get to eat soon and it won't be pretty at all," he exclaimed with mock agitation, lightening the mood.

Adam removed the fish from the coals. He un-wrapped the foil and displayed the baked whole fish on a bed of wild rice laid out on a large oval shaped platter from the cabin. Steam rose from the fish and the smell was divine.

"Adam, you gourmet chef; it smells so good," Mina complimented. The pineapple cores had tenderised the fish and added to the subtle lime flavour enhanced by the ginger and garlic. Adam pulled the skin back and poured the warm pineapple sauce over the steaming fish. Leah handed out the plates and took a moment to facetiously compliment Jack on the aromatic au-la-natural fern garnish, dramatically suggesting that this alone would be responsible for the feast to come.

They gathered around the camp table and filled their plates, then moved back to the logs that served as chairs. Never had they tasted fish like it. The garlic, ginger and subtle lime juice had lifted the fresh seafood flavour and this blended beautifully with the natural sweet pineapple sauce and exotic taste of the wild rice. "This is just magnificent," they all exclaimed over and over. There was very little conversation for some time as they savoured Adam's tropical seafood creation.

"You are not into conspiracy theories, Adam?" Jack asked while his hunger was being satisfied. Adam had never considered the question before and had to think a moment.

"Probably too busy with my studies to pay a lot of attention," he said easily, "I spend so much time researching my assignments, I don't bother to read much other stuff at present. I do know something is wrong with the crash of Princess Diana and Dodi because I studied that one."

"She was taken out," Leah interjected with absolute finality.

"I did an assignment on the detective work," Adam said, "Otherwise I wouldn't have even considered it. The investigation was a total mess, from every direction I looked at it. I couldn't believe Diana's 'stand in' chauffeur from the Ritz Hotel, Henri Paul, would have been allowed to write himself off with alcohol whilst on duty as we were told." A moments thought before he continued. "She was Royalty as well as a valued VIP hotel customer and as such, would have been allocated a professional driver, not some boozy slob with major issues that was portrayed to us by the media. That story cannot possibly be true and is not supported by the facts. Evidence has now come to light that the high alcohol, blood sample, with the high carbon monoxide content, was not Henri Paul's at all, but rather that of a suicide victim laid out in the same hospital who had drunk to excess before gassing himself with his car exhaust, which explains the carbon monoxide content. This can't be argued against, it is a fact. We were completely and deliberately led astray by the media stories."

Adam had amazing recall, "The errant pathologist who did the post-mortem, Dr Lecomte, as well as Dr Pepin who supposedly tested Paul's blood, covered up their deliberate error and continually misled the examining magistrates during the enquiry. It was not even subtle and was actually, quite apparent. We are then asked to believe that the Mercedes chauffeured car had been stolen and subsequently recovered and pressed back into service without a thorough check."

It could have had a bomb planted somewhere, the brakes could have been tampered with, or any other part for that matter, but they claim that wasn't even checked. The heavier armoured Mercedes was used as a decoy while Dodi and Diana were transferred to the lighter model to escape the paparazzi. This is palpable nonsense! Everyone agreed. "Then they wouldn't allow the Mercedes people from Germany to view the wreck; why do you think that was?

"Later, computer equipment and the case files belonging to Lord John Stevens, the man handling the investigation into the death of Princess Diana, were stolen from his offices at Scotland Yard, without any sign of a forced entry…it just goes on and on."

"I talked to my dad about it," Adam went on. "He says that in ancient times the 'sacrifice' day for the Goddess Diana was 31$^{st}$ August and annual sacrifices were conducted on that day. The Princess of Wales died in a location that in ancient times was a sacred grotto dedicated to the Goddess Diana, on the precise anniversary of that sacrifice day, 31$^{st}$ August. The name of the tunnel, 'Pont de L'Alma' even translates as, 'Passage of the Moon Goddess'."

"Is that right?" Jack exclaimed, "They're lying to us again. Wow! That makes it fairly apparent that she was actually killed as some sort of sacrifice."

"Yes, I believe you're right. This 'accident' occurred precisely on the 31 August 1997. How incredibly convenient! Was it an accident, or was she 'taken out'? You work out the odds. Do you need a calculator?"[16]

Mina squeezed Adam's arm, in a reflex action, thinking of the magnitude of the deception foisted on an unsuspecting public. She dwelled for a moment on the mass of floral tributes in London and all those folks who had mourned the Princess. *Many folks appear to suspect a conspiracy*, she thought, *but then I guess, a lot of others just don't want to know.*

"The 'official' inquiry like so many others, heard lies and innuendo," Adam went on, "The Monte Carlo jeweller, Alberto Repossi, claimed that the 'Operation Paget' detectives pressured him to change his story about providing a ring for the engagement of Diana and Dodi Fayed."

"Repossi now says that Diana and Dodi chose a £230,000 emerald and diamond ring. His evidence is hard to refute since Dodi can be clearly seen on the security cameras, in the act of purchasing it, with a date stamp showing the date and time. I viewed it on the web. Nevertheless, the 'official' enquiry then denied it and of course that makes it gospel!"

"I don't know if you read where a conspiracy author called Jim Keith revealed the name of a physician who disclosed that Princess Diana was pregnant at the time of her death. Keith then died under mysterious circumstances. He went into Washoe Medical Hospital outside Reno, Nevada for relatively minor knee surgery (after he fell from a stage at a speaking engagement) and came out dead in a box."

"The very same day, the web news service where he named the source became instantly inaccessible. For some reason, the coroner's report listed his cause of death as 'blunt force trauma' which had to refer to his knee injury."[17] There were exclamations of surprise as Adam shook his head in dismay at this apparent subterfuge.

Mina felt it was time to lighten up so moved into the cabin and returned a short time later with her interesting dessert concoction. She had continued the tropical theme with a large bowl of banana and pineapple pieces soaking in Malibu. She had placed toasting forks on a tray with a huge bowl of whipped cream laced liberally with Malibu liqueur and another small bowl of raw sugar and desiccated coconut. Another bowl held white marshmallows.

"What is it?" Leah asked.

"Well, it's my own special Mina-Pina Colada sweet," she explained, "…velly ancient secret recipe." This last bit sounded Oriental, but it didn't matter.

"Does it come with an instruction manual," Jack said feigning amazement.

"Well," Mina said dramatically demonstrating as if she were a TV chef, "You take a toasting fork, skewer a piece of Malibu riddled, pineapple and banana, (I usually use Coco Reibe, but we didn't have any), then stab a marshmallow on the end. You dunk it in the sugar and coconut to get a nice coating, then toast it over the fire till the sugar melts and the coconut browns. Next you smother it with the whipped cream; then you eat and enjoy. Here's one I prepared earlier!" She actually held up the one she had just assembled in front of them. "I won't be responsible for your actions when you taste this."

Mina was right, it was exotic, tasting of fresh piña colada and worthy of a top-class restaurant. They all laughed and joked as they enjoyed the unusual exotic dessert.

"Any one drops their fruit in the Malibu or into the fire has to run around the circle and skoal their wine," laughed Jack. Here it came again. He seemed to seek out opportunities to promote these silly games.

"It's either that or the whip," Leah exclaimed.

"The whip! The whip!" Jack screamed, in mock delight.

"Oh God, not more drinking games," Adam begged, but they played it anyway. It was really silly when Jack dropped his fruit in, three times in a row.

Just maybe, it was deliberate. The mood mellowed a little as they realised, they had to reluctantly leave Emerald Springs in the morning.

"This has been a wonderful time, Adam," Leah said, "thank-you for inviting us here." Everyone agreed.

"It's truly my pleasure," Adam said graciously, "Thanks for your company. I just love this place and I've enjoyed sharing it with you."

## Peaceful Easy Feeling

Jack had risen early that morning, so he and Leah retired to the cabin while Adam and Mina stayed out under the magnificent stars, watching some of the twinkling diamonds become obscured by gathering cloud. Not a word passed between them for quite some time. To herself, Mina mused that it seemed her stars had finally aligned.

In each other's arms, they found an intimacy that made words unnecessary. Mina was thinking about the spirituality that surrounded Adam as she snuggled close to him. It wasn't exactly spirituality, but she didn't know how else to identify it. Adam was just so serene and comfortable in his own skin and seemed to be immersed in an aura of peace. These quiet times with him were the ones that she loved the most.

"Are you actually a Buddhist?" Mina asked eventually.

"That's a very difficult question to answer," Adam responded. "For a lot of reasons, I don't actively follow any specific denomination but it's more complex than that. Firstly, it is not just Buddhists who follow the I Ching philosophy. It's a part of Martial Arts culture, then there's Taoism and other denominations. We find that because of our western style education, particularly in North America, we develop a mind-set that responds to rational structures. Things need to be verified by processes of supposed proof. We are encouraged to think in a particular way that started back when the ancient Greeks first dabbled in scientific explanation."

He paused to see if Mina was following. "The philosophy of yin and yang doesn't work like that and as a result, we Americans have trouble getting our heads around its concept. The Eastern thinking investigates the full environment of any action and its possible side effects within a harmonious dynamic. You understand?"

"Yes, I think so. It would be hard to pigeon hole specific beliefs with the mixing of Eastern religion and Western culture."

"Well yes, that's entirely true, but it's the harmonious interaction part that captivated me. That's what we are missing in this Christian country."

"As an example, the Book of Job in the Bible is pretty scary to me, because it shows God, egged on by Satan, torturing poor old Job, who has done nothing wrong and has not broken any of God's commandments. Here, God appears to be in league with Satan as he pits all his might against one man and reduces him to a pathetic creature eating dust.[18] Regardless of the feeble excuses of the clergy, there's no rational explanation for this behaviour."

"In the ancient versions of the Bible's scriptures, there was no Satan. He wasn't actually added to scripture until after the Council of Nicaea in 325 AD. Prior to this, the role of Satan was initially played by a character called Mastema. From its etymology, this word actually depicted the evil side of YHWH himself. As their tribal 'War-God', the Jews called him YHWH-Sabaoth, the 'God of Armies' or 'War God'.[19] To me, this demonstrates an imbalance in the whole thing."

"So, you see, contained within the good of YHWH, was originally the seed of the evil Mastema, as well as the bloodthirsty and warlike Sabaoth. This helps account for all the wrath, the killing, the cruelty, the demand for sacrifices and the bloody battles and so forth in the Old Testament. It flounders, however, when there is no allowance that good is contained in the sinners amongst his followers. Accordingly, the harmony is totally extinguished and, in my opinion, the whole thing falls apart."

"I never even considered it from that perspective, but I guess you are right," admitted Mina. "The Bible says in Isaiah, that even good Christians are all like unclean things, and their righteousness is like filthy rags; so apparently any spark of good within us, is not even recognised or acknowledged." Adam slowly nodded in agreement, somewhat sadly.

"Most Christians are totally unaware that when the Devil was introduced into the Bible, for the first thousand years, the death of Christ was originally documented as a ransom paid to the Devil. This is actually true, however; we don't know about it because there were no Bibles in English until about 1611. Nevertheless, this concept played a conspicuous part in the history of theology and the early church for over a millennium."[20]

"Is that right? This is really interesting," Mina said.

"Well, this entire scenario appears to stem from the ancient Sumerian epic traditions such as Gilgamesh and the Enuma Elish, where a ransom was required to affect escape from the underworld. It was, however, the Twelfth Century theologians Anselm and Abelard who decided that this scenario afforded too much power to Satan and altered the manuscripts."

"They were responsible for having that theology entirely turned around and re-written in the Bible. They documented that the death of Christ should not have been a ransom at all, but instead, that God must have had a requirement for the death of his own Son as a blood sacrifice, to appease himself.[21] This is the inane way it is now portrayed in the modified Bible and Christians have no inkling that it has actually been fully altered from the original."

Adam was certainly knowledgeable in spiritual things, thought Mina, but he was also gentle, sincere and caring…and tonight he showed that he could cook as well. What a catch!

## Spiritual Discussion

They paused to just look at the stars and noticed the clouds beginning to roll in. Adam sniffed the fresh air and sighed with satisfaction as he went on. "The conspiracy stuff that Jack talked about is pretty frightening, and Mina, you even mentioned the sense of betrayal when you can't trust your own government."

"Yes, I did say that and it's really not surprising that today's young people are seeking a more believable philosophy and abandoning the political parties and organised religions of their parents."

"Yes, and I mentioned before, the apparent effect that Nature has on our behaviour," Adam said quietly. "The I Ching introduces the interplay of eight sets of yin and yang that correspond to **heaven, earth, fire, water, valley, wind, mountain and thunder**. This further suggests a sense of the immense force of Nature, actively projecting its authority over the followers of this principle. Those who choose to reject it outright will likely remain totally oblivious." A moment's pause, "Those of us equipped with the capacity to understand, would be well advised to be receptive, attentive and humble."

Mina sighed gently, "I can see how that would work, but I'm afraid my education has been sadly lacking."

"Not at all Mina, you are far more spiritually aware than most people."

"Really? I just love hearing the things you are telling me, but it's like a whole new concept. Look at you, Adam; you have it all together so completely." Mina stated sincerely.

"Not true," Adam responded, "the first little trial I went through with the Police brutality thing, my confidence waned and I sat in my apartment, moping in self-pity. Two of my youngest students came around to coax me back to my class and to convince me that I was valued and needed. It was my father who brought me here to Emerald Springs and let the elements of nature do their healing work; the identical elements of yin and yang that I just mentioned. Maybe, Dad didn't consciously make that decision, it just happened. He is an amazing person and responds intuitively to his instincts; maybe he just subliminally knew that's what was required."

Mina reached up and kissed Adam, "I guess we also need the thunder in our lives to maintain perfect harmony."

Adam considered this and nodded. "I guess so. Do you see why I wanted you all to come here and experience this with me?"

"Yes Adam. Right from the first moment I arrived here, I viewed this as a spiritual experience, akin to visiting a sacred site. Now that I understand more, I consider our visit a privilege."

"Thank-you Mina; I'm certainly glad we were able to share this."

"Adam, where does that leave most Christians in this country?"

"Well, that is a very good point and worth considering. There was a major Gallup poll conducted back in the 50s or 60s that discovered the majority of practicing Christians in America could not name a single Old Testament prophet, they didn't know who preached the Sermon on the Mount and a substantial number believed that Moses was one of Jesus' apostles. These are the very people protesting about what Christian values are appropriate to be taught in our classrooms."[22]

"Their perception must be from a very limited viewpoint." Mina suggested.

"You are so right," Adam claimed, "It is not known whether the situation is becoming better or worse, but I suspect it would be no better today. As a vehicle of education and raising consciousness globally, the Christian Church has plainly failed, and failed miserably. They have knowingly taught guilt and dependency instead of peace and enlightenment."

For a time, they just rested in each other's arms, thinking about the implications and listening to the night sounds around them. Adam broke the silence, "To answer your observation, though, it has been stated that it would now be impossible to gain the Presidency of the United States without informing the voters that you are a Christian, but many of the politicians are hypocrites and most of the constituents are simply spiritually unaware, something like the icchantika. The Bible tells us that to identify Christians, you will know them by their actions. When it comes to political representation, the constituents seem to conveniently forget that, and are easily fooled by their words."

Adam shook his head as if in distress. "These politicians are the ones with their finger on the button. It is probably not an exaggeration to say that if the City of New York was suddenly replaced by a fireball, some significant percentage of the American population would see a silver lining in the resulting mushroom cloud. It would suggest to them that the best thing that is ever going to happen, was about to happen: the return of Jesus Christ, coming for the elect."

"It should be blindingly obvious that beliefs of this sort will do little to help us create a durable future for ourselves and our children. Imagine the consequences if any significant component of the US Government actually believed that the world was about to end and that its ending would be glorious. The fact that nearly half of the American population apparently believes in this doomsday Armageddon, purely on the basis of partially understood religious dogma, should be considered a moral and intellectual emergency."[23]

## Love Blooms

Mina had never actually identified that an intelligent, gentle and spiritual man was what she sought. She had articulated her feelings to her Guardian Angel and was now simply astounded with what had resulted. She smiled as she recalled what Leah had said about 'Girls and Apples' and particularly about finding a man who wasn't afraid to climb the tree for the best apple. Leah had said he would be special. Mina adored this wonderful man and being with him in this peaceful environment was a really special experience for her.

Adam must have been thinking reciprocal thoughts about how two kindred spirits had somehow collided.

"Mina, I really love you," Adam said quietly at last brushing her face with his lips.

"I love you too," answered the very contented young lady, with a trace of a tear in her eye. They cuddled a while longer as the night closed in around them. "We had better go in or we'll be wrecked in the morning," Mina said, taking Adam by the hand, kissing him gently and leading him inside. "Thank-you," she breathed, fondling her little crystal angel. Just then the first sounds of distant thunder sounded as a storm began to close in across the valley.

# Chapter 8
# It's About Respect

**Monday**
**Back to Europe**

"Hey wow! That was just the best time ever," Leah said in the taxi to the airport, checking out the pictures she had taken with Mina's mobile phone. "What a beautiful place and we had so much fun!" Mina nodded, it had been the best weekend of her entire life. She laid a friendly hand on Leah's shoulder, "Yes, wasn't it just amazing! I'm just so pleased Adam shared it with us. I asked him to thank the owner for us. It was so kind of him to let us use his wonderful place."

"Wasn't Jack incredible? I've been really underestimating him," Leah said, "…but whew, all the silly games. As I left he challenged me with an answer and I had to work out the question. I'd love to solve it and stick it to him."

"Well what's the answer?" Mina asked.

"It's 9W."

Mina looked thoughtful, "9W, Wait, wait, I think I have heard this one. It's about the German composer Richard Wagner."

"Really? Come on, share," Leah exclaimed with some surprise.

"Well it's pronounced Vagner, so the question could be, **'Herr Vagner, does your name start with a V'.** Answer – **Nein W**." Mina chuckled, while Leah looked astonished but pulled out her phone and started texting as a sly smile crossed her face.

"Thank you, thank you. Cop that, Jack." Then with a complete change of subject, "God, I don't feel much like arguing with Business Class today."

"I didn't want this stopover to end," Mina admitted honestly.

"That was fairly apparent, girlfriend," Leah said, "but not to worry, we'll have another break in about ten days."

"Leah, Adam was simply wonderful, I loved every moment with him, I think he's my soulmate. I think I'm really falling in love for the first time in my life."

When they landed in Frankfurt, Mina dropped into a Duty Free shop and spent some time buying an iPad. Leah was checking out perfumes nearby looking a little curious as she raised her eyebrows. "So I can talk with Adam on skype," Mina explained, "otherwise phone calls are so expensive from the Hotels."

"Gone a million, Mina-Pina," Leah said, "you're showing all the signs."

Mina couldn't wait to set up her new iPad and see if Adam was online. Eventually she made contact, "Adam, we're only just apart and I miss you already; how are you doing?"

"I'm missing you too Mina, my darling."

"The weekend at the cabin was just sensational. We all loved it. Thank-you so much."

"I loved it too, sweetheart," Adam said quietly.

"I feel like it's a sacred place. I'd really like to go there again, but I know we can't impose on Mr Winter. I hope you will tell him how much we enjoyed it and how much we appreciate his kindness."

"I made sure my dad passed on our thanks, but something interesting has just happened," Adam said, "Mr Winter is buying the big 60 foot, deep sea fishing boat they took out and he has now decided he won't use the cabin enough to justify keeping it, so he has given my dad first option on buying it. My parents are considering it. My fingers are crossed, because they just could end up owning it. If that happens, we can probably go there whenever we like."

"Oh Adam, wouldn't that be fantastic! It could really be our special place."

"When will you be back?"

"On the seventeenth. Nine days tomorrow."

"Adam I can hear you fine, but I want to see you as well. My IPad has a built in web-cam; could you get one?"

"Sure, I'll get one today, I've hardly ever used Skype before."

The call was terrific but if anything, it made Mina more lonely than ever. She had found something wonderful with Adam and it made the separation so much harder. She made a tough week of it evaluating her feelings and talking to Adam every chance she could. True to his word, Adam now had a web-cam, and their calls became a bit more intimate.

The ten days dragged, even though the girls were kept occupied and busy. One long haul was to Kuala Lumpur and on to Sydney again. They had both loved this trip the last time, and shopping was great in K.L. once you knew where to go. Unfortunately it was raining when they reached Sydney in the late afternoon and they went with a bunch of the girls to a friendly bistro for a light dinner and a drink.

They all talked about going up the tower but the rain kept up and visibility was hopeless. It was cosy in the bistro despite the rain lashing down outside. It was better to just relax and sip wine in front of the log fire and listen to the music of an acoustic guitarist at the far end of the room. Mina had a dual watch, one local and one set on LA time, since it was so easy to get confused with the time zones on the other side of the world. Adam would be sleeping now, she thought and her mind-picture brought a slight smile to her face.

## Captain Kangaroo

When they left in the morning, the rain had gone and it was a bright and cheerful city again. They journeyed from Sydney back to K.L. and on to Frankfurt. Then to London, Hamburg, Berlin, Stockholm, Düsseldorf, Munich, Paris, London again and on to Manchester then back to Frankfurt. Another trip went to Spain; the flights went all over Europe. Their flight to Madrid was certainly memorable because there was a particularly hard landing caused by wind shear, during a sudden and violent electrical storm that produced gusty crosswinds.

Really the flight should have been diverted, but the Captain realised the inconvenience this action would cause, and believed he could get the big craft down safely. He certainly did his best in the terrible conditions, but the wind shear gusted violently at precisely the wrong time and the aircraft bounced wildly. Soon after things settled down, the purser made light of it over the P.A. "Well ladies and gentlemen, you can stop clinging to the person next to you, especially if you don't know them. I'm not sure if we landed or were shot down but I think we're on the ground now. If you will please keep your seat belts fastened just a bit longer, Captain Kangaroo will bounce what's left of the plane to gate 29."

The passengers applauded, not really blaming the Captain, who had done well in the circumstances. They were just thankful to avoid being diverted to an alternate destination, which would have caused considerable inconvenience. Despite this, the name stuck, with the flight attendants now calling that German pilot, 'Captain Kangaroo'.

He took it in good fun and even seemed somewhat proud of the notoriety. Stories started to circulate within the airline about the Captain and he became something of a minor celebrity, the brunt of a hundred jokes. Fortunately, he had the good humour to laugh along with them, but he was also something of a practical joker himself, and assured the crew he would find ways to get back at them.

## Finally Flying Home

They say good things come to those who wait and finally, finally, after what seemed an eon to Mina, they were on the flight from Frankfurt back to LAX. She became preoccupied and nervous. Mina answered the hostess call button.

"You've got this wrong. I asked for dark rum, you've given me Bacardi. I don't like Bacardi…I expect…"

Leah was right there with the trolley to rescue her, using her sweetest voice, "Sorry Sir, here's a couple of dark rums for you and some mixed nuts. I have a pack of playing cards for you too. Will you need another cola with your drink, Sir?" (Just shut the fuck up and drink the stuff, will you. I hope it chokes you. You might as well be totally smashed as how you are now, you drunken lush.)

"Take it easy Mina, stay cool. It will be OK." Leah quietly comforted her friend, in the galley area, away from the passengers.

"I can't help worrying that the bubble might suddenly burst…I just couldn't take it this time."

"Come on Mina. Adam will be waiting at the airport just as doey eyed as you are. The two of you can head off into the sunset to live happily ever after. Well for three days anyway. Now get some coffee to these guys quick-smart, before they put you off the plane." Mina calmed down, got her head together and got back to work.

When they arrived at LAX this time, Mina dropped into the Duty Free shop and bought the beautiful Ralph Lauren—Polo jacket she had admired previously. "Shut up, you," she snapped at Leah, who had not uttered one word, but was doing things with her eyebrows that indicated something like, 'gone a million'. Mina's apprehension had been without foundation and Leah's prediction was entirely accurate. When the girls finally exited LAX, there was Adam waiting.

"I'll make myself scarce," Leah said waving 'hello' to Adam.

"Don't be ridiculous, you will not. I'm sure Adam will give you a lift home."

Leah moved towards a taxi, "Somehow, I don't think you'll be going home tonight, Mina-Pina, not to your home anyway."

## Meet the Folks

Mina and Adam woke late and had a wonderful day together, just lazing around then taking a casual drive to the beach, swimming and playing on the sand. They ate fish and chips in a park that looked out over the water and enjoyed the smell of the ocean and the fresh sea breeze. That evening, they visited the Mills residence in the LA hills. Dinner with the folks is supposed to be an ordeal, but it was not like that at all.

Adam looked fabulous in the stunning jacket Mina had bought for him and quietly watching him, she fell in love all over again. His parents appeared genuinely pleased to meet Mina. Sarah seemed delighted that Adam had found such a charming girl and was overjoyed that she fitted in so well with the family. Sarah was originally from Oklahoma City and was interested that Mina too, was an Okie and had moved to LA when she started High School.

They had heaps to talk about. Mina got along brilliantly with Sarah and thought Dr Mills was charismatic and very distinguished. There were no airs and graces in the Mills home, but there were good manners. Mina's impeccable manners and country girl charm won over both Donald and Sarah immediately; Adam, well he was already hooked. "Could you spare Adam for a moment," asked Dr Mills, "I need to talk with him."

"Certainly, but please bring him back soon," Mina responded, "He took some finding let me tell you."
Dr Mills looked back with a grin and retorted, "What do you think Adam?" He gave a wink and added, "We employed an entire Police force to find you, Ma'am."

Adam nodded knowingly, "Nothing but the truth." Dr Mills and his son went out on the front balcony chuckling while Sarah and Mina talked inside.

"I'll start serving dinner," Sarah said some time later, "would you like to go and find those males, dear, and tell them dinner is only a couple of minutes away." Meanwhile, on the front balcony with a view of the roadway, Adam and his father got a big surprise causing Adam to rush to the front door.

Mina was so happy everything was going so well. Adam's parents were marvellous. Adam was a truly wonderful guy and she loved everything about this new relationship and sincerely hoped it would last forever. It entered her mind that all the losers of the past were gone now and all the disappointments were over; she had found the very best.

It was a wonderfully welcome feeling. Mina entered the hallway and froze. No! This was not possible. She went cold all over and could not move, it felt like her heart had stopped. Adam had his arms around an attractive blonde girl and was kissing her fondly.

"Mina!" Adam exclaimed, finally spotting her standing there, "come and meet my sister Renee. She has been away and just dropped in unexpected. Come and say hello while I tell Mother we have one more for dinner. This is so great!" Mina had to pause a moment for her heart to start beating again.

"Hey Mina, I'm Renee," the lovely, blond girl said articulately. Mina was still breathing heavily, but forced herself to recover quickly, "Hello, you look so lovely, that's a great tan." *Mina, you are so stupid*, she said to herself, *where is your trust, where is your confidence, get your brain working.*

"I have just had three months in Hawaii with the University," Renee said, "it was so great...Dad!" Don Mills came in and hugged his daughter as Adam returned with Sarah.

"Mother!" she exclaimed as Sarah rushed in. They were a loving family and became involved in a communal hug for quite some time. Adam drew Mina into the huddle in a way that suggested she belonged there too. Mina felt really stupid for having doubted Adam even if only for a second.

"Darling, why didn't you call to say you were on your way," Sarah asked.

"Well I lost my cell phone; I think I left it in the seat pocket on the aircraft; I'll worry about it tomorrow; the pay phones at the airport were vandalised so I just grabbed a taxi and here I am."

"Welcome home, it is so good to see you," Dr Mills said, "Come on everyone and we'll eat now."

"Adam, you've brought a lovely young lady to dinner," Renee said hugging him again, then hugging Mina. "Goodness, what have I been missing; where did you guys meet?"

"Now that is a long story," Adam said moving with Mina to the dinner table.

There was no shortage of conversation. "Are you kidding me," Renee said a short time later, "this is the girl you needed to find to clear you from those stupid charges. Wow! That is so wild!" She took both Mina's hands in hers and shook them. She was lovely.

They finished dinner early as Renee was exhausted from her trip. "Trust me, it was the send-off party that did it," she insisted, winking at Adam and Mina.

Adam decided they should go too. Mina thanked them all and felt relieved that it had gone so well.

"They all loved you," Adam said, kissing her gently, "I knew they would." The night was still young so they decided to drop into Lo Stivale for a quiet drink before heading home. They were surprised to find Leah and Jack there.

"Do you guys live here?" Mina asked.

"Pretty much," Jack answered lazily, "They have food and alcohol so we see no reason to…" Leah slapped him playfully. They agreed to join them for just one drink.

"I shouldn't be drinking; I'm in a tournament tomorrow night," Adam shared with them some time later, "Tae Kwon Do championships. Would you guys like to come along…see me get my head kicked in?"

"Yeah! That would be neat. No, not to see you get your head kicked in, but I'd like to come," Jack said and Leah agreed easily.

## The Tournament

Mina, Jack and Leah had never before been to any event like it. Huge expanses of light timber floors with various 'rings' marked out in black and white. There were huge banners everywhere showing logos of different schools and codes of Tae Kwon Do. A real sense of awe, anticipation and excitement hung in the air in similar fashion to scenes of combat down through the ages.

A strange mix of raw emotion and camaraderie prevailed in the room enhancing the overall sentiment of respect that was ever present. This was evident in dozens of preliminary bouts as the combatants bowed to each other and then 'played fair' as they struggled to outclass their opponent. Some of the combatants were really good and it was a spectacular show.

Finally, towards the end of the evening, came the announcement from the M.C.: "Black belt open class, Corey James Daniels versus Adam Harper Mills." The three friends didn't really understand the rules, but it was still an entertaining exhibition. The two competitors looked amazing in the spotlights, coming out like ancient gladiators ready to do battle with chivalry and respect. Gladiators, however, didn't wear white doboks with coloured shoulder patches and gold embroided black belts.

There seemed no question these two were held in high esteem by a myriad of devoted, young martial arts enthusiasts and the applause for them was deafening. They faced each other and bowed deeply.

Both Adam and C.J. were brilliantly fit, highly trained and incredibly good. They punched, blocked, kicked and leapt incredibly high in the air with loud cries called 'kihop'. Adam had explained that this was partly for intimidation, but also expelled air to assist focusing power into a strike or kick. With one point each, they appeared to be in a fight to the death and though it was an exciting experience, Mina was a little concerned.

Adam had been under a lot of pressure and his training schedule had been severely interrupted by recent events. He was, however, marginally taller and finally gained the upper hand with a downward axe kick from a right leg that started from almost vertically above his head. A moment later C.J. Daniels was defeated. It had been a great match. The crowd loved the spectacle and broke into deafening acclamation, with Adam's youth club students in the lead. The combatants bowed deeply to each other and after they walked from the ring, Adam hugged his opponent showing they were just devoted to the sport and there was no animosity between them. Mina was quite relieved.

After Adam received his tall trophy amid more thunderous applause and camera flashes, they congratulated Adam on his win, then Jack and Leah left the stadium heading home. Adam and C.J. went to the showers. They were both then involved in some administration with the officials that detained them for some time. When Adam finally left with Mina, the spectators had all dispersed.

"That was so exciting and spectacular," Mina said, "but Adam I was a little terrified you would hurt each other."

"No," Adam said smiling, "C.J. is a good guy, but my mother used to give me worse whippings than he ever could."

"It didn't look like it," Mina said seriously. They walked hand in hand across the deserted car park. Adam paused and unlocked the passenger door of his RV for Mina.

"Freeze it right there, loser!" Came a sinister voice from the shadows that Adam recognised from the phone call some time ago.

## Deep Trouble

Four thugs appeared silently from the shadows. Two had guns; one was quickly pressed against Adam's spine and the other against Mina's cheek. This was uncharted waters for Adam, he didn't know quite what to do as the dirty creep's arm went around Mina's throat. The smell of him was not pleasant. He used some sort of powerful cologne that fought a losing battle with the odour of sweat and humanity, to a point where it would have been cheaper to just take a bath.

He believed the cologne he plastered on was just the thing to improve his sex appeal, however, he was such an ugly, obnoxious cretin that no female would knowingly choose to cohabitate with him, even if he smelt like new mown hay. In fact the puffery, 'makes you irresistible to females' on the scent's box, without an overrider for his particular situation, presented a strong case for getting his money back. Whoever had swung the ugly stick had been more than enthusiastic, and certainly hadn't missed. A second swipe would be unnecessary.

"Let the girl go," Adam said forcefully while sneaking a look around, "and we can talk. I take it you're Billy Flynn." This one had an oversized red nose that looked about as real as Mr Potato Head's, pinned roughly but not quite in the centre of his repulsive face. His greasy hair had been dyed with 'No more Grey' but the ugly was all natural.

"Give the man a cigar," the sinister voice came from behind him, whilst the gun barrel was twisted into his spine.

"Look Flynn, I am a student police detective and this is not a smart move. I don't know anything about your money. Opus left a note to say he was despondent because his mother wouldn't give him any more funds, so I don't think he had the money at all. Don't be stupid, we're not involved, and this will just get you loads of grief."

"Don't you call me stupid, loser. You took my money from Ronnie and now you took his girl as well. Get your knife Spud, we might carve up this little princess, then deal with the loser here."

Mina was terrified, she had little idea what this was all about, but recognised that these creeps had no scruples and no compassion. She and Adam were in serious trouble. Adam was amazingly good, but he could do nothing against four of them armed with guns and knives.

The dirty thug called 'Spud' approached her with a knife, grinning horribly, exposing his filthy teeth as he tested the point on his finger. Mina let out an involuntary scream. Spud's foul breath almost made her gag and the other foreign looking creep kept his free arm around her throat, with his gun now to her temple.

How was it that Mack couldn't locate these hoodlums, Adam wondered? Even a retired old bloodhound with a head cold could smell them at least four city blocks away. They certainly put no priority on personal hygiene. There was no way that little Christmas tree shaped air freshener hanging from the rear view mirror in their getaway car was up for the job.

Adam tensed not knowing what he could do. He knew then that somehow he would not let them cut Mina. He would die to prevent that. At the very least, he would leave a nasty body count if they tried. His mind focused. Tae Kwon Do was not just the training and fighting. It was a philosophy. It was observing, being aware. It was about sensing weaknesses and calculating odds. Adam had been staring into the eyes of the hoodlum who held Mina and he knew he had unsettled him, actually intimidated him. The creep couldn't hold his gaze. Adam also saw that the gun he held was an old model Browning and thought back to his weapon training.

He racked his brain, he could not afford to be wrong. Safety catch 'forward' to fire, he remembered. The safety catch was back. That gave him two or three seconds. The situation may well be pretty hopeless, but nevertheless, he prepared his body like a tightened spring, looking for an opportunity, getting ready for action when suddenly an ear-splitting cry rent the air. **'Kyung Yet!'**

### I'm No Loser

Adam bowed from the waist, just as the gun-loaded fist of Billy Flynn whistled over his head. His reflexes were amazing. He immediately slammed backwards with his elbow and connected with the gargantuan nose of a very surprised Flynn. It seemed that Billy's 're-education program' had commenced. Flynn let out a shrill cry as bone and cartilage snapped and claret flowed. He stumbled backwards, losing his gun which continued on its trajectory arc.

The coward had decided to pistol whip Adam from behind and was completely bewildered when the cry rang out and his target had quickly ducked. That had left Flynn totally off balance from the swing, and Adam very quickly capitalised on the situation breaking that magnificent proboscis. Now he had some real work to do, but it had all been rehearsed in his mind. In a fluid movement, he launched into the air with a lightning fast, split kick that took out Spud with the knife and knocked down the dirty thug holding Mina.

This one had screamed out something in a foreign language that could have been Iranian. Adam didn't speak any Iranian but would have bet all he owned that it wasn't particularly complimentary. In fact, it suggested the foreign creep was probably more than pissed about the kick to the head. Mina also fell to the ground and had the sense to stay down, rolling away from the action.

In the nick of time, the cavalry had arrived? C.J. Daniels had come out to the car park, heard Mina's scream and had immediately assessed the situation. He saw Flynn prepare to stave in Adam's head with his gun butt and had stridently given the Korean command. He knew Adam would understand and react instantly as he rushed to his aid. From his running start, he transferred the momentum into a perfectly placed crescent kick on the still staggering Flynn and one, two, three, front kicks and a massive side kick, on the grub who had been beside him, rendering them both unconscious.

Adam had made short work of Spud, but the creep who had held Mina, got to his feet and charged at him. In the fall, he had lost his gun and didn't look quite so tough right now. Adam fought a massive battle in his mind for that fraction of a second. He knew he could deliver strikes and kicks that could break bones and even kill and he badly wanted to take out this filthy thug for daring to put his grubby hands on Mina. That, however, would be purely motivated by revenge and wasn't the right way.

He instantaneously sidestepped, using the forward motion of the thug against him. He executed a perfect body throw that saw the creep hit the tarmac with a crash that knocked the wind out of him, allowing Adam to quickly apply an immobility hold, pinning his arms.

Mina was shaken but unhurt.

"Mina! Quickly! The handcuffs from the glove compartment," Adam yelled. Mina had been almost paralysed with fear, but now she sprang to her feet, finding the cuffs and bringing them smartly to Adam. He snapped them on the only conscious thug, securing his hands behind his back. He used his cell phone to call the Parker Centre for urgent backup. He checked that Mina was alright and hugged her to him and soothed her.

Adam then turned to C.J. they both adopted 'Ready Stance' then as one, bowed deeply to each other. Adam walked over and hugged him strongly, "Thanks C.J. They were armed and dangerous. You saved us and that took real guts, man." Adam stepped back and bowed again, "Ahn Young Hee Kah Say Yo."

C.J. returned the bow, "Wha; Chun Mun A Yoe."

## A Spoiled Evening

The tension was slowly ebbing away. Mina felt more relieved when the backup officers finally arrived and handcuffed the other three thugs. They sure were efficient. 'Junior officer needs urgent back up', sure trumps Mrs Jones' lost cat. At the Parker Centre, Adam had to make out a lengthy report and Mina gave a statement. C.J. would give his statement in the morning. Mack had been called in and he was stunned at the capture of the four hardened criminals by a student detective.

They had been on the wanted list for many months and Adam and CJ had done tonight what the entire force hadn't been able to achieve. "If this keeps up, I'll have to see if there's any wriggle room in the *'don't clutter up the neighbourhood with unconscious thugs'* policy," he breathed wryly; his blustering way of congratulating Adam on a job well done. Adam hugged Mina trying to erase the effects of the ordeal she had been through. Their evening had been spoiled, but they had been incredibly lucky. Without the intervention of C.J. it could well have been disastrous, even fatal.

Mina had been almost speechless for some time now. As they finally headed for home, she quietly asked Adam to explain what it was all about and what had actually happened. Adam told her briefly how Flynn ran a drug ring and he and his thugs were wanted on various drug related charges and for a number of assaults. On this occasion, Mack might even see it as attempted murder. Ron Opus had peddled drugs for Flynn and owed him money.

Mina gasped as she recollected how once Ron had taken money from her; she had been a fool to ever be involved with him. She had thought he was 'misunderstood' and that she might be able to reform him. Now she had to admit that he was consorting with hardened criminals and had been totally beyond help or rehabilitation.

Adam went on, "It seems Opus stalled Flynn by saying he had the money, believing he could eventually get it from his mother. He was desperate and when she refused, rather than face Flynn and his thugs, he committed suicide."

Mina shuddered deeply. She was ashamed that she had ever been associated with Ron and that she had inadvertently involved Adam in this dreadful mess. She was, nevertheless, saddened and felt a tinge of sorrow for the predicament so insurmountable that Ron had found no other way out. Flynn and his thugs certainly played for keeps and instilled fear in their unsavoury colleagues.

"It seems likely that Ron Opus was after money when he attacked you and Leah," Adam observed. "Anyway, he told Flynn he was bringing him the money. When he didn't arrive, Flynn saw all the publicity and decided that I must have taken it from him."

"My God, Adam, coming to my rescue at the coffee shop involved you in all of this. I am so very, very sorry."

"It's fine. Put it all in the rear-view mirror," Adam quipped.

"No Adam, I am really sorry you became involved because of me."

"Want to clear the slate?" he asked brightening visibly.

"Yes Adam, I'll do anything to try to make it up to you."

Adam stopped the car, "Well I hurt here," he said pointing to his neck, where a red mark remained from Flynn's fingers. Mina rubbed it, snuggled up and kissed it better. "And here," he pointed to his cheek where one of C.J.'s strikes had got through his guard in the tournament. She kissed the spot. "And here," he pointed to his lips. This time Mina didn't hold back. She kissed him passionately, then more gently as all the tension and shock began to ease away. It felt like that wasn't enough so Mina repeated the dose. They finally came up for air and eventually continued on their way home.

"OK, all's forgiven now." Adam smiled at her.

Mina smiled back and finally began to relax. After some thought she asked, "What was that cry that C.J. made?"

"We follow the Korean form of Tae Kwon Do and for authenticity, learn the Korean commands. 'Kyung Yet', is the Korean for 'bow'. C.J. gave it as a command. It was his way of saving me from getting my head bashed in with Flynn's gun butt. Pretty clever, huh?"

"Both of you were incredible. What was that ritual you did before he left?"

"The bow is the strongest form of respect," Adam said sincerely, "it conveyed to C.J. that we may have been opponents earlier tonight but we are forever friends who love and respect each other within the sport and outside it. I then gave him my sincere thanks."

"But what were the words you spoke to him? They seemed to impress him greatly."

"Ahn Young Hee Kah Say Yo," Adam repeated, "Well it loses a little in the translation, but it means something close to 'Go in Peace', but it actually conveys much more. We competed tonight and I was able to defeat C.J. and he may have been a bit miffed because he has been training hard and knew I was a bit below par from my suspension and he probably hoped for a win."

"He helped us out of a hell of a spot back there and I was just conveying to him, look don't accept our earlier bout as a defeat, don't beat yourself up about it, what you just achieved is pretty amazing, you're the man, you sure nailed this one when it really counted, now be calm within yourself, my friend, and go in peace with all my thanks. You understand?"

Mina nodded. "What was it he replied?"

"Chun Mun A Yoe, is like 'you are welcome'," but he added, "'Wha', which means sort of, 'togetherness in harmony' just suggesting it was a team effort, we did it together for what was right to maintain peace and harmony."

After a few minutes silence Mina asked, "Adam, where are we going?"

"I'm taking you home to your place sweetheart."

"My place is with you tonight, Adam, I'll get my things in the morning."

## Saying Goodbye

This time there were some tears when Mina had to leave. Being with Adam was so exhilarating, so natural, so wonderful that she hated to depart. The silly shock she had received when his sister Renee arrived, just made her realise how much this relationship meant to her. The terrible fright she had received from the encounter with Flynn and his thugs, did so even more.

She always seemed safe with Adam and he came through with the aid of C.J. even when the situation looked so bleak. In some ways, she had been responsible for bringing all that trouble on Adam, but he just took everything in his stride. He was just amazing. Now Mina felt she could not live without him and she didn't want to leave.

Once she was on the aircraft, however, it was like instinct totally kicked in and she was again the smiling, friendly, professional flight attendant.

"Let me help you with that."

"I'll just hang your jacket up the front."

"Here, let me take your little girl."

"Yes, 27-F is just through here."

She got the job done, and no one knew she was suffering.

## Get Your Head on Straight

Next day in Hamburg, when they reached their hotel, Mina went without Leah, to the heated pool on the hotel's upper floor. She swam a lot of laps then rested beside the pool, tiny droplets of water cascading from her healthy, lithe body. She swam some more. Mina knew it was time to get her act together and told her Guardian Angel about it. Surprisingly, she was the only one in the complex but splashed water showed where others had used the facilities earlier.

She ran the entire courtship with Adam through her mind like a newsreel, actually pausing to smile at tiny memories that would likely stay with her forever. "OK, Mina," she said to herself, speaking aloud and with conviction; "you are a complete person who just happens to be in a relationship with the most adorable guy on the planet. You're not going to blow this one and nothing is about to go wrong. You like him and he likes you."

"There just isn't anything to be miserable about. You wanted it, you deserve it and you have it. No more anxiety and nonsense now, relax and enjoy the feeling, because you are a strong and together person. You can live your own life singly and you can happily bolster it with a brilliant developing relationship with a wonderful man. None of the stuff with Ron Opus or Billy Flynn was your fault, it just happened."

"Adam doesn't hold you responsible. Now get over it. Naturally, you and Adam will be together when you can be, but you will also spend time apart when you must." She disciplined her mind, confirming that she could operate this way, with gratitude for the relationship she had, with happy thoughts of the times they would be together again. "Be happy for all that you have, not miserable for what you don't have!"

She affirmed that she would never again bury herself in needless concerns or self-pity just because for a time, it was not possible to be with Adam.

Mina did a lot more laps and was happy. She left the complex with a new resolve, softly humming the old standard, *'I Can See Clearly Now the Rain has Gone'*.

Leah noticed the change immediately. "You were gone a while. Were you swimming all this time?"

"Yep, to L.A, and back," came the quick reply.

"Was the weather nice?"

"Yeah, pretty much...It's gonna be a bright, bright Sunshiny day."

Presently, "Let's do some stuff. I want to go and see where the Beatles played," Mina said. "We've been here often and we've never taken the cruise of the harbour or toured the lovely canals. I want to visit the Alster to see some of Hamburg's mansions and the magnificent Alster Park."

"How do you know it's magnificent if you've never seen it?"

"I sent the same postcard home that you did, smarty," laughed Mina.

"Where did the Beatles play?"

"Well back in 1960, they started in Hamburg at the Indra Club which still exists today. Not long after, they moved to the Kaiser Keller in the notorious red-light district of Saint Pauli, where they played seven nights a week. After a trip back to Liverpool, they returned to Hamburg in 1961 and appeared at the Top Ten Club then in 1962 they were at the Star Club."

"I didn't know you were a Beatles fan; how could you possibly know all that?"

"Look right here, I read it on the tour brochure."

"WOW, did you see the offer on the front? Buy three tours and get a fourth one free! Is that a bit like getting two bonus tracks on a Yoko Ono album?"

"You win Mina, I'll get ready. Now wish me luck," she waved her hair comb as a wand, "**bed hair be gone, ugly duckling to swan.**" She made a sad face, "Darn, didn't work, OK, I'll just put on some makeup and we can go."

"That process can take longer than painting the Golden Gate Bridge."

"Look who's talking, you little skank; I won't be a minute."

# Chapter 9
# A Few Loose Ends

### Criminology Lecture

"Today we will touch on an amazing case that occurred recently, right here in Los Angeles," stated the lecturer, pacing up and down, with a self-satisfied look on his face. "It's the case of Ronald Opus...Is anyone familiar with this case?" Murmuring and a couple of affirmative reactions. It caught Adam's attention and he looked up in surprise. "I'll give you a brief summary now and provide a handout at the end of class. OK? In this unusual case the Medical Examiner concluded that the deceased had died from a shotgun blast to the head. The problem was that Mr Opus had written '666' on his forehead before jumping from the top of a ten-story apartment block with the intention of committing suicide. He had a note in his pocket that was considered a possible 'suicide note', but it was initially missed in the body search and not found until later."

Here Adam groaned audibly as if in some pain. It was an automatic reaction as the suppressed feelings were resurrected and the memories flooded back. The lecturer turned sharply, suddenly realising that Adam, along with his father had been closely involved in this case. It had not occurred to him when he prepared the lesson. He now proceeded with more caution out of respect for the feelings of his student and didn't touch on the beating Opus received and the part Adam had played. Fortunately, the other class members weren't aware of this and didn't seem to even notice.

"By a one in a million chance, after Opus jumped, a shotgun blast killed him instantly, as he fell past a ninth-floor window. Now right here, this strange case gets quite bizarre. The jumper was apparently not aware that building workers had installed a safety net at the eighth floor level, which would have normally rendered the suicide attempt, unsuccessful." There was some murmuring from the class. "Pay attention to this people, because there will be an assignment on this case."

*An assignment, I could write a whole damned thesis on it!* Adam thought, rolling his eyes.

"Ordinarily, a person who sets out to commit suicide and ultimately succeeds," the lecturer went on, "even though the cause of death might be different than what was intended, is still defined as committing suicide. So...here we have Mr Opus jumping to what should have been 'certain death', when he is taken out, with both barrels of a shotgun. This caused the Medical Examiner to believe it was a homicide but that's not the end..."

There were more murmurings from the class. The lecturer waited for his dramatic pause to gain full effect. Now in a ninth floor apartment, an elderly couple were arguing and the man had threatened his wife with a shotgun. Believing the gun was not loaded, he cocked it to scare her and finally pulled both triggers as he turned away. He missed her and accidently shot right through the window and by a freakish coincidence, caused the instant death of Ronald Opus as he passed by the open window.

By the letter of the law, if this man had actually planned to kill his wife, but instead accidentally killed the jumper, then he would be responsible for the second degree murder or manslaughter of that second person. When confronted with a murder charge, the elderly man was adamant that he believed the shotgun was not loaded. His wife reluctantly supported him so there was no pre-meditation or intent against the jumper. It was considered that there was also, no real motive. It seemed that it was a regular occurrence for this jerk to threaten his wife with an unloaded gun, so since it appeared he had no actual intention of shooting her, the killing of Mr Opus was considered accidental. Again the class broke into murmurs.

"The investigation then turned up a witness who claimed he saw the old couple's son purchase shells for the shotgun, some time prior to the shooting. It transpired that the wife had cut off her son's financial support and knowing the propensity of his father to threaten her with the shotgun, he had clandestinely obtained shotgun cartridges and loaded the weapon so his father would shoot his mother. He figured the father would then go to jail and with his mother dead, he would inherit the money." A long pause while the class settled.

"So, in the eyes of the law, the son who loaded the gun with this specific plan in mind, was guilty of the premeditated, attempted murder of his mother and by default the accidental murder of the jumper Opus, even though he had not actually pulled the trigger." Again the murmur of voices as the class expressed amazement. They had never heard of a case like this one with all its twists and turns. "Now people, I couldn't write this case history even as a hypothetical example, because in a final exotic twist, the baffled investigators discovered that the victim, Ronald Opus, was in fact, the old couple's son who had loaded the shot gun!" There was an uproar.

"Opus had pressing money worries and became distressed at the inability to engineer his mother's demise and as a result, jumped from the roof above the tenth floor of the building. Since he had loaded the shotgun, it meant that he had actually engineered his own death, so the DA and the Chief Medical Examiner had no option but to give a final verdict of suicide." The class erupted!

Adam had always kept a fairly low profile in his classes and it seems no one, apart from the instructor, even knew his family name or identified his part in the case. He shook his head. Even with all the publicity, no one else seemed aware of his involvement in the bizarre events and he was thankful that the instructor had not drawn attention to it. It seemed to Adam, that this case had occurred years ago and now hearing the re-cap summary, some discrepancies triggered in his agile brain.

The lecturer summarised quickly, "In case you missed it, take note that the old man actually killed his own son with the shot gun blast. Because the son had loaded the shotgun to implement the death of his mother, he was guilty of the attempted murder of his mother and ultimately, the killing of himself. Whether it's right or wrong, it turned out that he became the victim and actually murdered himself, so accordingly, it is now recorded as a suicide. Weird case!"

There were exclamations and questions from all over the class and the lecturer had to raise his hands for silence. "One of our lessons from this case is that you must always look at what would be considered 'normal behaviour' before you start considering the really bizarre. This was a very bizarre case, but the motivation and actions were actually quite conventional. I personally believe a lot of time was wasted on this case because it had so many twists and turns which bogged everybody down. Let's write some of them down." He moved to the white board and commenced recording the 'bullet' points:

- The suspected involvement of drugs and cults wrongly indicated a ritual killing or sacrifice.
- The '666' was a red herring and far too much was made of it.
- The basic suicide note was not initially found so it was uncertain if the victim had jumped or had been pushed.
- The body wasn't identified for more than a week.

- The case went from suicide, to homicide, to accidental death, to murder, to suicide.
- The mother had information that police initially failed to realise. Mrs Opus may have cracked the case wide open had she been questioned in a different manner.

"There's heaps more information, but you will have to search that out for yourselves." The lecturer produced a neatly stapled, typed hand-out and went on to outline the assignment of researching the case and writing an essay arguing whether the investigation could have been handled better, whether the conclusions reached were correct and what additional factors should have been considered.

As he listened to the precis of the unusual case, something twigged in Adam's mind and he was visibly shaken. 'You must always look at what would be normal behaviour before you start considering the bizarre'. Another thing triggered his curiosity; what was it that Jack had said at the lake about the Twin Towers coming down. Adam thought deeply. After class, he went home and switched on his computer.

### The Home of Dr Don Mills

It was the weekend and Adam turned up at his parent's home. His mother immediately ushered him in for coffee and raisin toast. She hugged him and inquired after Mina. His father joined them. Renee was out catching up with friends and Adam was really sorry he had missed her. He remained quiet for some time focusing his thoughts and finally it all burst out as he explained about the assignment he was doing on the Opus case and what was bothering him.

They discussed it for some time. "We had better talk to Mrs Opus first," Dr Mills said, thinking deeply and looking more owl-like than ever. "Barry Hannaway is moving back to San Diego today and he is taking her things in a trailer. We promised to help her move out of the apartment so I was going there anyway. You can help us carry a few boxes down. OK?"

Barry Hannaway had arrived first, with a U-Haul trailer hitched to his vehicle. He had moved some of the cartons down already. They all chipped in with the rest of the boxes and some furniture and had the job done in quick time. Mrs Opus was holding up well considering the loss of her son, the failure of her marriage and the ordeal she had been through. She informed them that Clive had attended the cremation service and had not been seen since. Good riddance! He was a missing person who nobody missed, she claimed with a slight wry smile. She was moving to San Diego to be with her sister.

She had no idea where Clive might be or how he was supporting himself. He had always been very secretive and accordingly she knew nothing at all about any of his dealings. She was quite happy that should he return, she would be long gone and her apartment would be rented out with the locks changed. He had told her nothing and he had now been missing for almost two weeks. Mills and his son discussed some of Adam's concerns with her and checked a few angles.

Barry would head off presently, accompanying Maggie Opus to San Diego. He had previously arranged the sale of Ron's car and his things, and had brought Maggie the money. Right then Hannaway called Dr Mills aside and handed him a box containing a few things he didn't want Maggie to see. Mills saw a bag with traces of white powder, a Browning automatic, a flick-knife and Ron's mobile cell phone that he had found in the glove compartment. A large '666' was emblazoned across the back of the phone in black marker pen. Dr Mills discreetly placed the box in his vehicle, to hand on to Mack's office.

Mrs Opus was very grateful for their assistance. She profusely thanked Dr Mills and Adam, but she reserved special status for Barry Hannaway; she thought he was an angel. Father and son said their goodbyes and were touched by the sincere thanks of Maggie. They were to feel the firmness of Barry's handshake for the next fifteen minutes.

Dr Mills borrowed his son's cell phone, "Mack, we'd like to meet with you right away, if that's convenient."

## Another Story

Quite often when Mina and Leah did a crew change, they were able to catch up with Claire, in the crew lounge. Claire was a vivacious person and always had all the latest gossip and loved sharing it. At times, she seemed a little gullible and Mina thought she spent more time passing on these stories, than actually evaluating if the information was true and believable. That was just Claire, and they loved her anyway. Her stories were always entertaining and delivered at break-neck speed. Leah ran into her at Hamburg Airport as the girls were flying out. Soon after, Mina could see that Leah was busting to share the latest story.

"This is priceless," Leah exclaimed, "Claire got this from the receptionist at the hotel in Paris." It seems, Captain Kangaroo was in the same hotel as the Flight

Attendants and must have been feeling a bit lonely so he thought he'd call an escort girl he saw advertised on a card in his room. A particularly pretty girl calling herself 'Erogonique', was shown in a photo, bending over, displaying her ample charms. She had all the right curves in all the right places, beautiful thick wavy blonde hair extensions and long graceful legs. So, the Captain picked up the phone and called the number listed there. 'Hello, can I help you?' a sultry voiced woman answered.

"'Well, hello, I read that you give a great massage and I'd like you to come to my room,' he started, 'No, wait, I want to be entirely honest with you. I'm in town all alone and what I really want is sex. I want it hard; I want it hot, and I want it now. I'm talking all night long. You name it, we'll do it. Bring handcuffs, gags, toys, everything you've got in your bag of tricks. We'll go hot and heavy for hours. Tie me up, cover me in chocolate syrup and whipped cream, anything you want, baby. Now, how does that sound?'"

"The sexy voice answered, '…actually, that sounds pretty nice, but for an outside line you'll need to dial 9 first!'"

Mina tried to visualise Captain Kangaroo's face and just cracked up, regardless of whether the story was true or not.

### Ironing out Some Wrinkles

There was a large, framed picture of a derelict Irish Castle on the back wall of Mack's Office. Adam hadn't ever noticed it before and guessed it might be a recently installed symbol of Mack's Irish heritage. Perhaps the castle had been owned by a distant ancestor. If so, he thought, you might be somewhat reticent to advertise this fact, since the thing was parked precariously on a precipice overlooking an angry sea and didn't look all that permanent.

Adam found his concentration wandering as a weird thought crossed his mind. Mack loved to promote his Irish ancestry and he was proudly vocal about having kissed the Blarney stone. Knowing Mack as he did, Adam wouldn't be at all surprised if he had actually bitten off a chunk and swallowed it.

"Tell him Adam." Mmmmm. Silence for a beat.

"Well it occurred to me sir, that for Ron Opus to let a pusher know that he was buying cartridges to load the shot gun, would be pretty stupid. We should not lose sight of the fact that he was actually setting up a murder. His profile indicates that he was not the brightest crayon in the box, but he was street smart, and to let a pusher have something on him like that, would be needlessly creating a witness who could send him to jail."

"A pusher is not the most reliable person in the world, now is he? At the very least, he would try to lever some advantage from that information, particularly if Ron Opus inherited money as a result of his mother's demise. It could be money, more drugs, or something a lot more serious, like blackmail. I just don't believe a street-wise Opus would expose himself to that situation; it is not normal behaviour."

Mackenzie winced and tried a few experimental scratches. He seemed agitated, Adam thought, maybe because of the interruption, however, he really couldn't have looked more uncomfortable if the Irish Castle above his head, was about to fall on him. Mack tried another scratch, made a steeple with his hands, bowed his head slightly and moved his lips almost like he was praying.

His concern was likely warranted since he had just heard that the pusher had blown bail and was now missing in action with skip-tracers after him. Jesus! What if he was lying and hadn't seen the purchase of shotgun shells at all. What if the father planned the whole thing and got Ron to relay that particular story. The wife had the money and they both wanted it!

Adam continued to look at his superior, waiting for him to break the silence. Right now Mack didn't inspire much confidence and Adam had a hard time getting around the lack of support over the past several weeks. The blinkers fell off. Adam had been brought up to be respectful but now he saw Mack in a new light. Mack was overweight and dressed like a slob and really, was not much of a leader or role model. He appeared to become more nervous and began to squirm in his swivel chair, causing an immediate struggle between burgeoning flesh and the blue wool knitting of his stretched and frayed ski jumper.

The line of penguins displayed across the front appeared to be waddling towards an icy pool located somewhere below the 9 millimetre holster in the vicinity of his left armpit. Adam watched their progress, quite fascinated, expecting to see the whole line enthusiastically dive in at any moment. Mack's appearance took weekend casual dress to a whole new level but he seemed blissfully unaware of his lack of sartorial elegance. He was a man with concerns on his mind.

Dr Mills had been silent for some time but fired up now, looking for answers. "What if Clive Opus was dealing drugs himself. What if he had a falling out and actually planned to kill his son and have it classed as an accident?" he stated, "Why has he now disappeared?"

"Oh Christ, are you telling me Clive Opus is missing?"

"From right after the funeral, Mrs Opus just told us. Come on Mack, he wouldn't be likely to abandon his meal ticket if something wasn't wrong. So what's the best guess. He's been murdered or he's done a runner or what…Mack?"

Mack groaned in exasperation; he had no answers. The stretched penguins looked almost as forlorn, especially the one in the middle with the gravy stain across its white chest plumage.

"Next," Adam continued, "we have accepted that Clive Opus accidently fired a double barrelled shotgun, which has an extremely wide cone of fire, near his wife standing in the same room, yet somehow he missed her entirely. He missed her at point blank range and yet with extraordinary precision, the double charge almost took the head off the jumper who happened to be passing the window."

"Coincidence only stretches so far, Sir. Mrs Opus didn't even get one pellet burn yet a direct hit was scored on the human missile going past the window. The adjacent windows were not broken either. That has got to be close to impossible!" Adam had done some serious checking on the case.

"It seems to be fairly apparent that there are still some wrinkles to iron out here, Mack," Dr Mills stated bluntly, "Perhaps the son was the target all along. Maybe they were together in drugs and had an altercation. Maybe the son wasn't driven to suicide; maybe he was forced to write the note and then pushed. Look, the chance of an accidental shot from a supposedly unloaded gun, killing a jumper passing the window at that instant, is just astronomical odds."

After the lesson, Adam had recalled what it was Jack had shared with them, at the lake, about falling structures from demolition. He then spent an hour on the internet and more time with a calculator. He joined in now, "Sir, a falling human body accelerates at about 36 feet per second, every second, until terminal velocity is reached. Terminal velocity is when the downward force of gravity is equal to the upward force of drag and no more acceleration is achieved. These are fixed laws of physics."

"For example, the terminal velocity of a skydiver in a free-fall position, jumping feet first, with less drag, is a bit faster. Things like the clothing worn and the shape and orientation of the body would make some difference, but in the first second of a jump a body falls something close to 36 feet. I believe that the window in the Opus apartment is no more than 6 feet high. So after just one second, a body falling from the roof at 36 feet per second, would pass a 6 foot window in under one-sixth of a second."

"We are being asked to believe that as the jumper flashed past the window in something under one-sixth of a second, a shotgun blast, with unerring accuracy, hit him in the head. Since he had his hands up to his face, it almost obliterated all fingerprints and killed him instantly. We are literally looking at split second timing." He paused, "The odds must be billions to one against it." The senior Mills remained silent considering this and Mack looked very unhappy. "Add to this the fact that the window panes around it were not blasted out by the double shotgun blast it gets more and more implausible."

Mack had gone about as pale as a White Pointer in Winter, but out of habit, quickly reverted to his usual arrogance, to look about as menacing as one. "Where's your damn 'Cosmic Joker' now," Mack spluttered somewhat bitterly to Dr Mills.

"Well you are right Mack, but coincidences do happen. I've been looking into it since we spoke. There was a situation where a man called Joseph Figlock was walking down the street in Detroit in the 1930s when a baby fell on him from a high window. He broke its fall and saved its life. A year later he was showing a friend where it had happened and the same child fell on him again from the same window and he saved it again."[24]

"That was an amazing coincidence with astronomical odds against and I am the first to agree it is uncanny, although it actually happened. This Opus case, however, is bizarre, it fractures all forms of coincidence. You must agree that there is still some serious investigative mopping up needed here."

Now Mack looked like he had copped a bad oyster. With his known love of country music, you might have told him Willie Nelson's latest album had stiffed. Not only that…Gary Glitter was making a comeback with his cover of 'Blue Eyes Crying in the Rain' now sitting at number one. Mack's pained look remained fixed as he thought a long time, scratching his stomach at infrequent intervals, and his voice went dry and raggerty like he had swallowed a sock, "Look gentlemen, no thinking person on the planet still believes that Lee Harvey Oswald shot President John F. Kennedy with a 'magic bullet'. Before he could blow the whistle on the conspiracy, the patsy Oswald was silenced by Jack Ruby who just happened to be dying of cancer. After the murder of JFK, about thirty-something people connected to the case died under mysterious circumstances but nothing was ever done about it. You understand; the real perpetrators were never identified and got off scot-free?"

"Regardless of how implausible the media explanation was, the public swallowed it. Since then, theories have been voiced, books have been written and films have been made that juggled the evidence in various ways, but at the end of the day, it all came to naught. The Warren Commission may have been an ongoing joke but its conclusions were accepted as fact and that's the way history records it."

He thought some more, "I'm not saying there is any conspiracy behind this Opus case, but it's still exactly the same situation. I don't have the manpower or the desire to go tilting at windmills. Suicide or Murder, that's what it comes down to, and really, what the hell does it matter which is written on his tombstone or which is documented for posterity, it won't bring Ron Opus back. Clive Opus may have gotten away with something, he may not have. He may have done something wrong and he may have even paid with his life."

"Possibly it even happened in my precinct, but there's virtually nothing I can do. Unsolved files are a fact of life. We all try to change the world or at least to make a serious mark on it…" He searched for agreement. "Don, you do that as much as I do, and Adam you are turning out to be exactly the same. The way you handled Flynn is a remarkable example."

"That was incredibly good work. So we try hard, we give it our best shot, sometimes we're successful, sometimes we're not. At the end of the round, there are some things that could have been handled better; and some things that are better left alone. We'll just leave this one as a suicide; OK." He shook his head dismally.

"Adam, you are due some considerable back-pay for the time you were suspended. I was able to arrange the top rate, I'm just sorry it took so long to come through. I also approved some 'expenses money' for the Flynn arrest, in your own time. You deserve it." Having got that off his chest, Mack appeared to brighten up considerably as he handed Adam a bulky envelope. "You've had a rough time. I've approved some leave. Why don't you take a break and enjoy yourself, son!"

Adam understood what Mack was saying but he remained somewhat annoyed. He was training to be a detective for goodness' sake and so felt the cost of enjoying himself was to dismiss all the discrepancies in this case. He was disappointed with the way the case had been run and the class assignment he was doing would certainly reflect that. He was distraught with the way he had been treated along with his suspension and right now he was specifically pissed off with Mack for all he was sweeping under the carpet. Mack might be entirely right, but he didn't have to be so blasé and smug about it.

"Thank you, sir." Adam got up without another word and left the precinct.

He felt very confused and wondered what Mina would do in this situation. She was a Libran and always balanced the scales. Mina had an uncanny sense of what was fair and just. She had been in his thoughts constantly; he needed to talk to her. He thought of something really wild. Just maybe he could use this break to arrange a surprise…

# Chapter 10
# A Neat Surprise

**Somewhere in Europe**

Leah received a call on her cell phone, raised her eyebrows to Mina and stepped outside the hotel room to take the call. When she returned, Leah went back to working on her nails. Leah's 'cover up' was a bit strained, "Claire told me another story about yesterday's flight with 'Captain Kangaroo'; wanna hear it?" she said.

"OK, but I think these stories are mostly urban myth," Mina said stifling a yawn.

"Well, the girls were on the Madrid run again. The captain really is a fun guy, and believes he sounds delightfully 'Continental' on the P.A. He loves the microphone, as you know. The Flight attendants had been sending him up as usual and he must have decided to get back at them. Soon after the evening take off, he came on the P.A. system saying, 'Ladies and Gentlemen, this is your Captain speaking.'"

"We have reached cruising altitude of 30,000 feet and the weather ahead looks good indeed. We have a tail wind and hope to have you on the tarmac in Madrid just before 9 p.m. We hope your flight is enjoyable. Thank you for choosing Lufthansa, we pride ourselves on having the prettiest Flight Attendants in the business, but…unfortunately…well, none of them are on this flight. We will be turning down the cabin lights in just a moment. This is for your comfort and safety, but in addition it is our own attempt to hide the appearance of this particular crew."

"OK!" Mina said giggling, "I believe he would say that."

Next morning before the flight out, Leah slipped away to the Lufthansa counter at the airport. "Just checking on something," she told Mina. As usual Leah could not keep a secret very well and her body language and overacting made Mina think something was up, but she dismissed it in an instant, believing Leah had a hot date or was arranging a secret rendezvous or something like that. Actually, she was.

## Some Turbulence

Adam parked his RV in the long-term car park at LAX and headed for the International Terminal with some trepidation. What he was about to do was crazy and he hadn't really thought it through properly. He had lost faith in his job, in his boss and in the entire system. What did he believe in right now…he believed in Mina. The lovely girl had touched his very soul and Adam was wholly smitten. He wanted to see her, he needed to be with her, he realised just how much he loved her.

Everything had been arranged for him, and Adam boarded the plane with time to spare. The Lufthansa service was brilliant but the flight was not an enjoyable one as Adam turned things over and over in his mind. He considered several scenarios. As a detective he always asked 'what if?' and now he was plagued by the negative thoughts that came with this exercise. What if he had misread Mina's intentions? What if he was moving too fast? What if he was only reacting to the ordeal he had just been through? What if…? It went on and on for hours…churning…churning in his mind.

He couldn't watch the 'in flight' movie and he only picked at the airline food. He had a fitful sleep and kept torturing his mind until, eventually, the aircraft began to lose altitude and he heard the landing gear extend. A perfect landing followed and then a taxi along the minor runway to the disembarking gate. Adam held his nose and blew strongly to clear his ears. With this, he seemed to clear his mind a little.

Through the aircraft window, he finally saw the sign for 'Charles de Gaulle Airport' in French and English. The French customs and immigration were thorough but polite and courteous. Adam retrieved his luggage and caught a taxicab to the hotel Leah had mentioned, where the Lufthansa crews chose to stay.

## What Goes Around…

It was a charming old stone building adjacent to a well-tended park and had been magnificently restored to its former glory from an earlier era. Adam noted particularly, how this hotel oozed an elegance and charm that could not be replicated with modern chrome and glass. He paid off the cab and as he turned to approach the entrance, a well-dressed older lady passed him on the sidewalk that was bordered by a thick hedge along the front of the park. A bellhop headed for his bag as Adam cast an eye over the Paris skyline from this elevated position, taking in the ambiance of the city, bathed in glorious sunshine.

While he was taking in some deep breaths, from the corner of his eye, he saw the old lady suddenly set on by three scruffy looking muggers, one of whom was grabbing at her handbag, wrestling it from her grasp and knocking her to the ground. It seemed like this creep was up for the job too, looking to be about three times her body weight. This hairy monster would fill a phone box and for the sake of humanity, you prayed he wouldn't reproduce.

It was like that 'evolution of man' cartoon, with the last frame saying, "Go back." The assailant had almost no forehead and was so overweight and ugly that he would be a shoe-in for the gig, if ever they needed another gorilla at the Ménagerie du Jardin des Plantes Zoo just visible in the distance. Considering his apparent, limited intellect, it was probably a good fallback for him in the medium term, if the crime thing didn't work out.

Along with his two skinny sidekicks, he made the mistake of running Adam's way planning to escape into the park through a break in the hedge where the cobblestone pathway entered. Even though Adam was tired and cramped from his long flight, he sprang into action with an agility that simply defied description. He was on them in an instant operating from well-honed instinct and training.

One twisting karate punch and the unkempt giant with her handbag went down, like a cold beer at a bushfire. Faceplant. The bigger they are the harder they fall…It seemed, the ground shook from the impact. Isaac Newton's first law … effectively proven. Adam noted the expensive Hi-Top Nike's he was wearing, which he had likely stolen, because for this creep to require such sporting footwear would be a bit like street racing in a dump truck.

The other two grabbed for Adam, one pulling a flick-knife and clicking the blade out menacingly. Adam launched high into the air; his flying body almost horizontal. An effective mid-air kick put the second assailant down. The knife clattered along the pavement. The third attacker turned to retrieve it, yelling obscenities in French, but his legs were taken out from under him with a well-executed sweep. He struggled to his feet and tried to eye gouge Adam, until a slamming forearm block protected Adam's face and almost removed the assailant's chin. This one folded like a bad poker hand. Adam was fast, God he was fast; the entire incident took just seconds and three bag snatchers were effectively curtailed, giving a whole new meaning to 'down and out'.

As Adam helped the dazed lady to her feet, the hotel's concierge, dressed something like an Italian Admiral, gold braid flashing, complemented by a heavy fake tan, rushed over and began protectively checking her welfare, whilst sucking air through his commercially enhanced, pearly white teeth. Ignoring her thanks as if he had done nothing, Adam retrieved her handbag and brought it to her. Though badly shaken, she paused to thank him profusely in French, before she was escorted back to the hotel.

She looked like a really nice, dignified lady, Adam thought as he turned towards the hotel entrance. The two less corpulent assailants were struggling to regain their feet, no fight left in them, as two sturdy, security men rushed over to take charge of the situation. The gorilla was still out for the count. Many of the staff members were now watching from the hotel steps as Adam entered. He was approached by a petite check-in receptionist.

"A room monsieur?" Adam nodded and couldn't help but note the plunging neckline with a couple of outstanding features on display; also commercially enhanced, if the truth was known. She too, displayed magnificent white teeth. The HR people at this particular establishment certainly had an eye for personal aesthetics.

The bellhop, not a blemish on his baby face, had collected Adam's bags and was hovering nearby. Adam commenced explaining to the receptionist that he wanted a nice room but he was a student on a budget.

*"What the hell am I doing here then?"* he muttered to himself looking at the opulence around him. The hotel's chief security guard came back in, still puffing from his exertion.

"We thank you, monsieur, you save special lady," he hesitated searching for words the American would understand, "…you save also, (how you say)…my ass." Adam couldn't help but smile at the sincerity of his mangled English.

Having escorted the lady upstairs, the concierge with the dark tan and light teeth, returned and rushed over. Adam had noted that outside, he had beaten the security men to the scene by a full minute.

"Thank you, monsieur, you are the hero!"

"Not at all," Adam said, "I was just trying to help."

"Monsieur, I am Jon-Pierre. Can we get for you, the room?"

"Yes please," Adam said looking around at the luxurious decor, "but something reasonable please, I am on a budget." Some rapid-fire French followed between Jon-Pierre and the receptionist and despite heavy gesturing, Adam did not understand a word of the dialogue.

"Monsieur, you will have a suite at no charge. We cannot thank you enough."

"Really?" Adam said astounded, "Why are you doing this, Jon-Pierre?"

"Monsieur, the lady you help, she is the manager of some special guests who stay in hotel; she is very grateful. We also want no publicity that the muggers operate near our hotel and our security guard he is, how you say, goofing off!" Adam was still chuckling about this as they moved to the elevator and up several floors. He still held a smile until the concierge opened the ornate double doors to his suite.

"Stone the bloody crows!" he exclaimed in awe, imitating the crusty Australian who had recently helped him off the hook, back in LA.

"You are Australien, no?" asked Jon-Pierre, who was a bit of a character it seemed, "Blooty good show mite!"

"No, no, I am from Los Angeles," said Adam overwhelmed at the opulence of the suite, "I just know an Australian who talks that way." The concierge was adjusting the thick velvet drapes of the amazing room, "First time in Paree?"

"Yes," Adam said, "I am meeting my girlfriend here."

"Is the city for romance, monsieur. You need anything at all, you just let Jon-Pierre know, you hear." He winked and exited.

## Gay Paree

Adam was astonished as well as overjoyed at his luck. He had never seen a luxurious suite like this before. The plush carpet was over an inch thick and the double bed covered about an acre. Adam moved around the suite and decided to try out the fancy shower. The bathroom alone was about the size of his apartment in LA and the shower was like a carwash.

It was certainly impressive in rich marble, with about ten bottles of shampoo, conditioner, body lotions and bath oils lined up on a shelf with soft waffle weave towels that would dry a good-sized elephant. All the fittings were gold and crystal and the overall effect was simply spectacular.

He enjoyed the shower and let the hot spray wash away his drowsiness. Adam couldn't help noting that it wasn't all for show. The sparkling gold multi-showerhead had more firepower than the dull chrome one in his LA apartment. He felt invigorated and greatly refreshed but now he had better get to work. He had a few hours to prepare his surprise and set about making the necessary arrangements.

Adam had dreamed about seeing Mina again and wanted this evening to be perfect. Picking up the elaborate house phone, he tried to make a booking at the hotel's main restaurant, but 'special guests' were staying in the hotel and the two restaurants were both fully booked out. He made a few more calls but mainly because of the language barrier was not having much luck. Adam used the elevator, obtained a map in English from reception, then exited the hotel, turned left and walked smartly with a purpose.

Jon-Pierre was not in sight, probably checking on the lady. Adam was thankful because he was still a bit embarrassed by all the fuss, they made of him. He did, however, really appreciate the room and the saving of his meagre funds. He could never justify the cost of an extravagant room like that and he guessed Mina would be blown away. He thought about how much she would love this suite.

Adam would find another suitable restaurant, and he really wanted to surprise her with a night at the ballet, knowing how much she would enjoy it. When he arrived at the theatre, a smartly dressed receptionist apologised profusely, that no tickets remained for that evening's performance. This was not going well at all.

"Tomorrow night?" he asked and from the French gestures and her pointing to a computer screen, he understood they were booked out for a week or more in advance with no cancellations likely.

Adam was dismayed, he hadn't allowed for this and nothing was going right. Maybe this spontaneity hadn't been such a great idea. He was a bit dejected as he walked back to the hotel.

"Sir, you are not happee?" it was the check-in receptionist with the magnificent front.

Adam explained his problem, "Is true Monsieur, you must book many days in advance."

Adam looked crestfallen. "I so much wanted to take the lady I am meeting, to dinner and to the ballet…"

"She is your fiancée Monsieur?"

"I am going to ask her to be," Adam said pensively. He couldn't help it. Mina was on his mind and he told the receptionist all about her. She seemed to understand and in an instant Jon-Pierre was summoned and the girl explained the problem in French. There was much waving of arms and animated speech. The concierge turned to Adam, mouth agape looking horrified, "Monsieur! Did Jon-Pierre not explain; you want anything at all, you just ask?"

"I didn't want to bother you," Adam said truthfully.

"Now Monsieur, you go and rest, Jon-Pierre will fix."

"No," Adam said, "I have to make some arrangements."

"Monsieur, please no insult Jon-Pierre. Go! Go! Jon-Pierre will fix."

"Really…?"

"You go!" Adam was dismissed.

He left, but he did not rest; he walked a few blocks and did some serious checking and haggling. Despite the language problems, he eventually made a purchase, spending a lot of the money he had converted to traveller's cheques.

## Flight into Paris

"I know you're up to something," Mina exclaimed from the jump seat, "I can see that look in your eye." Leah tried to play dumb, but excitement showed on her face and a smile touched her lips. Nevertheless, Mina really had no clue what was in store for her.

All that afternoon Jon-Pierre had been in deep discussion with various hotel staff members and a few guests. He visited the lady Adam had rescued for a long discussion and made a myriad of phone calls, chuckling quietly the whole time, thoroughly enjoying himself. He was very good at his job and thought of everything. When the flight crew finally emerged from Charles de Gaulle Airport just on dark, the hotel's limousine was waiting.

Obediently standing on the pavement alongside, was Adam, dressed very smartly, looking quite handsome but very confused and just a bit anxious. Mina let out a cry, dropped everything and ran to him almost smothering him with kisses.

"Oh Adam," she cried. "How did you get here, I had no idea, this is the best surprise ever." She turned to her friend, "Leah you were in on this…" She smiled, even though tears were running down her face. She gave her friend a conspiratory wink and mouthed a sincere, "Thank-you!"

Leah walked discreetly to the Citroen that was to transport the crew, leaving Adam and Mina to travel in the hotel's stretch limo. Mina chatted nonstop all the way to the hotel and hugged Adam to herself as if frightened he may get away.

Adam was almost overawed by the beauty shining like a beacon from Mina's lovely face.

He felt some trepidation about the night ahead and just a little nervous about asking this beautiful girl to spend the rest of her life with him. He wanted this evening to be perfect. He would finish University at the end of this year and very much wanted Mina for his wife. God, he hoped she would say yes.

Mina took a call on her cell phone. She had cause to appreciate Leah more than ever. Her friend was a treasure, she had arranged one of the other girls to work Mina's final shift leaving her free to share another two days with Adam in Paris before heading home to LA. They travelled through the City's streets towards the hotel, resting in the luxurious red velvet upholstery of the gleaming white limo.

Adam had underestimated the contacts and talents of the wily Jon-Pierre; true to his word, he had indeed, arranged everything. A quick cocktail at the bar together, then Mina was whisked away to the room to bathe and change. Adam was escorted to a transit room downstairs where he was fitted with suitable formal attire from the hotel's suit hire.

## Cinderella

Mina was clearly stunned. The luxurious suite exuded elegance far beyond anything she had ever experienced before. A very sweet French maid had run a bath for her and it was simply divine soaking in the warm water with bath salts and sweet perfumed oils. She was allowed to relax there for some time before the maid brought her a robe then showed Mina the magnificent gown she had laid out on the bed. "For me?" Mina was now past being stunned. "But how…!" All the accessories were there and it was like she was dreaming, with her own maid and wardrobe mistress.

A French hairdresser appeared and a makeup artist and Mina had to pinch herself as they swiftly and professionally went to work pampering her, putting her hair up and applying makeup, crooning away in French the whole time. The maid assisted her to dress and when she finally looked in the full-length mirror, Mina was transformed, she hardly recognised herself, wearing a tiara and matching necklace that looked like real diamonds.

"Oh, la-la! Mademoiselle looks very beautiful," hamming it up and blowing kisses on his fingertips, Jon-Pierre arrived right on cue, ready to escort Mina downstairs.

"How is all this possible?" Mina asked, almost unable to speak.

"Your beau, Ad-am want best for you, Mademoiselle. You not to worry; they are all friends, they stay in hotel," Jon-Pierre told her without further explanation. The maid appeared and adjusted Mina's outfit. She snapped on a pashmina cloak with faux ermine trim, completing the outfit and making Mina feel like a fairytale princess. Like most true romantics, Mina had often dreamed of a dramatic entrance down a gilded staircase. She had really hoped that this dream would come to fruition at least once in her lifetime.

It was a shock to realise that out of the blue without explanation or fanfare, the stage was all set and the time was right now. It didn't exactly occur as she had dreamed; however, she had to admit this was pretty special as she was escorted by the beaming Jon-Pierre in his full concierge regalia, down in the elevator, to the head of the grand staircase.

When she left on the flight earlier that day, Mina had no inkling that something wonderful like this was predestined for her in Paris. Now here she was dressed up like a princess with not one clue what was going on, except that somehow, Adam was here and some surprise had been mapped out for her. It was mystifying, but it was also exhilarating and really nice.

*"Well OK, ready or not people, here I come, Cinderella is going to the ball."*

As she paused at the head of the stairs, she spotted her handsome prince, standing in a smart tuxedo with a velvet collar and colourful matching cummerbund and bow tie, waiting for her with his jaw dropped and his mouth open. God, he looked handsome; dumbstruck, but still handsome. As she descended the stairs with poise that would make her high school personal development teacher proud, Mina looked absolutely radiant and her smile warmed his heart as she gracefully made her grand entrance. Adam was plainly gob smacked. Mina wasn't just glamorous and beautiful; she was hot, like whitehot nuclear heat.

## A Night to Remember

Arm in arm with no idea what was happening, Adam and Mina were escorted on a gentle stroll through the stylish foyer, along the sidewalk and into the adjoining park to the surprised stares of several patrons heading into the hotel. The park was a sight to behold; the actual picnic area had been transformed, especially for them. The table was covered with a starched, white linen cloth resplendent with coloured napkins while a multitude of candles caused reflections from the sparkling glasses and fine silverware.

Dimmed coloured lanterns hung from the trees and this natural décor had more ambience than the finest Paris restaurant. Under the stars on this perfect evening, they were seated to dine al fresco. Chatting happily, they were served elegant French cuisine and fine champagne by a happy and willing chef. Never had they tasted entrées so magnificent and their eyes were only for each other. A very discreet photographer caught all the action and apart from a few flashes they would never have known he was there.

"Adam, how on Earth did you do this," Mina asked for the third time. Adam couldn't answer that particular question, because he honestly didn't know. He was as surprised as she was. He just smiled to see her so happy and glowing.

As the entrée dishes were cleared away, from out of the darkness, violin music wafted towards them, sensual and sweet. It came closer and Mina immediately recognised the ballet piece. It was live music and she was also aware this was no amateur musician.

"Oh my God," she exclaimed in delight as she recognised the maestro. "Adam this is not possible; that is Emile Le Chevalier, the lead violinist with the French Ballet." Adam was concerned. He attracted the attention of the concierge, who was acting as a very capable maître d'hôtel.

"Jon-Pierre you have excelled, and we thank you, but we cannot possibly pay for all this."

"You worry too much Monsieur; relax, enjoy. They are friends, they stay at hotel. You help us very much; we help you but a little. The lady you help; she is manager-patron of the ballet and sends her thanks. There is no charge, Monsieur; it is our pleasure."

Adam and Mina relaxed and they did enjoy. The violinist continued to play classical ballet pieces and a totally delighted Mina, recognised each one. Then dinner was served under stylish silver covers.

"Tomorrow night we can have your favourite, Macca's with fries," Adam said, showing he still remembered their first date, "but tonight, I guess this will have to suffice." This brought a smile to Mina's expressive face.

"Bon Appétit!" Jon-Pierre exclaimed, as he removed the covers with a flourish. They say you can't get a bad meal in Paris. Both Adam and Mina believed they had never before, in their entire lives, tasted food so superb. Romantic violin music and soft lighting, fine French Champagne and elegant cuisine made this the most memorable dinner ever. The smiling couple enjoyed it immensely.

The dishes were eventually cleared away and right on cue, the sweet violin launched into the unmistakable music from the ballet, Swan Lake. Mina could not contain her appreciation. This was one of the finest violinists in the world and he was playing dinner entertainment just for them. Jon-Pierre turned up the lanterns and as the soft lighting penetrated the darkness, a prima ballerina moved effortless from the shadows on to a small timber square prepared for her. Mina hugged Adam as the disciplined artiste performed the 'Dying Swan' excerpt, for her utter enjoyment, right there in the park.

"She is from the French Ballet, she is quite famous," Mina breathed, totally overwhelmed. She was captivated and entranced by the gorgeous and talented ballerina. It was a magical, once in a lifetime experience and Mina followed every movement from their 'front row' seats. The superb dancer made the piece come to life. Magnificent! All too soon it was over as the ballerina took her bows. Their energetic acclamation did justice to the amazing impromptu performance. The lanterns were dimmed again as Peach Melba sweets were served. They looked sensational, consisting of a ripe peach, poached in vanilla syrup, presented in a fancy cup of vanilla bean ice cream and covered with crushed ripe raspberries.

"Oh Adam, this is all too incredible, I just can't believe it is happening to me. It's like a fairy-tale…Thank-you! Thank-you…! I love you so much." Adam's heart leapt. Gourmet 'fromage blanc' and steaming coffee followed after sweets and Mina was hoping this wasn't the end of the magical evening. She wished it could go on forever.

"Please tell me, tell me, tell me. How this all came about," Mina begged.

"I really tried hard to secure tickets to the ballet," Adam explained, "but they were totally booked out. I wanted so much to take you."

"So, you brought the ballet to the park, you crazy man. Oh Adam…" Mina had never felt so happy and so loved. This was truly special.

Jon-Pierre had discreetly moved away but now that they had finished their dinner, he was back, "Monsieur, Mademoiselle, your carriage awaits!" God he was a dramatic showman and just a tad corny but so very cool.

"What now…?" Mina was breathless.

"We'll just have to wait and see," Adam confessed. They were escorted to a princess coach pulled by two grey horses and they settled back comfortably in the rich leather, cushioned seats. The photographer snapped some pictures as they set off. They travelled through the streets of Paris, performing 'Royal waves' from the coach, laughing freely.

"Where are we going?" Mina asked.

"I'd only be guessing," Adam stated honestly, nervously fingering the gold box in his jacket pocket.

"Adam, what did Jon-Pierre mean you helped a lady?"

"Oh! She was a young, blonde nymphomaniac from the Moulin Rouge, and I helped her out of a long dry spell," Adam said, straight faced, the twinkle in his eyes making it hilarious.

"Adam!"

He told her briefly about rescuing the lady from the purse-snatchers, considerably down-playing the part he had played.

"I think it might have been a bit more than that, to warrant all this."

"You worry too much Mademoiselle; relax, enjoy," Adam said, with a hilarious overdone French accent, actually sounding a lot like Jon-Pierre. "Mademoiselle; it is our pleaseuuure!" The flourish he placed on the last word made Mina crack up, till tears appeared in her eyes. She dabbed them quickly to ensure her makeup didn't run.

Their destination soon became obvious as they stopped right near the base of the softly illuminated Eiffel tower. Mina gasped in delight since she was finally seeing this icon up close; she would remember this night forever. It was just perfect. The sightseers at the Tower were stopped in their tracks as Adam in his fancy tuxedo and his stunning princess in the flowing gown and jewelled tiara, alighted from the carriage.

"They must be in a movie," they heard American voices exclaim from the crowd and indeed people were looking around for the cameras. The fast elevator took them to the top with its stunning view of the lights of Paris. Mina thought her heart would burst when Adam kneeled right there at the top of the Eiffel tower, pledged his undying love and asked her to be his bride.

This time the tears flowed freely, as emotion overcame her. Her friend, Leah, had been so right when she declared that all her dreams would come true when the time was right. Adam was the perfect partner and she loved him dearly; in fact, she could no longer envisage life without him. "Yes, YES, **YES!**" she answered. She knew now that she wanted this more than anything in the world.

Adam took out the gold case. He spared a moment to be grateful for all the help Leah had provided, over the phone.

Baguette diamonds were Mina's favourite, she had told him, she even knew the correct size. *Well let's hope so, here goes*, he thought. Mina saw the sparkle in the subdued lighting as Adam opened the case and slowly placed on her finger the magnificent diamond ring he had bought earlier. It was a simple gold setting with a massive central baguette diamond and two tiny baguettes set in the shoulders; not ostentatious, but a spectacular ring. "Adam, how did you know…it's, it's…just so beautiful…it's beautiful!"

Mina was overcome with emotion as Adam embraced her and kissed her fondly in the romantic setting, with the lights of Paris reflecting in the river Seine below. She had enjoyed every moment of this memorable evening with its mystery tour and she silently thanked her Guardian Angel on the coach journey back to the hotel with her new fiancé. This is what she had always wanted and this was the man she had searched for so diligently. Earlier in the park, it had never occurred to her that this evening was to be a proposal. Yet again she noted that every moment she spent with Adam always seemed so exhilarating and so special.

Back in the magnificent hotel room, opulent waffled robes were laid out on the bed and on the table were chilled French champagne, strawberries and chocolate truffles. Mina really didn't need more champagne. She had made the decision to be Adam's wife and going a little out of character, she swept the robes to the floor as she threw Adam on the bed and dimmed the lights.

### An Amazing Day

Next morning there came a discreet knock on the door and a late breakfast in bed was served by a beaming waiter. When the silver covers were lifted, they saw smoked salmon omelette, with toasted crusty French bread. The aroma was divine. There were also mugs of rich, milky coffee.

"I could get used to this," Mina exclaimed. A note on the tray said they were booked on a late morning cruise along the Seine, a cruise promoted by the hotel.

Soon after breakfast, "I have a million phone calls to make," Mina said, "I have to call Leah, my mother and my Aunt Margaret and all my friends. We'll have to do the rounds when we get home, so you can meet them all." Adam winced, "It's OK, I promise they're all civilised. Nobody bites, but I do have to show you off; ladies' prerogative. Wait 'til I tell them we were engaged in Paris and about Swan Lake in the Park and everything, they'll just die." Mina commenced making calls.

Her mother was just ecstatic at the news. "When we get back, could you come to dinner with my mother and my aunt on Sunday night," Mina asked Adam, with her hand over the mouthpiece.

"No way!" Adam replied, "Sunday nights, I get drunk with my buddies and play poker." He dodged the thrown pillow and ducked quickly behind the bedpost to avoid another missile before he headed for the shower.

"Well, you'll have to get used to it, Sweetie." Mina called loudly, "My mother holds a 'command performance' every Sunday so we can have dinner with the family, without fail, no exceptions, right after the church service." Mina looked so sincere. Adam pulled up dead and groaned; what had he got into here?

"Gotcha Dude…" She cracked up. It was so unexpected, Adam laughed too. God, he loved this woman.

Sometime later they were picked up from the hotel by the cruise company and commenced a memorable look at Paris from the river. It was interesting to note how the ancient part contrasted, yet blended with the modern architecture. Landmarks dimly remembered from High School history lessons, were brought alive by the multi-lingual commentary.

They viewed the golden dome of Les Invalides, the slender spire of Saint Cappelle, the sinister looking Conciergerie, dominating a large portion of the Ile'de la Cite, with the Gothic towers of the amazing Notre Dame Cathedral set in a stately manner on its little island in the Seine. In the distance, they saw the white domes of Sacre' Coer, the highlight of Montmartre. When they passed the Port de la Bourbonnais Bridge at the foot of the Eiffel tower, Mina couldn't contain herself, thinking about the romantic proposal the night before and how this man had changed her life; just then Adam pulled her close, kissing her fondly.

"What was that for?" Mina asked.

"Just for being wonderful and not making me have dinner with the folks every Sunday."

A light lunch was served on the cruise boat, but Mina and Adam were still satisfied from the previous night's feast and the amazing gourmet breakfast and opted for just mineral water and some fruit. After the cruise, they visited the Louvre, and then strolled along the bank of the Seine, arm in arm studying the paintings by the myriad of artists. On their eventual return, there was another note in their room advising a complimentary restaurant booking had been secured for them for that evening.

"This is just amazing," Mina said, "we are being treated like celebrities but if we keep up with all this eating, I'll have to live at the gym. The French certainly love their food." They rested in each other's arms and talked about their plans for a life together, until it was time to prepare for dinner. They arrived at the restaurant punctually at 7:45 p.m. and were shown to a table by a gracious maître d'hôtel. The celebrity status had preceded them and he insisted on treating them like royalty. It was a sumptuous affair and they sat overlooking the park where they had enjoyed the magical dinner and entertainment the previous evening.

They talked with excitement about their engagement and Mina could not take her eyes off her new fiancé and the beautiful ring he had chosen for her. She asked how Adam had selected such a magnificent design. Mina's heart melted as Adam offered his explanation, "You are my dream girl Mina and the choice was easy. The two small baguettes represent you and me. We came together as one," he indicated the main diamond, "the sum is greater than the single parts and we both became more complete and whole. The ring has no ending, it goes on forever and that is my troth and my pledge to you." Mina was overwhelmed. She was the luckiest girl in the world and she just adored this romantic, spiritual man.

For dessert, they were served a French favourite, a sumptuous Crème Brûlée Caramélisée à la Vanille. After they laughed and joked their way through this delight, Mina broke the following silence with a sudden exclamation, "Oh my God!"

"What is it?" Adam said slightly concerned.

"Mina Mills! Oh goodness, that sounds a bit like Minnie Mouse."

"That's not a deal breaker, is it? You won't back out just because of that…?" asked Adam bringing a smile to the face of his fiancée.

"Look! It's really Harper-Mills if that helps," Adam said, "…I don't like to flaunt airs and graces but would you prefer 'Mina Harper-Mills'?"

"Indeed yes!" Mina said with an English accent, "Announcing, Mrs Mina Harper-Mills." She stopped dead and went serious. It was amazing how her thoughts changed so quickly with different associations. "Adam, remember what you said about Princess Diana?"

"Yeeees?" he replied searching her face for the connection.

"I thought about it a lot and I think she was a pretty amazing person. She started out as a shy unsophisticated girl and as she matured, I think she really tried hard to help where she could. She tried to make a difference in the world and made good use of her position. It's just not fair that she's gone, and I would like to go through the 'Pont de L'Alma' where she died, sort of as a small tribute, to show we remember and that we care."

"What right now?" Adam asked.

"No in the morning before we fly home."

As it happened, after the elegant dining, they left the restaurant just before 10 p.m. and from the foyer noticed a row of cabs waiting outside the hotel. It was a beautiful night with a big moon so they spontaneously decided to go right then. The cab driver understood English fairly well and they went through the tunnel sparing a silent thought for Diana, Princess of Wales and the good things she had accomplished before her life was terminated so tragically. The mood was fairly sombre. Adam said gently, "Want to go back, now?"

"No, let's drive around a bit." They went on viewing Paris by night, drove down the Champs Elysées and saw the Arc de Triomphe de l'Etoile. The city was so alive and vibrant that soon they were captivated by its charm and their mood became jovial once more. Sometime later, they were becoming tired from all the excitement and decided to return to the hotel. There they held each other tightly and embraced the love they had both sought for so long. They fell asleep and woke still in each other's arms.

## Engagement Present

After breakfast, Adam checked the time zone and called to tell his parents that he and Mina were engaged. He couldn't help but add that he thought she was the most wonderful girl in the world. Adam's mother was plainly overjoyed at the news and added that she and his father had recognised the signs some time ago and yet it was still a big surprise. Sarah actually became a little teary as she wished them all the very best.

"I think your father has a surprise for you," she added, "...but first can I please speak to Mina."

Mina talked seriously for some time before there was a break in the conversation, "Sarah's just getting your father..." she said with her hand over the mouthpiece.

"Congratulations Mina, we are so happy for you and Adam and let me take this opportunity to roll out a metaphoric red carpet, and welcome you to the family. We are so glad to have you and hope you will make each other happy and have a long, prosperous life together. We wish that sincerely."

"Thank-you Dr Mills, I am very happy and will do everything in my power to make Adam happy. That is a promise I intend to keep, Sir."

"I'm sure you will Mina, now if you will put Adam on the phone, I have a surprise for you both." Mina handed the phone to Adam.

"Congratulations Adam, and well done," the older Mills said, "we couldn't be more pleased. Your Mother and Renee are now crying hysterically in each other's arms, so I guess that means they're happy. You have our blessings of course."

"Thank-you Dad, I value your support. What's this about a surprise?"

"Two surprises actually," the Doctor added, "I noticed how frustrated you became during our talk with the Lieutenant and I must confess, I admired your stand. Things weren't handled well and you had reason to be bitter at the alienation and lack of support. You took it on the chin and I was proud of you. Of course, we discussed your future briefly when you and Mina came to dinner. Well, I had a call yesterday from a Mr Jonathan Rylah who is in charge of intelligence and security at LAX, and we had quite a talk."

"We'll discuss it when you get home Adam, because it's entirely your decision, not mine. Actually, I was fairly impressed. Mr Rylah was very professional and he is interested in having a talk with you sometime next week, with a view to recruiting you for employment with his department in Airport Security. Nothing is certain and it may not become permanent until you finish your course but it seems a huge step forward to me. The pay scale is way better and that industry would appear to be fairly exclusive and certainly has a strong future."

"That is amazing Dad and of course I'll meet with him. Thank-you so much."

"I did little enough, I believe he knows Barry Hannaway through Rotary, so I guess Barry recommended you."

"I am so grateful."

"The second surprise is for you and Mina and we'd like to discuss that with the two of you when you arrive home."

"Can you give me a hint, Dad?"

"Sure! It's no secret. As you know, the Ronald Opus case was quite weird with all its twists and turns. I chose to précis this case in my talk about the most bizarre case we had ever encountered, at the AAFS annual awards dinner for our 25th anniversary, on Friday night. My talk was reported in the press, it actually caused a bit of a stir."

"Later, I was approached by a media network and contracted to give a couple of exclusive re-cap specials on the role of the Chief Medical Examiner as it applies to this wacky case, with live questions and answers etc. For this, they offered me a ridiculous amount of money. Adam, I didn't feel good about profiting from a situation that caused you so much hurt, so after some soul searching, I think I arrived at the right solution."

"Go on..." Adam was intrigued.

"Well, you know Carl Winter bought the Ocean 60. He was overjoyed that you liked the Emerald Springs cabin so much. Of course, you know he is a widower and has no heirs. He shared with me that as your godfather he really wanted to leave you the Emerald Springs property in his will. I happened to know that he has extended himself a fair bit in buying the boat and likely needed the money from the sale of the cabin. So, I discussed a solution with him and he accepted."

"Yes?" Adam hardly breathed and Mina watched him, wondering what had caught his attention so intensely.

"I offered him the substantial TV network money and we will split the balance 50/50. This can now be an engagement present from Carl Winter and from your mother and myself. We will arrange the title transfer of the property so you and Mina can have it now."

"Oh Dad...that's incredible...thank-you...and thank Mr Winter...that's amazing!" was all he could get out. Adam was dumbfounded. Unable to speak, he slowly passed the phone to Mina for Dr Mills to explain the situation to her.

"Thank-you we are just astounded..." was all Mina could say, "Thank-you so much, we certainly appreciate it."

"It's ours," they repeated over and over, "we can use it whenever we can get away."

"When we decide to purchase a home in the future," Adam stated, "that property is solid collateral...but it's too beautiful; we could never sell it."

"Never!" Hearing this would have made Carl Winter very happy indeed. Mina called Leah, now back in Hamburg, to share her joy, "I just cannot believe all the wonderful things that are happening to us."

"I am so happy for you Mina-Pina. You truly deserve it."

"I remember what you said about dreams coming true when the time is right."

"I just sort of made that up," Leah said a little sheepishly, "I didn't entirely believe it, or really feel sure it would happen."

"I did!" Mina said.

## Shop till You Drop

"I had better get moving if we are to fit in some shopping and get some gifts and souvenirs," Mina laughed as she rushed for the opulent shower. Jon-Pierre wouldn't hear of them using a taxi and arranged a driver to take them to the shops, in the hotel Citroen. They had a fun morning scouring the shopping areas of Paris. Adam guessed that shopping must actually be a national pastime here, with boutiques and stores everywhere. They saw high-end designer goods in Emporio Armani and Louis Vuitton.

They visited Hermès and saw impeccably crafted items that subtly promote good taste and sufficient means. No VW's in the carpark. They then headed for Boulevard Haussmann and ventured through the City's prestigious department stores. Mina discovered Galleries Lafayette which boasted good shopping amidst stunning architecture and Forum des Hales, which occupied the site of the age-old markets, and offered a plethora of separate venues in a fascinating, underground complex.

It was an amazing shopping experience and within their moderate budget, they were able to purchase wonderful gifts for everyone who had been so kind to them. They say shopping is therapeutic and Mina noted with some satisfaction that every trace of previous disquiet and nervousness was now removed forever. Adam had been correct; this relationship was perfect for both of them. The individual parts had become a complete and more confident whole unit. Perhaps for the first time in her life, Mina was at peace and totally content. She was just truly, madly, deeply, in love.

After a little more sightseeing, they finally headed back to their marvellous suite to pack before their transport to the airport and the Lufthansa flight that would take them home to LA.

"Paris will always be Fantasyland to me, now," Mina said quietly. "Adam, I kinda like you a lot, my handsome fiancé and I really appreciate all your care and thoughtfulness. It was a wonderful surprise that I will cherish forever. Thank-you for indulging me and making all my dreams come true." She cuddled him fondly, feeling totally fulfilled, perhaps for the first time ever.

## Goodbye to Paris

"I can never thank you enough Jon-Pierre for all your help. We will never forget Paris, and we will never forget you," Adam stated earnestly.

"Monsieur, we are glad your American President is gone, we not like him very much, but you…we like," stated the concierge simply, with brutal honesty.

"Yeah…well we didn't like him much either," Adam stated with a grin, "I didn't vote for him."

Adam presented Jon-Pierre with the gold cuff links he had bought as a token of their appreciation and Jon-Pierre received them with obvious delight. He gave Adam a box that contained a set of the magnificent 'his and hers' waffle robes with the hotel's logo emblazoned on the pocket and a whole assortment of hotel merchandise.

"To help you remember your stay with us, Monsieur," the hammy concierge added, pearly teeth flashing. He then left them for a moment, moving swiftly to the elevator. When he returned, on his arm was the dignified lady Adam had helped, now looking much better.

"Permit me to present Madame Miquette St. Claire, from the French Ballet," he said regally and with great affection. The lady hugged Adam crooning 'Merci' over and over in French.

"I did very little," said Adam, "thank-you for all you did for us."

Jon-Pierre translated and Madame St. Clair hugged Adam and Mina in turn. There was some rapid-fire French and Jon-Pierre translated. "Madame want to know how you meet," he asked Mina.

"Easy," Mina told them sincerely, "…he rescued me."

Jon-Pierre translated for Madame St. Claire who responded with a chuckle, "She say, he rescue her too. He is good man."

"Yes, he is," Mina agreed, "the very best."

Next Madame St. Claire had a surprise for Mina. She presented her with the framed and mounted ballet slippers worn by the prima ballerina when she had danced for them in the parkland. Also mounted in the display was an autographed photograph of the violinist and the dancer herself.

"Merci beaucoup!" Mina said curtseying to Madame St. Claire, "Thank-you so much, you are so thoughtful. Oh my God, I will treasure this forever!" she exclaimed, the sincerity and delight showing in her face. The old lady hugged Mina again and said to Adam in broken English.

"Belle is so beautiful!"

"I know it," Adam replied bowing to her and nodding his agreement.

Jon-Pierre made a production of presenting a velvet covered photo album of their wonderful night in the park. Mina had only spotted the photographer once or twice yet there was a whole assortment of photos, right from her dramatic entrance, the walk through the foyer, lovely shots of the table setting, Mina and Adam seated, the maestro violinist, the amazing ballerina, the princess coach and photos of them at the Eiffel Tower, and the photographer had even captured Adam's proposal. All these memories were hers to keep in this magnificent compendium and tears came to Mina's eyes.

"Thank-you all very much, you have been so kind."

"Thank you, Jon-Pierre, you are a good man," Adam said sincerely hugging him.

"Please thank all your friends again for us, you made this really special for us! We certainly appreciate all you did," Mina stated with genuine appreciation.

"You most welcome, Monsieur, Mademoiselle. For your help Ad-am, we thank you also."

There were more hugs and handshakes all around and fond goodbyes.

"You will call your first son Jon-Pierre, Monsieur?" the concierge asked suddenly with a straight face. Adam considered it, but didn't answer, looking at Mina who was decidedly non-committal.

## To the Airport James

The hotel's limousine had been arranged to take them to the airport in style. The receptionist and most of the staff, plus several of the guests were there to say goodbye. They finally left, waving like celebrities.

"No way!" Mina shrieked from the plush velvet seat.

"No way—what?" Adam asked looking concerned.

"Jon-Pierre! Oh, yuuuck!" Mina said laughing. "Absolutely, no way."

"He was a sweet guy," Adam said simply.

"He was amazing, I will never forget him," Mina said appreciatively. "Oh Adam, I am so happy and just look what Madame St. Claire gave me. I just can't believe it. She was so lovely." She though a while, "Perhaps there was a lot of money in her purse that you retrieved or something like that. They were just so kind to us."

"Yes, maybe there was…but perhaps they are just genuine French romantics," Adam suggested.

In the airport waiting lounge, Adam was lost in his thoughts. He was finally disturbed from his daydream with a kiss from his lovely fiancée, "Penny for your thoughts, Sweetie."

"I was just thinking about our discussion at the lake, about dualism, about yin and yang and about how the pendulum swings one way and then back the other. It seems that as you go through life, you can try hard to do what you think is right, but regardless of your intentions, sometimes you are punished and sometimes you are rewarded. I'll tell you about it sometime." Mina nodded. She understood the balance perfectly and squeezed his hand. She was that kind of person. "Rewarded is better," she whispered.

"Don't I know it!" Adam breathed.

Thoughts of the first altercation involving Adam at the coffee shop, the second in the car park with Flynn and what she knew about the third with the muggers in the park, flashed momentarily through Mina's mind. Yet again she was amazed and thankful at how these negative things had occurred in a way that had changed her life so positively. She had to admit that had it not been for the dreadful first incident, in all likelihood she would never have met Adam.

The terrible exchange with Flynn and his thugs had served to draw them even closer together. Then the dreadful episode with the purse-snatchers, was responsible for the wonderful, memorable time they had shared in Paris. The interaction of something good resulting from something bad in each of the cases was pretty much in line with Adam's explanation of Yin and Yang. It was something Mina would consider for a long time.

*"Dopo la pioggia viene il bel tempo,"* she muttered to herself involuntarily. Noting Adam's raised eyebrows, she whispered, "Calm comes after the storm. Even dark clouds can have a silver lining." She snuggled up and kissed him passionately. He understood.

Before the flight, Mina was able to catch Leah and the crew for a moment. She flashed her left hand and caused shrieks from all the flight attendants. Leah hugged her and rushed over to hug Adam. Mina quickly showed them the photo album and there were exclamations all around. The girls were just blown away and the girl-talk could have gone on for hours. "Go, go! We have to board now," Leah finally exclaimed, drying her eyes with a tissue, "and Mina …Congratulations, you did it so well. I am soooo jealous."

Mina quickly boarded the flight with Adam and found they had been secretly upgraded to Business Class. For perhaps the first time, she felt her life was complete and truly fulfilled. Adam's trip to Paris and brilliant surprise had given her immense joy and she hugged his arm. He really was considerate and special. Once they were airborne and the safety demonstrations were over, a Flight Attendant arrived with champagne and strawberries.

"Leah!" was all Mina got out, before a message came over the P.A. in Captain Kangaroo's fruity tones: "We have an urgent message for the passenger in seat 5A…" Adam glanced at his boarding pass and came to attention, looking concerned.

"Passenger 5A, would you please…take special care of our favourite Flight Attendant, Mina, for all the years to come. Passengers we ask you to please join with us in wishing Adam and Mina all the best in celebrating their engagement on our flight to LA."

The flight attendants were right there to fire 'party popper' streamers all over them, making a dreadful mess in the aircraft. The whole plane erupted in applause!

The smiles on the faces of Adam and Mina were a joy to behold.

# End Notes

[1] Wikipedia Free Encyclopedia http://en.wikipedia.org/wiki/Coroner.

[2] 'Spray on Pants' recorded by Kisschasy. Lyrics by Kisschasy.

[3] This was covered in Ian Ross Vayro; *'They Lied to Us in Sunday School'*. Joshua Books, 2006.

*"The Name of seventy-two triplets is derived from three Biblical verses; Exodus Chapter 14: Verses 19, 20 & 21. Whether by coincidence or design, each of these verses contains exactly seventy-two Hebrew letters. These verses then form the basis for the seventy-two triplets in the name."*

(i) Take the letters of the first verse in direct order
(ii) Those of the second verse in reverse order
(iii) Those of the third verse in direct order

Begin with the first letter of the first verse, which is W (Vav). Then take the last letter of the second verse, which is H (He), and finally, the first letter of the third verse, which is W (Vav). The first triplet is, WHW. In order to construct the second triplet, one proceeds in the same manner. Take the second letter of the first verse, Y (Yod) the second last letter of the second verse, L (Lamed), and the second letter of the third verse, Y (Yod). The second triplet is, YLY. This method is continued until all seventy-two triplets are recorded.

Exodus 14: 19
WYSO MLAK HALHYM HHLK LPhNY MChNH YShRAL WYLK MAChRYHM WYSO OMWD HONN MPhNYHM
WYOMD MAChRYHM:

*"And the angel of God, who went before the camp of Israel, moved, and went behind them, and the pillar of cloud moved from before them and went behind them."*

Exodus 14: 20
WYBA BYN MChNH MTzRYM WBYN MChNH YShRAL WYHY HONN WHChShK WYAR ATh HLYLH WLA QRB ZH
AL ZH KL HLYLH:

*"And it came between the camp of Egypt and the camp of Israel, and cloud and darkness were there, yet it gave light in the night, and one did not come near the other all that night."*

Exodus 14: 21

WYT MShH ATh YDW OL HYM WYWLK YHWH ATh HYM BRWCh QDYM OZH KL HLYLH WYShM ATh HYM LChRBH WYBQOW HMYM:

*"And Moses stretched out his hand over the sea, and God caused the sea to go back with a strong East wind all the night, and it made the sea into dry land, and the waters were parted."*

Using the directions contained in the Jewish Zohar (The Book of Splendor) this calculates God's complete name of 72 triplets:

WHW YLY SYT OLM MHSh LLH AKH KHTh HZY ALK LAW HHO YZL MBH HRY HQM LAW KLY LWW PhHL NLK YYY MLH ChHW NThH HAA YRTh ShAH RYY AWM LKB WShR YChW LHCh KWQ MND ANY HOS RHO YYZ HHH MYK WWL YLH SAL ORY OShL MYH WHW DNY HChSh OMM NNA NYTh MBH PhWY NMM YYL HRCh MTzR WMB YHH ONW MchY DMB MNQ AYO ChBW RAH YBM HYY MWM

It is the actual ineffable, unpronounceable, sacred name that is shortened to YHWH.

[4] This was covered in Ian Ross Vayro, *'They Lied to Us in Sunday School'*, Joshua Books, 2006.

[5] This was covered in Ian Ross Vayro, *'They Lied to Us in Sunday School'*, Joshua Books, 2006.

[6] A 'drongo' is actually a noisy and conspicuous Australian bird, however, a race horse was named 'Drongo' and due to its lousy form and continued losing streak, that cost punters a lot of money, anyone classed as a totally useless loser is now called a 'drongo' in Australian slang.

[7] Stanislav Grof and Hal Zina Bennett, *'The Holotropic Mind: The Three Levels of Human Consciousness and How They Shape Our Lives'*, page 5, 1993, HarperSanFrancisco; Reprint edition. I believe however that it was Fred Hoyle who first postulated this example and it was accordingly attributed to him by his colleague Chandra Wickramasinghe.

[8] This point was made by Richard Dawkins, *'The God Delusion'*, 2006, Bantam Press London, a division of Transworld Publishers.

[9] See Plato, *'The Crito'*, trans. Benjamin Jowett, Walter J. Black Inc., Roslyn, NY, 1942, 44d.

[10] This point is made in Heng-ching Shih, 'T'ien-T'ai Chih-I's Theory of Buddha Nature—A Realistic and Humanistic', Page 168–9.

[11] For this information, I am indebted to Heng-ching Shih, 'T'ien-T'ai Chih-I's Theory of Buddha Nature—A Realistic and Humanistic', Page 168–9.

[12].The Christian Bible carries many passages such as the following:

*Exodus 22: 29–31 "Thou shalt not delay to offer the first of thy ripe fruits, and of thy liquors: the firstborn of thy sons shalt thou give unto me. Likewise shalt thou do with thine oxen, and with thy sheep: seven days it shall be with his dam; on the eighth day thou shalt give it me. And ye shall be Holy men unto me."*

*Numbers 8: 17–18 "For all the firstborn of the children of Israel are mine, both man and beast; on the day that I smote every firstborn in the land of Egypt, I sanctified them for myself and I have taken the Levites for all the firstborn of the children of Israel."*
Just what is the purpose of all this ritual murder?

*Ezekiel 20: 26 "I let them become defiled through their gifts—the sacrifice of every firstborn—that I might fill them with horror so they would know that I am the Lord."*

[13] Bongolese—A fictional tribe invented by Richard Dawkins in his book "The God Delusion" to make fun of cultural relativism. *"You are only truly 'in' a place if you are an anointed elder entitled to take snuff from the dried scrotum of a goat." (Dawkins, Richard. 2006 "The God Delusion", Bantam Press).*

[14] This was covered in Ian Ross Vayro, *'Tears in Heaven'*, Joshua Books 2008.

[15] This was covered in Ian Ross Vayro, *'Tears in Heaven'*, Joshua Books 2008.

[16] This was covered in Ian Ross Vayro, *'Tears in Heaven'*, Joshua Books 2008.

[17] This was covered in Ian Ross Vayro, *'Tears in Heaven'*, Joshua Books 2008.

[18] The founder of modern analytical psychology, Carl Jung points out in his commentary, *'Answer to Job'* that for all his might and power, YHWH actually damns himself in humiliating Job. The integrity and fortitude of Job, stands in sharp contrast to the rage and reproach of YHWH, emphasised by the disparity of all His might pitted against the impotence of Job. As Jung notes, by His grotesque actions, YHWH unwittingly reveals deep flaws in His own character.

It is this somewhat evil nature that the ancient Hebrew named 'Mastema'. Prior to the documentation of Satan as an entity, the dark and evil nature within YHWH was identified and called 'Mastema'. The only tenable explanation is that it is this evil nature of YHWH-Mastema that was responsible for the revolting torture of Job in this mismatched power struggle.

[19] YHWH-Sabaoth was considered the God of War by the Hebrew people and the word *'Sabaoth'* meant something like army; hence YHWH was a War-God or God of armies. When the first English Bible translators encountered the word Sabaoth, they created a new English word 'Host'. Accordingly, the 'heavenly host' is now taught as angels when in reality it is a heavenly army. This is confirmed when the same Hebrew word 'Sabaoth' is used in the following passage:

*Exodus 14: 17 I will harden the hearts of the Egyptians, and they shall follow them: and I will get me honour upon Pharaoh, and upon all his <u>host</u>, upon his chariots, and upon his horsemen.* (It is not difficult to see that this refers to Pharaoh's Army.)

[20] This was covered in Ian Ross Vayro, *'God Save Us from Religion'*, page 54, Joshua Books 2007.

[21] This was covered in Ian Ross Vayro, *'God Save Us from Religion'*, page 54, Joshua Books 2007 and Ian Ross Vayro, *'They Lied to Us in Sunday School'*, page 195, Joshua Books 2006.

[22] This was a Gallup Poll taken in 1954, reported by Robert A. Hinde, *'Why Gods Persist: A Scientific Approach to Religion'*, 1999, Routledge London.

[23] These thoughts are taken from Sam Harris, *'Letter to a Christian Nation'*, 2006, Knopf.

[24] Telephone interview with Mrs Arthur Figlock, Harper Wood, Michigan, *'Mysteries of the Unexplained'*, Readers Digest General Books, 1982, page 181.